# PROLOGUE

DECEMBER 25, 2:37AM


Dr. Christopher Nestrom couldn't sit down.

He had a stool at his workbench that he'd designed himself. He'd had it manufactured by hand in Germany and flown to his home at a cost of fifteen thousand dollars. It was designed specifically for his body shape, his work habits, the specific height of his workbenches.

It was the perfect stool. And in that moment, he was too excited to use it.

This was the moment he'd been waiting for, the moment he'd been working toward every single day for the last eighteen months.

For the last sixteen years.

Innumerable false starts. Countless failed prototypes. Endless iterations. Designing. Tweaking. Testing. Redesigning. Re-tweaking. Re-testing. Night after long night. Month after infuriating month.

He couldn't sleep more than a few hours a day. He could barely eat. He'd lost twenty-five pounds in the last year alone.

All of this was normal. Par for the course for Dr. Nestrom when he was working on a new project.

It was the same process he'd followed for the Nestrom 1, which had established him as the premier industrial designer of his age and made him a multi-millionaire at the age of thirty.

It was the same process he'd used for the Nestrom 2, which had made him a multi-billionaire at the age of forty-two.

And it was the process that was about to push technology into a new era, redefining the hardware people used every single day around the world.

Money had become meaningless to Dr. Nestrom by this point. Except as a way of keeping score.

The one with the most money wins.

And who knows? The Nestrom 3 could make him the world's first trillionaire. Because this prototype, this iteration, was going to work. This was a moment that would be remembered for generations to come.

This was the one.

He was sure of it.

Nestrom tilted the overhead light to the side and bent low over his workbench, pulling on his magnifying glasses so he could see more clearly. This was fine work, detailed work, with delicate components and little tolerance for error.

Chips, wiring, heat sinks. Everything had become so small that they could barely be seen with the naked eye anymore, and certainly could not be manipulated by hand. First he'd needed tools, then nano-tools. Dr. Nestrom spent more time between projects designing and building new tools than he did designing and building the next device.

The light shone bright on the workbench, a spotlight on the most important thing in Dr. Nestrom's world—his work. He made the last adjustment, checked all the fittings. Plugged into his laptop and checked all the power sources and connections one more time.

The new chip design was perfect. A breakthrough revolution in its own right that had taken Dr. Nestrom years to perfect. Transistor nanoscaling, intelligent architecture, and silicon compilation had made chips that were orders of magnitude faster than older designs. But they all still relied on the transmission of electrons through silicon channels, a process which became unreliable at atomic scale. Nestrom had thrown out the approach altogether, running smaller, faster photons through more reliable carbon nanotubes instead of silicon channels. That innovation alone would make Nestrom the richest man in the world and alter the course of technology for the next fifty years. But it was just one part of Nestrom's newest project.

The code for the operating system was rock-solid. Tested literally millions of times, with test suites running twenty-four hours a day in parallel on a bank of servers for the last three months, the OS had been run through endless AI-generated test cases, variations on every possible scenario an end-user could push the hardware through, and a whole bunch they couldn't possibly come up with. The new OS was bombproof, bulletproof, and dishwasher safe, to boot.

Compared to the chip design, the optical tech had required only minor breakthroughs, but it had been difficult to design. Wearable technology had to handle the intersection of every possible human body shape with every possible way to wear the device and every possible environmental condition, whether rain or snow or bright sun or city lights at night. The combinations were infinite, so the design had to be infinitely flexible. Not an easy task, but hardly revolutionary. All it took was old-fashioned innovation, and a hell of a lot of prototypes.

After all that, the design and manufacture of the hardware itself had been trivial. All it required was a sturdy housing to protect all of the components and shield the wearers from harm, using lightweight, comfortable materials that would eventually allow for customization to suit the inevitable whims of fashion.

All of that had been done. All of those problems had been solved.

All that remained was the final hardware test.

Dr. Nestrom slipped the device on over his ears like a pair of eyeglasses, then tapped one side of the thin resin frame to turn on the power and authenticate the system.

The lenses lit up before his eyes.

After the splash screen with his company logo faded from view, Nestrom saw a white-on-blue wireframe version of the room directly in front of him, then all around him, above and below, the operating system presenting him with a 360-degree view of his space in a way that felt completely intuitive, despite the fact that it was wholly unnatural.

Unlike the Nestrom 1, which had been a breakthrough in industrial design, and the Nestrom 2, which had been a revolution in hardware-software integration, the Nestrom 3 was a quantum leap into the future. It was the first production-ready integration of hardware, software, and the human brain.

From all appearances, it was just a simple pair of glasses. But there was nothing simple about them. These glasses pushed far beyond augmented reality and virtual reality. They created a new reality, an interface between the sensors in the hardware, the software operating system, and the human brain itself that extended the human mind and the human senses.

Where augmented reality used sight and sound, and virtual reality added touch, the Nestrom 3 leveraged, extended, and surpassed all of the human senses. It was the first true augmentation of the human mind, one that could reach deep within the brain and generate patterns that resembled actual human thought and intuition.

In the scientific literature, it had been thought impossible. Unimaginable.

But Nestrom had not only imagined it. He'd built it. He'd made it possible.

And for the first time in human history, he was using it.

The 360-degree wireframe view of the room quickly resolved into a full model in three dimensions, with real-time accuracy in shading, texture, and position. Nestrom turned his head from side to side. The image of the room moved with him, smooth and completely natural, as clear and natural as if he were seeing them with his own eyes.

Which, of course, he wasn't. The image before him was photo-realistic, but the lenses themselves were opaque. From the front, to an onlooker, they would show an image of Nestrom's eyes, as real as if he were wearing normal eyeglasses.

This was configurable, of course. The appearance of clear lenses was the default, but he could choose to hide his eyes, as if he were wearing dark sunglasses, or choose any opacity in between. He could change the tint or color of the appearance. Since it was just a projection, he could even change his eye color, change his eye shape. Hell, he could play the movie Bambi for the world on the front of his lenses if he wanted to. It was just a screen, like a computer monitor.

The inside of the lens was the same, just a screen that could show anything. But the default state was to show the world around him. All the way around him. In hyper-realistic, extrasensory detail. In a way that the human brain could easily assimilate.

In just the way you could walk through a room and have a mental image, an innate sense of what was behind you and above you, as well as a visual image of what was in front of you, Dr. Nestrom had figured out how to project that same sense into your mind when you were wearing the Nestrom 3.

And the sense wasn't limited to the room you were in. With enough sensory data, which was easily obtained these days from the ubiquitous cameras and sensors in the world, including the devices we all carried around every day on our wrists and in our pockets and handbags and backpacks, you could have an innate sense of the entire house, the grounds, the city, even the whole world, if your mind was capable of assimilating that much information without going completely mad.

It truly was a breakthrough. Dr. Nestrom's greatest achievement.

Through the glasses, the room around him resolved. Even though the actual physical room was mostly dark, lit only by the light over Dr. Nestrom's workbench, the image in the lenses was lit as if the room were bathed in full daylight.

A figure walked into view in front of him.

"You did it."

A sensor warning popped up. It wasn't visible, but Nestrom felt it. As if it were whispering into his left ear.

*Heart rate elevated.*

"You startled me," said Nestrom.

"You brilliant asshole. You actually fucking did it."

Nestrom extended his senses. Just by thinking the commands, the system would respond. He pushed the operating system to bring in more information. About the room. About the house above him.

About the person standing in front of him.

The operating system overlaid a heat signature on the person, as well as vitals it could glean from a distance. Facial recognition pulled up an array of biographical details.

Nestrom didn't need those. He knew the person standing before him all too well.

"Language, please," he said, "But, yes. I did."

"Amazing." The figure reached up to take the glasses from Nestrom's face. "Do you mind?"

"They won't work for you," Nestrom said quickly, leaning away from the outstretched hands. "They're keyed to my bioidentifiers."

"Of course." The person lowered their hands, a soft smile on their face. "Security, above all else."

"It's very late," Nestrom said. "What do you want?"

The person smiled, their teeth bright and clear in the light from the overhead lamp, the rest of the face shadowed, giving the impression of a Cheshire cat hovering in the darkness.

"It doesn't matter what I want, does it? You never seem to let me have it." They stepped into the light, that Cheshire grin joined by bright, predatory eyes. "But I'll take what I can get."

Nestrom sensed movement behind him.

Another person.

He vaguely wondered why he hadn't sensed it earlier, why the glasses hadn't highlighted the second person in the room. He'd have to check on that in the code.

Always optimizing. Always debugging.

The person before him leaned in close, their face filling Nestrom's view.

There was no mistaking the look in their eyes then.

*Heart rate elevated. Approaching clinical levels.*

Nestrom didn't need the glasses to tell him that. He could feel his heart pounding in his ears.

He'd built a self-defense module into the system, but hadn't spent enough time learning how to use it yet. He didn't think he would ever need it.

Instinctively, his hands groped around him for a weapon, but found only air.

He thought about lashing out, striking the person with his fists and running for help.

He might be able to get past one of them, but not both.

Too much younger. Too much stronger.

And far too angry.

"Why are you doing this?" Nestrom asked. "Don't you have enough?"

The person's smile disappeared, replaced with a sneer.

"What is it you always say?" they said as Nestrom felt cold metal press against his temples from behind. "Oh, right. 'Whoever said there are no stupid questions'"—their sneer morphed back into the Cheshire grin—"'was an idiot.'"

Nestrom had one last thought before the voltage from the leads flowed through his brain, jolted his synapses, and started an electrical cascade. One last thought before his mind seized and the electrical cascade stopped his heart.

His last thought was that his new device, the Nestrom 3, worked beautifully. Simultaneously, exactly as designed, Nestrom could see in his mind both the killer standing before him and the killer standing behind.

# 1



Cameron Hauk waited in the back of the cab while it idled in traffic, the blasting heat bringing out the smell of sweat soaked into the cracking leather of the back seat. It filled Cam's nostrils with a skunky, fungal smell. The heat condensed on the inside of the windows, fogged Cam's view. The drip of the condensation only enhanced the image of sweat in Cam's mind, as if the car itself were sweating.

The endless files of cars outside were nothing but blurred smudges of red light on both sides of the car, the jam of rush hour made worse by the coming holiday. Everyone was trying to get out of town early for Christmas, and everyone was trying to do it at the exact same time. The crush of cars felt silly, yet another symptom of a mindless mob refusing to question their own assumptions and think for themselves, blindly doing what was expected, what everyone else expected of them, without thinking about what they wanted, and what might be a reasonable way to get it.

But the weaknesses of society weren't Cam's concern at the moment. He had much more important things on his mind.

He'd done his research. He'd made a plan. He'd laid the groundwork as best he could. All that remained was to do the job.

As the cab approached the train station, Cam slipped into character, as his parents had taught him and he'd practiced so many times. The secret was to commit, fully and completely. To inhabit the character. Actors called it method acting. Cam thought of it more as a means of survival.

The first step was to choose a name. Cam had already done that: Sam Davis, a name from another job, another phase of a larger plan. Forgettable and ubiquitous, it would be hard for someone to remember a name like Sam Davis, and even harder for them to track down, if Cam didn't want to be found. The fact that it was similar to his own name was coincidental, but helpful. Easier for Cam to instinctively respond when someone called him.

Cam swiped his credit card, thanked the driver, and exited the cab. The afternoon air was crisp. Cam welcomed it against his flushed face. It may have been filled with car exhaust, but at least the outside air was cold and didn't smell like flop sweat. The air carried the sharp smell of approaching snow, with its promise of beauty and danger and excitement, three words that described the same thing in Cam's mind.

As hordes of passengers streamed into the train station around him, their energy swept into Cam, the energy of all of humanity, of a thousand human minds, human hearts, human lives. Silly and mindless they may be, but in that moment they were all Cameron Hauk, and he was all of them. Cam closed his eyes and drew in a deep, cold lungful of beauty, of danger, of excitement. Clouds of exhaust and a chorus of honking cars formed a soothing backdrop to the mantra Cam looped in his mind.

*I am Sam Davis.*
*I am Sam Davis.*
*I am Sam Davis.*

**2**

The humming quiet of the train car.

The rhythm of the wheels as they thumped along the tracks.

The damp coolness of the window as Sam leaned his temple against it.

The soft scratch of his graphite pencil across the rough texture of the cotton drawing paper.

At this hour, the train was usually filled with people commuting home from work.

Today, it was full of people heading home for the long Christmas weekend.

Sam was doing neither.

He leaned against the cool window and sketched the face of the man across the aisle, sitting backward against the direction of the train, facing toward Sam.

The man was oblivious to Sam's attention. He had long hair down to his shoulders, well-trimmed and healthy. That suggested a certain counter-culture hippiness, but the man wore a blue suit and brown dress shoes under a light-brown overcoat. Neither the suit nor the overcoat looked cheap, but they were hardly tailor-made. They weren't flashy enough for it to be a part of his personal brand, some kind of ironic statement that might cause his counter-cultural friends to break into half-hidden hysterics. And the way the suit rumpled around the man made it seem like he wore it out of duty and routine, not from any real desire to dress well.

His dark round glasses and patchy, three-day stubble combined with his long hair to give Sam the impression of a part-time beat poet or maybe the lead singer in a punk band. But the suit implied he was trapped into a corporate gig in the city to feed his barefoot suburban kids and pay the mortgage he never thought he'd have.

Sam worked all of that into his sketch as he leaned against the cool window, rocking gently in time with the train.

"You need to put more sadness into his eyes."

A woman's voice.

Sam couldn't tell where it was coming from. For a quick moment, he wondered if the voice were inside his head, a voice from his memories.

Then someone shifted from the seat behind him, came around into the aisle, and sat in the empty chair beside Sam. He quickly moved his shoulder bag to the floor so she wouldn't sit on it.

"More desperation," she said, pointing to Sam's sketch. "That man is one spilled coffee away from shooting up a day care center." She tapped his sketch book. "I want to see that in his eyes."

Sam eyed the woman.

"You an art critic?"

"Just critical, in general," she said. "And, uh,"—she eyed Sam slowly from head to toe—"I know talent when I see it."

Sam ignored her implication.

"Not talented enough to put the right amount of horrific future carnage into the eyes, though?"

She paused only for a moment, clearly unused to having her implications ignored.

"I'm sure you would have gotten there, eventually," she said, a slight smile at the corners of her lips. "I'm critical, and I'm also impatient." She lay the fingers of both hands flat under her chin and batted her eyelashes prettily. "It's a winning combination."

Sam couldn't help but smile.

The girl was pretty. Borderline gorgeous. The kind of woman who was always good-looking, but rarely chose to go so far as to be intimidating.

And then every so often, on special nights, she'd come out and knock you dead with her show-stopping looks.

Sneaky good looks. The kind that creep up on you out of nowhere.

But more than that, she was forward and funny. Sam liked people who didn't bullshit around, putting too much store on pleasantries or social boundaries. There's no need to get all up in other people's business, but if you've got something to say, just say it. Don't beat around the bush. That just makes everyone hot and itchy.

Sam went back to his sketch. He had been working his way back to the eyes. And he was planning to put more emotion into them. Not just sadness and desperation, but also optimism and hope. The guy was slogging back and forth to work every day, but he was doing it for some reason. He had something he'd rather be doing, for sure, but he also had something—probably someone, his wife or his kids—that he was slogging for. Someone that was worth the slog.

"You're a real artist," said the woman when Sam held out the finished sketch to her. He fidgeted with his pencil in his fingers, twirling it between his thumb and forefinger like an airplane propeller as the woman glanced from the sketch to the man and back, several times. "Damn." She nodded her head. "I feel like I know the guy already. Like your art reveals his truth."

"Isn't that what art is supposed to do?"

The woman shrugged. "I thought art was supposed to make money."

Sam folded up his sketch pad and put it in his bag with his pencil. "Not in this world," he said.

"You don't sell your stuff?"

"I guess I never thought anyone would want to buy it."

"I would."

Sam sniffed a laugh. "Thanks."

"No, I mean it. How much for that sketch?"

"It's okay. You don't have to do that. Thank you, though."

"I'll give you five hundred dollars for it right now."

"Five hundred?" Sam laughed. "Well, I was hoping for three mil at Sotheby's next week."

The woman dug in her bag for a moment and came back with five crisp, new, one-hundred-dollar bills. She held them out to Sam.

"Jesus," he said.

"Money for work," the woman said. "That's normally how it's done."

Sam took out his sketch book, signed the corner "Sam Davis" in a compact scrawl, and carefully tore it from the book.

"Here," he said, holding it out to the woman. "Take it. Free of charge."

"I can't do that," she protested. "Take the money."

"Call it an early Christmas gift," Sam said.

She stubbornly held the bills out, but Sam just as stubbornly stared back at her, smiling sweetly.

Reluctantly, she put the bills back in her bag, then regarded her new sketch.

"I'll just have to find another way to pay you back," she said, glancing at Sam from the side of her eyes.

As she put the sketch carefully into her bag, a shiver ran up Sam's spine. It wasn't often that a beautiful stranger on a train propositioned him twice in five minutes.

"Where are you headed?" she asked.

"Rockford."

"Seeing family for Christmas?"

"My mom lives up there."

The woman peered out the window and up at the sky. She leaned across Sam to wipe a circle of condensation off the glass, leaned more than she had to. Sam could smell the faint floral scent of her perfume, warmed by her skin. Her hair pooled on his thigh.

"Hope you get in before the storm hits," she said.

She turned her head toward him, still leaning across his lap.

Their lips were only inches apart.

Sam watched as she slid her gaze from his eyes down to his lips, the tip of her tongue wetting her own lips until they glistened.

Sam felt a thrum throughout his body, like his nerve endings had come to life all at once.

The woman pulled away, smiling to herself.

Sam turned away, looked out the window to hide the flush he felt on his face and to focus his mind on something else, anything else.

The sky had been a light grey when Sam got on the train. But outside the window, it had turned leaden as the sun went down. In the dim remaining twilight and the passing glow of the lamps lighting the track, Sam could see light snow beginning to fall.

"It's gonna be a good one," the woman said.

**3**

By the time the train reached Marlon, the light snow had become a blizzard.

By the time they made it to Temper Junction fifteen minutes later, a full inch had accumulated on the ground at the station.

Temper Junction was only halfway to Rockford. Sam still had more than an hour left on the train.

"You're not going to make it," said the woman beside him.

They'd been chatting for almost an hour. The man in Sam's sketch had gotten off long ago, replaced by a dowdy old lady. Sam and the woman beside him had taken turns inventing stories about her.

She was a grandmother visiting her daughter and grandkids, said Sam.

She was a secret Russian agent, scouting ways to cripple American infrastructure, said the woman.

She was the owner of a cookie bakery heading home after closing shop, said Sam.

She was a former Israeli assassin, now elderly, off on one last job on Christmas Eve, just to feel that old thrill again, said the woman.

At the next stop, the lady got up and paused beside their chairs on her way out the door.

"Maybe you're both right," she said with a wink.

Sam and his seat mate laughed for a long time.

"Attention," came a staticky voice over the loudspeaker. "Due to inclement weather, service on the Carlin line is suspended after Bridgeton. Repeat. Service on this train will end at Bridgeton due to inclement weather creating unsafe track conditions. We apologize for any inconvenience. Authorized MTA employees will be available at Bridgeton station to advise on alternative travel options and local accommodations."

A collective groan came up from a few passengers in the train car.

Sam looked out the window and sighed heavily.

"Looks like Santa's bringing me something for Christmas after all," said the woman.

Sam looked at her, confused.

"He's bringing me you."

She flashed a full smile so dazzling, so bright, so drop-dead beautiful, that Sam was momentarily stunned.

The woman laughed. As if she knew exactly what effect that particular smile would have.

There was a sleek black car waiting at the curb outside the station at Bridgeton. A tall, thin man in a stately overcoat and black leather gloves stood beside it. As they approached, he opened the door. Steam billowed out as the heated air from inside the car met the increasingly frigid air outside.

"Good to see you again, miss," he said, his smooth, deep voice somehow conveying politeness without betraying even the slightest hint of true emotion.

"Hello, Carlton," the woman said as Carlton held the door, one hand behind his back. Her voice was just like his, friendly and cold at the same time. "This is..."

She sat down in the car and looked up through the open door at Sam.

"...my friend," she continued. "He'll be spending the holiday with us."

"Very well, miss," Carlton said. "I'll inform the house."

"You really don't need to do this," said Sam, standing on the curb with his small duffel bag in one hand. "I'm sure I can find a taxi or something."

"You'll never make it to Rockford, taxi or no taxi. Even a helicopter wouldn't get you there before this storm gets really bad. You'll end up staying in some shitty motel for god knows how long until the storm blows over." She gave him that smile again, the one that made Sam break out in a sweat, no matter how cold the air was becoming. "You might as well come home with me."

"But it's Christmas Eve. I don't want to intrude."

"All the more reason," she said, "and I promise you won't be intruding." She slid across the back of the car and patted the seat.

Carlton nodded solemnly as Sam slid into the car beside the woman, leaving his bag on the curb beside the woman's suitcases. The leather of the back seat was warm against Sam's palms. He could feel the heat of the seat warmers through his clothes.

When Carlton shut the door beside him, the sounds of the outside fell immediately silent, like Sam had been sealed inside an air-tight container. Albeit an air-tight container that was perfectly heated, gloriously comfortable, and inhabited by a gorgeous woman who was currently reaching over to grab Sam's hand in his lap.

"I suppose if you're going to spend the night at my house, we should at least introduce ourselves," she said. "I'm Kat Nestrom."

She squeezed Sam's hand, rubbing the back of her own hand very distractingly against Sam's thigh as she did. The car shook softly as Carlton loaded the luggage into the back with a soft thunk. Sam jumped and glanced over his shoulder out the back window.

"Sam Davis."

The car shook as Carlton slammed shut the trunk. Sam jumped again.

Kat squeezed Sam's hand once more and released it, running her hand slowly down his thigh to his knee, before Carlton opened the driver's door and slid into the front seat.

"Fifteen minutes to arrival, miss," he said.

"Thank you, Carlton."

Kat stared out her window as the car pulled away from the curb. Her flirtatious manner dropped from her tone.

"Is he... civil... today?"

Sam saw Carlton's eyes flick up to the rear-view mirror, then focus on the road again.

"Your father is aware of your arrival," he said.

Kat snorted and stared out the window.

Despite the warm air, to Sam the car suddenly felt cold.

Then Kat turned from the window and put her hand on his thigh again, this time sliding slowly up from the knee.

"Sam Davis," she said, and again flashed him that high-wattage smile as Sam's entire body tingled like a string of Christmas bells jingling. "We're going to have a very merry Christmas this year, you and I."

**4**

From the way she dressed, Sam wouldn't necessarily have guessed Kat was from a wealthy family. But you could never tell these days. With half of the billionaire CEOs out in California sporting hoodies all the time, the standard of dress for wealthy people had become unclear.

The five crisp hundred-dollar bills were a clue, though, as were Carlton and the expensive-looking car.

Expensive-looking *electric* car, no less. It slipped through the snowy night like a thief, smooth and quiet, the crunch of the new-fallen snow beneath the tires the only sound, its headlights the only illumination that Sam could see around them as they left the small town of Bridgeton far behind.

But when they pulled off the road, through an automatic gate, and down a drive, any doubt about Kat's financial situation disappeared from Sam's mind.

The house they pulled up to was nothing short of a palace. Massive and modern, the sprawling complex rose three stories high and curled around to either side, forming a cold embrace around the circular driveway. All concrete and wood and glass, the building looked like a tech product, like one of those smart home devices or a next-gen smartphone.

The last house lights Sam had seen were at least five miles back down the road. Out here in the middle of nowhere, in the inky dark night, the first thought that came to Sam's mind was that the enormous house seemed like the perfect place to rob. Elegant and impressive, it reeked of cool, effortless money and cold, calculating intellect. And places like that usually had glaring holes in their security, holes that you could drive a rich man's ego through.

Kat Nestrom.

Subconsciously, Sam's hand touched his pocket.

Touched the phone in his pocket.

Touched the Nestrom 2 phone in his pocket.

Kat was the daughter of the billionaire Christopher Nestrom, the guy who invented the smartphone in Sam's pocket. In everyone's pocket. Or he invented the tech behind it or something like that. Sam didn't exactly know. But Christopher Nestrom was fucking rich. That much, Sam knew.

"Home, sweet home," said Kat in a way that made it sound like anything but.

Sam had encountered a few very wealthy people in his life, and none of them had seemed happy. He was sure there had to be some happy rich people out there somewhere, but in Sam's experience, money wasn't what led to happiness. Happiness came from somewhere else. Sam hadn't quite figured out where, but he knew it didn't come from a bank statement.

Money didn't hurt. Not at all. It just wasn't the main answer.

Carlton opened Kat's door for her as Sam got out of the car on the other side. Kat came around the car and stood beside Sam as he gawked at the estate, his head tilted back to stare up at a spire that peaked at least fifty feet above him.

The entire front of the building was lit with a thousand soft yellow lamps. Sam felt like an ornament in a Christmas tree. Or, with the heavy snowfall quickly getting worse, maybe it was more like a snow globe.

The front door swung open, sending a blade of yellow-white light knifing along the snowy ground until it touched their feet. Sam felt Kat stiffen beside him. She squared her shoulders and gripped Sam's hand tight, her leather gloves creaking and cold around his bare skin.

She turned on that high-wattage smile again and pulled him toward the door.

"Miss Katerina." The man at the door had a bearing so regal it made Carlton seem like a stable boy. He tilted his head in slight bow. "Welcome home."

"Thank you, Phillip," said Kat in a drawl that made Sam wonder if she was intentionally mimicking the characters on Downton Abbey or if this was just the way rich people were taught to speak to their staff. "Is he here?"

"Dr. Nestrom is in his workshop at the moment."

"Of course he is. Will he be coming up anytime soon?"

"Dinner is scheduled for eight o'clock, miss."

"You mean he's not coming to say hello?" said Kat, her voice dripping with sarcasm.

Phillip paused for a fraction of a second, the tasteful rebuke of the professional server. "He has been informed of your arrival," he said, his tone betraying nothing but helpful competence.

Kat snorted as she peeled off her gloves.

"This is my friend, Sam," she said as she looked around the foyer, her boot heels clacking against the slate flooring.

Sam stepped through the door into a cavernous space, sparsely decorated, with smooth wood appointments along the walls and a muted painting or two. Probably original Michelangelo's or something equally extravagant. Doors led off to either side, and a wide staircase ascended before them, rising to a balcony that wrapped around the walls of the room one story up, leading to parts unknown.

"Have his bags brought to my room," said Kat.

"Of course, miss," nodded Phillip.

Sam reached out to shake Phillip's hand. Phillip stared at it as if Sam were holding the rotting head of a fish as a gift for him. Face of stone, aura of disgust.

The professional server.

"Madam and Mister Crowell are in the study enjoying cocktails with Master Brandon," said Phillip after closing the front door behind them.

"Thank you, Phillip," said Kat over her shoulder. "That will be all for now."

Phillip nodded solemnly, as if he could now die happy having fulfilled his purpose in life, and disappeared into the shadows.

There one moment, gone the next. Without a trace.

Sneaky like a thief, that Phillip. Just like the electric car.

"Come on, Sam," said Kat, slipping her arm through his. "Let's go meet the family."

The stiff rich lady was gone. The cool, interesting woman from the train was back again.

Sam wondered if Kat was even aware of this social schizophrenia she had, or if it was all just second-nature by now. Rich people were a different breed. It may be America, but it still had royalty. The only difference was that crowns in America were bought and sold with money, not blood. Mansions and staff and Madam this and Master that.

Different world. Different language. Different way of life.

Kat led him down a curved hallway to a set of doubledoors that were thrown wide open. The room was large, decorated like the foyer with more sumptuous, tasteful, largely colorless furnishings and appointments. Overstuffed couches and chairs arranged before a stone hearth with a sumptuous dark-wood mantle, a pool table in one corner, a tall bookshelf in another.

Leather and wood, stone and steel. It was like the middle ages, reforged with diamond-chamfered edges and high profit margins. It reeked of wealth and boredom.

A fire blazed in the hearth. As they approached, Sam could see a man and a woman seated on a luxurious leather couch before it. A second man, tall and muscular, stood by the hearth, arguing with the woman. The first man sat beside her, lost in his smartphone, seeming for all the world as if the other two didn't exist. They all had drinks in their hands, in crystal tumblers that sparkled in the firelight.

"Don't bother to meet me at the door," announced Kat as she released Sam's arm and entered the room two steps ahead of him. "It's not like you haven't seen me for a whole year or anything."

The man with the smartphone leapt from the couch, his face beaming, and practically ran to Kat, giving her a big hug.

"Sam, this is my brother-in-law, Thomas Crowell." Kat's smile seemed mostly sincere.

"Great to meet you, Sam."

His grip two-handed and mushy, Thomas worked Sam's arm like he was pumping water, grinning widely.

"And my sister, Cruella— I mean, Christa."

"There's that rapier wit again," said the woman, standing from the couch. She didn't smile, but pulled Kat into a long embrace. She broke the hold and studied Kat from arm's length, then held out her hand to Sam.

She looked older than Kat, but had the same deceptive features, the kind that could masquerade as merely beautiful but, at the flick of a switch, could become deadly gorgeous.

At that particular moment, they were in the deadly gorgeous configuration.

Her long red hair curled around her neck and rested over

one shoulder like a lazy cat. Her long bone-white dress rode the curves of her body like a sculptor working a pottery wheel. She wore a long white glove that extended to her elbow, and shook Sam's hand with only her fingers, bent at the knuckle. Sam didn't know people actually wore those kind of gloves anymore. And with the way she took his hand, he wasn't sure if he should shake it or kiss it.

This really was starting to feel like Downton Abbey.

"And that little punk by the fire is my ne'er-do-well twin brother, Brandon."

Brandon threw back the rest of his drink and set the empty tumbler on the wood mantle with a thunk before stalking toward his sister. He threw his arms around her in a great bear hug and spun her in a circle, Kat's laughter spilling out like diamonds on a stone floor.

Thomas and Christa returned to their seats with bored expressions on their faces.

When he put her down, Kat put her hands against her brother's cheeks and studied his face for a long moment.

"You're drinking too much," she said. "I can see it in your eyes." She sniffed the air around her brother. "And I can smell it all over you."

"Too much is a relative measure," Brandon replied. "One man's too much is another man's pour-me-another." He turned his head toward Sam. "I've always thought of myself as the other man," he said.

He reached out a hand to Sam.

"Brandon Nestrom."

"Hi," said Sam, taking Brandon's hand. "Sam Davis."

Brandon clamped Sam's hand in a vice grip. Sam was sure he could feel hairline fractures forming in his metacarpal bones. Brandon's stare was so intense that Sam felt his own brain might melt from the heat of it and ooze out his ears.

Kat came up behind and put her hand on her brother's shoulder. "Let him go, Brandon," she purred in his ear.

Brandon continued to melt Sam's brain with his glare.

"Yes, Brandon," drawled Christa from the couch. "You mustn't damage Kat's Christmas present before she's had a chance to unwrap it."

Brandon scowled, but released Sam from both his grip and his stare. He stalked to the sideboard and refilled his drink, leaving Kat looking at Sam with the kind of gaze that filled most men's wet dreams. Like a cat watches an unsuspecting mouse, imagining the meal it would make.

But Sam hadn't decided whether he wanted to be eaten.

Brandon returned with three glasses. He handed one to Kat and held another other out to Sam.

Sam took it, vaguely wondering if Brandon might have laced it with iocaine powder.

No. That would be inconceivable.

He noticed that his glass and Kat's each held two fingers of what smelled like bourbon, while Brandon's glass had the whole hand.

Brandon lifted his tumbler. "Merry Christmas," he said.

"Merry Christmas," said the others, even Thomas and Christa, in chorus, like the kind of conditioned response you hear from the congregation in a church service.

"Merry Christmas," said Sam a moment later.

But the others were already drinking.

# 5

DECEMBER 24, 6:19PM

"So, Sam, what do you do?" asked Thomas with a level of amiable interest that formed a stark contrast to the studied boredom of his wife.

"I'm a student," Sam replied, "at City College."

"Little old to be a student, aren't you?" said Brandon.

"I came to it later than most."

"Good for you," said Thomas. "What are you studying?"

"Criminology."

Brandon coughed and spluttered his drink. He swatted at the front of his shirt with annoyance.

"Don't you think you've had enough?" smiled Kat, soaking a napkin in tonic water from the sideboard. She dabbed at her twin brother's shirtfront. "It's not even seven o'clock and you've already forgotten how to swallow."

"Don't mind my brother," drawled Christa from the couch. "Alcoholism is his latest hobby. Like most of his other hobbies, he's not very good at it."

"What do you hope to do with your degree?" asked Thomas, his friendly smile completely unflappable.

Sam shrugged. "Maybe work for the government. FBI. CIA. DOD. Something like that might be interesting."

"I didn't realize the defense department hired criminologists," said Thomas.

"My focus is on computers. Data analysis, data science, that kind of thing. They're hiring for that skill set."

"Everyone is hiring for that skill set," said Brandon, refilling his glass again. He dropped heavily into the leather chair beside Sam. "It's the latest trend."

"Are you hiring data scientists, Thomas?" asked Kat. "Thomas runs my father's companies," she said as she sat on the arm of Sam's chair, holding her drink in one hand and wrapping the other arm around Sam's shoulder. She leaned close against him. Sam could feel the heat of her body, could feel the swell of her breast against his cheek.

He could feel something else start to swell, too.

He took a swallow of his drink.

"Thomas runs our father's errands, you mean," said Christa. She smiled sweetly at her husband.

"We're always looking for promising young talent," said Thomas.

"I suppose the young part is out," said Brandon.

"Are you promising?" asked Christa.

"Yes," smiled Kat, pressing herself more firmly against Sam. "Are you?"

"Are you talented?" asked Brandon.

"Yes," said Kat, her voice husky and low. "Are you?"

"Criminology is an interesting subject," Sam replied, doing his best not to think about what Kat was doing. Or what it was doing to him. "And the computer angle suits me well enough."

"'Suits me well enough'? Doesn't sound like Grade A material to me, Thomas," said Christa. "You'll have to shop elsewhere for fresh meat."

"I'm happy to chat with you, Sam," said Thomas. "Whenever you're ready."

"Phillip!" shouted Brandon.

The butler's form appeared in an instant, as if he'd been hiding behind a curtain the entire time.

"Can't you bring us some food, Phillip? I'm starving."

"Dinner is scheduled for eight o'clock, Master Brandon, but I will ask the staff to provide light refreshments for you."

"Thank God," Brandon muttered. "And tell them to bring up some of those little sandwiches I like. The ones with the cucumbers and the crusts cut off."

Phillip nodded as solemnly as if he'd been entrusted with state secrets, then evaporated once again.

"Crustless cucumber sandwiches?" scoffed Christa. "You're a child, Brandon."

"It's not my fault our dear father insists on eating dinner so late."

"Eight o'clock is not late."

"It is for dinner. I haven't eaten since lunch."

"Most people don't eat between lunch and dinner."

"Most people aren't forced to wait until eight o'clock."

Christa opened her mouth to say something else, but glanced at Kat and closed it again. Sam couldn't see Kat's expression from his position beneath her breast on the chair. There were worse problems to have, he had to admit.

Brandon downed his drink and bounced his knee, then shot to his feet.

"You shoot pool, Sam?" he said, walking to the pool table.

"A little."

"Get over here and shoot some nine-ball, then," said Brandon. "We've got to do something to pass the time before we're granted our audience with Dear Papa." He nodded toward a group of pool cues hanging in a rack on the wall. "You can pick first. You're the guest, after all."

Sam inspected the cues. They were all high-quality, hard maple two-piece cues, laser-straight. All had a similar shape and design except for one on the very end, which sported a gold-flecked ivory ferrule and a pressed Irish wrap, useful for players whose hands had a tendency to sweat.

Sam picked up the special cue. It was very heavy, and unlike the other cues, which had the common Pro taper, this one had the more conical European shape.

"That one's mine," said Brandon.

Sam glanced over his shoulder to see Brandon glowering at him, as if he would rip Sam's arms off to get his favorite cue from Sam's clutches.

Sam doubted Brandon would win in an actual fight, but he shrugged anyway and set the cue back in the rack. He hefted a few of the other cues. There was a variety of weights, ordered left-to-right in the holder from light to heavy. He chose a mid-weight cue, took a cube of blue chalk from the shelf, and stepped back from the rack.

Brandon quickly retrieved his cue. He took two balls from the rack and handed one to Sam. They each scraped some chalk over the tip of their cues, put their balls on the table, and shot the lag without another word.

The lag in pool determines who plays first. Two players stood shoulder to shoulder at one end of the table, simultaneously shooting one ball along the length of their side of the table, bouncing it against the far rail and letting it roll back to the rail in front of them. The player whose ball was closest to the near rail would play first.

Sam intentionally hit his lag heavy. He wanted Brandon to shoot first, to get a feel not just for his playing style, but also his competitiveness. Would he be a sore loser? Was he trying to prove something, to put Sam in his place? Or was he just looking, as he said, for a fun way to pass the time until dinner?

When the two balls came to rest, with Brandon's ball about an inch closer to the near rail, Brandon swept the two balls off the table. "You break," he said.

That surprised Sam. The winner of the lag won the right to choose who would play first. Most of the time, they would choose themselves.

By letting Sam shoot first, Brandon ran the risk of Sam, if he were a very good player, pocketing every ball and winning the game without Brandon even having a turn.

That meant one of two things. It could mean that Brandon was very kind to guests.

From the cue selection and Brandon's general attitude, Sam already knew that wasn't true.

It could also mean that Brandon was very confident in his playing abilities. Or that he figured Sam was not a very good player.

Either way, Sam was happy to play along. He wasn't there to piss anyone off. If all went well, once the storm blew over and the train lines opened in the morning, he'd be on his way again.

Brandon racked the balls into a tight diamond-shaped formation at the far end of the table. Nine-ball, as the name suggested, was played with nine balls, numbered sequentially from one to nine. They were racked in a diamond shape with the number-one ball at the front tip of the diamond, the number-two ball at the back tip, and the number-nine ball at the center. The remaining balls were randomly distributed to fill out the diamond shape.

To start the game, one player would hit the cue ball with force into the front ball, crashing into all the others and sending them flying around the table. Some would usually roll into pockets on the side of the table while the others caromed around until they came to rest. Then, players had to hit each remaining ball into the pockets. With each shot, the first ball struck by the white cue ball had to be the lowest numbered ball on the table.

If, during their turn, a player failed to pocket a ball, or if the cue ball went into a pocket, or if any one of a variety of other, more technical rules was broken, the second player would have a turn. The game would alternate back and forth in that way until the eponymous nine ball was pocketed.

Whoever sunk the nine ball was the winner.

Thomas and Kat stood behind Sam and Brandon, watching. Christa leaned over the back of the couch.

A crack rang out like a gunshot as Sam slammed the cue ball into the tip of the diamond. The balls ricocheted like agitated bees in a hive, back and forth around the table, bouncing off of the felt-covered rails, banging off of each other. One rolled into a pocket with a thunk, then another, then a third.

When they had all come to rest, Sam surveyed the table and turned to Brandon.

"Another game?"

Brandon's eyes rounded for a moment as he scanned the table, searching for the nine ball.

It wasn't there. It had rolled into a pocket after Sam's break shot. That meant Sam was the winner.

Brandon's face immediately darkened. Definitely competitive.

"Another of Brandon's hobbies, obviously," called Christa from the couch.

Brandon glanced at Kat, who hid a smile behind her tumbler of whiskey. "Rack 'em," Brandon snarled at Sam. He stomped to the sideboard to pour himself another drink.

He didn't offer to get one for Sam.

Definitely a sore loser.

As Sam gathered the balls and reset them into their diamond shape, a staff member came into the room through a door Sam hadn't even noticed. Even as he watched the man enter, Sam could barely make out the edges of the opening, so cleverly and invisibly was it built into the wall.

That must have been how Phillip magically appeared and disappeared.

The staff member pushed a small cart draped with a table-cloth. On the cart were two silver platters. One platter held a variety of crackers and crostini loaded with intricately carved or arranged foods. One had what looked like thin-sliced lox twisted to look like a pink rose, with little squares of green cucumber underneath like petals, all set into a bed of herbed soft cheese. Another had some kind of goat cheese spread topped with avocado and herbs.

The other platter held cut vegetables and dip, hummus and pita, squares of hard cheese, and bunches of red and black grapes.

Between the platters on the cart was a silver coffee pot and several ceramic mugs, along with a pot of cream and a bowl of sugar.

"Where are the fucking cucumber sandwiches?" cried Brandon from the sideboard.

His tumbler was filled nearly to the rim. Sam was starting to wonder how Brandon was still standing after drinking so much whiskey.

"My apologies, Master Brandon," said Phillip.

Again, Phillip had materialized from thin air. He hadn't come through the hidden door. Sam had been staring right at it. The man was a wizard.

"The kitchen staff were unable to prepare the sandwiches you requested," Phillip said. "I do apologize for the incon-venience."

As he glared at Phillip, Brandon's face turned blood-red. Sam waited for it to explode.

Phillip stared back at Brandon, his face impassive and cool.

Cool as a cucumber.

Brandon sighed heavily, his shoulders rounding and sagging, all menace draining from him in an instant. "Fine," he said sulkily.

"There are cucumbers included with the crudité, Master Brandon," said Phillip. "I hope they are to your liking."

"Okay," mumbled Brandon. He seemed more like a chastened child before a strict parent than a grown man speaking to his butler. "Thank you, Phillip."

Phillip nodded solemnly. With a quick gesture to the other staff, they left the room through the hidden doorway.

No one moved or said anything. They just stared at the cart laden with food. Even Brandon didn't move toward the snacks, though he'd been the one to request them. He just gulped his whiskey, his hand in his pocket.

"Are you two going to play pool," said Christa at last from the couch, "or should we stare at each other until dinner?"

**6**

Sam and Brandon played three more games.

Brandon had declared Sam's first victory a fluke, so Sam let Brandon win the next game.

When Brandon offered best two-out-of-three, Sam took the second game for himself. He didn't want Brandon to catch on that Sam was letting him win.

Brandon was not a good pool player. He talked a good game and he had a fancy cue, but his technique was unstudied. His cue ball leaves were inconsistent, his spin control was atrocious, and his understanding of strategy was non-existent.

He was all talk and no walk.

If they were in a pool hall, Sam would be playing Brandon—not just playing against him, but playing him—all night long, milking the rich dilettante for all he was worth.

And Brandon would be too insecure, headstrong, and arrogant to notice.

But they weren't playing for money, and Sam wasn't there to make Brandon feel foolish in front of his family.

He tried hard to let Brandon win the third game, but Brandon made things difficult. When it finally came down to the last ball, Sam intentionally missed his shot and left a perfect setup for Brandon. All Brandon had to do was hit the cue ball straight with just a hint of backspin and he'd win the game.

Unfortunately, that easy setup was not easy enough. Brandon got too excited. He hit the nine ball into the pocket, but he hit it way too hard. He screamed in anger as the nine ball went into the pocket, bounced off the back, and popped onto the table again.

Sam managed to keep himself from sighing out loud as he moved to set up for another shot.

"That was in," said Brandon.

"It has to stay in for it to count," said Sam, quoting the rule without thinking as he bent over the table to line up his next shot. His focus was on finding a way to somehow make Brandon's next shot even easier.

"The ball was in," said Brandon again.

He stepped up close to Sam.

Sam glanced beside him and saw that Brandon was holding his pool cue upside down, with the thick end up. Brandon's knuckles flushed white as his hand gripped the cue like a bludgeon.

Sam stood straight and looked Brandon in the eye.

Brandon's face was impassive. There was no flush of anger like there had been with Phillip and the cucumber sandwiches. Brandon's eyes were not wild with rage like they had been when the ball bounced out of the pocket.

All Sam saw in Brandon's eyes was cold observation. He watched Sam like a hawk watches a mouse.

Sam felt his own indignation rise. He didn't like assholes who twisted the rules to suit whatever insecurity they were trying to hide. He didn't like spoiled rich kids who were used to getting their own way. And he didn't like bullies who used intimidation to win.

But what was the point of standing up for the rules of a pool game when nothing was on the line? No money, no pride. There wasn't even an audience, beyond a bored heiress, her lap-dog husband, and Kat, who had been undressing Sam with her eyes all night long and clearly didn't give a shit about pool.

"Okay," said Sam, setting his cue on the table. "It was in. Congratulations." He held out his hand to Brandon.

Only then did the cool impassivity in Brandon's eyes waver, replaced with a flash of anger, like Sam had deprived Brandon of the game he really wanted to play—a brawl with Sam.

Brandon didn't back down. Even as Sam held Brandon's gaze, he could hear Brandon's fist tighten on the cue, could feel the menace thicken in the thin space between them.

"Oh, goody." From the doorway behind them came a voice dripping with boredom and sarcasm. "The next of kin are all here."

A shadow seemed to flick across Brandon's eyes and he stood confused for a moment, as if he were waking from a dream.

"Auntie," called Christa as she stood from the couch. "I didn't realize they were disinterring you tonight."

"Time for my annual dusting, I suppose," said the woman.

Brandon set his cue on the pool table and backed hurriedly away, scurrying to the sideboard and pouring himself yet another drink.

From Christa's comment, Sam expected the new arrival to be an ancient relative. But he turned to see a woman at the door who, while certainly older, was anything but old. She looked to be in her early fifties, tall and thin, with long legs and smooth skin. Her short, white-blond hair was close-cropped underneath and poured over the top and down to her ears like a frozen waterfall.

She wore tight black jeans and leather boots, a loose black top cut in a deep V-neck, and a large gold belt buckle with two overlapping circles, some logo that Sam assumed represented an expensive clothing brand. While understated in design, her clothes reeked of money in their materials and the way they flattered the woman's figure.

Christa gave the woman an air kiss beside each cheek and a hug that lasted too long to be anything but sincere. Thomas pecked one of the woman's cheeks with a broad smile.

"Katerina," the woman cooed as Kat approached. "You look lovelier each time I see you."

"I've got your genes, Aunt Cress," said Kat as she gave the woman a hug. Sam had never seem Kat's high-wattage smile brighter than in that moment.

"You certainly didn't get it from your father," said the woman.

"Sam," said Kat leading the woman toward him, "this is my Aunt Cressida."

"Well, well," said Kat's aunt, scanning Sam slowly from top to bottom and back again, "you've outdone yourself this year, Kat."

The woman held out her hand to Sam, palm down, fingers bent. Sam had no idea what to do with that gesture except to take the woman's hand in his and kiss the back of it like she were the queen of England.

"And a gentleman, as well." Kat's aunt purred. She pulled him toward her and ran her hand over Sam's arm, stopping to feel his biceps. "Mmm, mmm," she said, practically curling up in Sam's lap. "I may have to take a turn with him first."

Sam had never been discussed like a sex toy in a display case at a kink shop before. Not to his face, at least. He wasn't sure whether to feel offended or amused. For the sake of civility, he put an amused smile on his face.

"It's nice to meet you, Aunt Cressida," said Sam.

"I'm not *your* aunt, honey," said the woman. "When you're screaming my name later tonight, you can call me Cress."

Sam's amused smile faltered.

Kat removed Sam's hand from her aunt's grip and slipped it around her own waist, pulling herself close against him. "This one's not for sharing, Auntie," she said.

Cress arched one eyebrow, never taking her eyes from Sam's. Her eyes were a light, crystal blue, clear as diamonds.

"We'll leave that for him to decide," she said with a wink as she spun on her heel, watching Sam's reaction the entire time.

"No hello for your dear Aunt Cress, Brandon?" she said. "What is it this time? Did Phillip hide your dollies again?"

Brandon set his drink on the sideboard and dutifully gave Cress a hug. Despite the harsh words, Cress held him tightly, rubbing her hands against his back, then held his cheeks in her hands, peering into his eyes.

"Brandon, honey, what are you doing to yourself?" she murmured.

Brandon shrugged.

"Come on," she said, throwing her arm over his shoulder and steering him to the couch, "come sit by me and tell me what's going on with you."

"My father's older sister," said Kat.

"Older? How young is your dad?"

Kat arched her eyebrow at him and smiled, just the way her aunt had done a moment before. "You're not the first one to be fooled. Aunt Cress looks like she's forty, but she's almost seventy."

"That number counts all the things I've learned how to do," called Cress, turning to look over her shoulder from the couch. "I'll be happy to show them to you tonight." She winked at him again. "You'll be very happy when I do, believe me."

This time it was Sam's eyebrows that arched high. He shook his head. Almost seventy or not, Kat's Aunt Cress was a gorgeous woman. Despite himself, he couldn't help picturing what things she might have to show him. It wasn't an unpleasant image.

Kat scowled at him. Her expression was playful, but her eyes were fierce.

Sam opened his mouth to say something, anything, to diffuse the tension.

Phillip spared him the trouble.

"Ladies and gentlemen," Phillip said as he appeared in the doorway, a clock striking the hour somewhere in the background, "dinner is served."

# 7

DECEMBER 24, 8:23PM

The dining room was huge by any standard, but the massive table in the center made it feel long and narrow. There was enough space around the stone dining table for the bustling staff to do their work, but little else. The dark wood walls, punctuated by chaotic pieces of abstract art in scuffed metal frames, like portholes to madness, only deepened the cloistered feeling.

The feeling was offset only by the ceiling, which had to have been at least twenty feet high and was composed of a series of long windows arranged in a rectangular pyramid above them. Soft lights illuminated the scene outside the windows so that even in the dark night, despite the reflections from the light inside the dining room far below, Sam could clearly see the blizzard raging outside, the driving snow a sheet of white beyond the glass.

He wondered how it was that the glass was still clear when he could see snow already accumulating on the rooftops of the rest of the house around it.

"It's heated," said Thomas.

Sam glanced to his left and saw Thomas looking up at the ceiling, too.

"Blew my mind the first time I saw it. They light the area around the windows at night and heat the glass to keep the snow off in the winter." He smiled at Sam. "So you always have a perfect view of the world through the glass."

Sam could smell food nearby, hot and rich. It set his stomach rumbling, but there was no food to be seen. Only a vast table filled with glasses and dishes and surrounded by sullen people.

Half of the table was empty, with the sullen group arranged at one end. The head of the table remained open, presumably for Kat's father. Thomas sat on Sam's left with Christa across the table from him. Kat took the seat to Sam's right, with Brandon across the table from her. That left Cress seated directly opposite Sam, holding him in a predatory gaze as they waited for Kat's father to arrive.

Waited.

And waited.

And waited.

"I thought dinner was supposed to be at eight," growled Brandon.

In front of Sam on the table was more china and cutlery and glassware than Sam had ever seen before. The place setting had enough equipment for four people, at least.

A large platter sat in front of him with a bowl on top. To the left were two forks, the outer fork smaller than the inner fork. On the right were two knives and two spoons, descending in size as they worked away from the plate. All were perfectly straight, perfectly spaced, as if the place setting were set down with a stencil.

Above the plate were another fork and spoon, facing in opposite directions from one another and laying perpendicular to the other cutlery. Beside that, on the left, were a small plate with a knife laid across it and a coffee cup on a saucer. On the right were four crystal glasses. One was a champagne flute and the other three looked like wine glasses.

Why anyone would need three separate glasses for wine was beyond Sam. The only thing that seemed normal to him was the napkin, which he spread onto his lap. Everything else seemed ridiculously extravagant.

"Do you eat like this all the time?" said Sam to Kat.

She shook her head. "When we eat together its usually only three courses. And father never eats with us. This is only for Christmas."

"His gift to the family," muttered Brandon.

"Usually only three courses? How many courses are we having tonight?"

Kat's lips twisted into a cringing smile. "Nine."

"I hope you're hungry," said Cress across the table to Sam. From the tone of her voice and the look in her eye, Sam didn't think she was only talking about food.

"I'm sure he'll get his fill," said Kat back to her aunt, her eyes steely as she stared across the table. Her hand slipped along Sam's thigh under the table, nestling itself close to his crotch. Parts of Sam began to reach for Kat's hand of their own volition.

Maybe he was hungry after all.

"When the fuck are we going to eat?" said Brandon. "Phillip!" he shouted, holding up the empty tumbler he'd brought from the billiard room. "Bring me another drink."

"You've had quite enough, Brandon," came an imperious voice from Sam's left.

The first thing Sam noticed was the change in everyone's attitude at the sound of the voice. Where before there had been smirks or looks of irritation, now there were blank expressions. Where before people had slouched in their seats, now they all sat straight. Even Cress cast her eyes downward in deference at the sound of the commanding voice.

Sam turned to see a man stride into the room and fought to

stifle the gasp that tried to escape. He was sure that the look on his face was one of poorly-concealed surprise and delight.

Dr. Christopher Nestrom was as well-known for his reclusiveness as he was for being one of the richest people in the world. Half of the people in the world carried a device of his design in their pocket, including Sam. The other half wished they could afford to.

Powerful in both build and carriage, the man held an aura of strength and authority about him. He wore a black t-shirt over black jeans and black sneakers. His full head of hair was black, shot with just a hint of grey, and trimmed long on top, giving him an air of both sumptuous elegance and vivacious youth.

His face, however, was deeply lined around his mouth and his eyes. His cheeks were hollow, carving down to a sharp jaw line and a pointed chin.

But his eyes.

Those were what caught Sam's attention.

They blazed with an arresting intensity. They seemed to see everything, understand everything, all at once, to peer through the masks of deception and politeness everyone wore and perceive the truth of the world.

And to find it wanting.

"I apologize for making you wait," he said as he sat, drawing his napkin across his lap with a snap.

Immediately, Phillip and an army of staff appeared with water jugs, wine bottles, soup tureens and ladles, filling two of their glasses, one with water and the other with white wine, and spooning some kind of green soup into the bowls that sat before them. One staff member would spoon a ladle full of soup into the bowl, a second would follow with a dollop of cream, and a third would add a drizzle of olive oil. Two teams of servers worked each side of the table, providing everyone with their food in a remarkably efficient manner.

"Who is your guest this year, Katerina?" said Kat's father as he leaned over his bowl and brought a spoonful of soup to his mouth. His voice betrayed no particular emotion beyond polite interest, but Sam still felt an air of disdain at the comment.

"This is Sam Davis," Kat said. "Sam and I met on the train from the city this afternoon. When the storm closed the track, I invited him to stay for Christmas until it opens again."

"Very kind of you," said her father, his words again carrying that hidden payload of disapproval.

"Sam," said Kat, "this is my father, Dr. Christopher Nestrom."

Sam could see from his surroundings that Kat was wealthy, but her father was next-level wealthy. Nestrom was wealthy *and* powerful. The kind of power that controls heads of state.

The kind of power that usually turns people into insufferable assholes.

"It's a pleasure to meet you, sir," said Sam, "and thank you for your hospitality. It's very kind of you to allow me to join you during your holiday."

Nestrom set his spoon down in his bowl and stared at Sam. It was the first time Sam had felt the power of the man's gaze, and it was all he could do to keep himself from looking away. The intensity in his eyes was a weapon. Sam felt as though the backs of his retinas were being pummeled by a thousand tiny bullets of judgement, like buckshot from a shotgun. It felt like Nestrom were probing Sam's mind through that stare.

Sam stared back.

Dr. Nestrom was probably used to people cowering before him, shrinking away from that powerful gaze. That meant he probably didn't have his own defenses in place. Sam fought the instinctive urge to cower and studied the man, looked deep into his eyes, trying to find out what made him tick. Sometimes first impressions say the most.

But from this distance across the table, Sam could see only cold curiosity. There was passion there, too. Anger, even. But it seemed muted, like coals banked in a fire. Like sitting to dinner with his family on Christmas Eve was the last thing Dr. Christopher Nestrom wanted to do.

Nestrom closed his eyes, his cheeks twitching. Sam was afraid he'd somehow upset the man, angered him with his stare, perhaps. He didn't want to make an enemy of Nestrom, if he could avoid it. Though that was probably impossible.

Nestrom pulled in a deep breath. By the time he let it out, the twitching in his cheeks had stopped, and he opened his eyes again. They were even more intense than before. As he stared into space, they slowly came back into focus.

"Thomas, did you sign the papers for the Questron acquisition yet?" he said, resuming his eating without further comment to Sam.

"Our lawyers are still going back and forth with them on a few things."

"Our lawyers are idiots."

"Our lawyers are the best in the world. I hired each of them personally. They're protecting our—"

"Never mind," said Nestrom. "I'll sign it myself in the morning." He took another swallow of soup. "How are you, Trucky? Any venereal diseases this year?"

Trucky? Sam looked around the table, unsure who Nestrom was referring to.

"There's still time, Richard," said Cress with a slow drawl. "I'm still hoping for another shot at the prize." She looked across at Sam as she brought a spoonful of soup to her mouth, somehow managing to make the gesture feel seductive.

"Just try to keep it out of the papers this time."

"Father," said Christa, "I'd like to use the jet next week. I want to ring in the New Year in Tenerife this year with Thomas. All of this cold weather is making me dreary."

"Thomas can't even close a simple acquisition deal. Now you want me to reward him with a jet ride to Spain?"

"I want you to reward *me* with a jet ride to Spain," replied Christa. "Thomas can stay behind if you need him to."

Sam felt Thomas stiffen beside him, but he didn't look up from his soup.

"And what have *you* done that merits reward, Christa? Hmm?" Nestrom stared at his daughter as he swallowed another mouthful of soup. "Most money wasted on unnecessary clothing? Top spender on jewelry? Most efficient waste of space?"

Christa's face reddened and Sam thought he saw a glint in her eyes as she turned her gaze down to her lap.

"No, Christa," said Nestrom, his spoon scraping against his bowl as he finished his soup. He wiped his mouth with his napkin and sat back in his chair, signaling to Phillip with one hand. "If you want to go to Tenerife so badly, you can find your own way to get there."

The army of staff emerged again, removing everyone's soup bowls whether they were finished with them or not. Sam had his spoon halfway to his mouth when a staff member swooped in from his right and lifted his still half-full bowl. The man hovered patiently until Sam realized he was waiting for the spoon. Sam pulled it from his mouth and set it in the bowl. The staff member whisked away.

As one phalanx of staff filed out of the room with the soup bowls, another entered carrying small plates of food and set one before each of them. Sam looked down at his to see charred broccoli with peppers and pink onions, along with mushrooms stuffed with cheese and bread crumbs.

He looked at Kat, who held up the small fork on the outside. Sam smiled, thankful for the pointer, and scarfed the food before the staff could come and take it from him again.

It didn't take long to finish the small plate of food, and Sam ended up finishing well before the others, giving him time to sit and observe. Despite having her request so brutally denied, Christa reinstated her smiling countenance, quite different from the snarky, world-weary socialite she'd seemed in the billiard room. And Thomas remained polite, but quiet, in front of his boss. An interesting switch from the way both had behaved before dinner.

Brandon and Kat stayed mostly silent at the ends of the table. Brandon, in particular, seemed to want to hide. He ate his food quickly and quietly and kept his eyes mostly on the table before him, looking like a child who had been punished.

Or who might be punished at any moment.

Kat had removed her hand from Sam's leg as soon as her father walked in. Aside from the introductions, she hadn't said a word since, and had only picked at the food on her plate.

Cress was already on her second glass of white wine. Aside from a few spoonfuls of soup, she was ignoring her food entirely, so far.

No one spoke with anyone but their father. And, aside from Christa's request, no one spoke unless first spoken to by Nestrom.

It was definitely not the very merry Christmas celebration Sam had been expecting.

It felt more like the last supper of the damned.

**8**

Three more courses passed in near silence, the only sounds the clink of cutlery against china, the rustling efficiency of the staff. A mixed-green salad dressed in bright, fresh lemon. A crispy fish with the head still on, the dead fish eye staring up at Sam, shocked at the audacity of its slaughter for his enjoyment. A tender lamb chop served with mint and slim fingers of roasted carrot, accompanied by red wine in the third wine glass set before them.

Staff members came to clear the table and present the next course the instant Dr. Nestrom finished his portion, or when he signaled them, whichever came first. There was no consideration whatsoever for the other people at the table. It was clear to Sam that, from the point of view of the staff, the others were Nestrom's dinner observers, not his dinner companions. The fact that the observers were fed while they observed was merely an annoying inconvenience.

After the lamb, as the butler, Phillip, directed the staff in clearing the plates and glasses, filling the champagne flutes, and

50

delivering the smallest bowl of sorbet Sam had ever seen, Dr. Nestrom leaned back in his chair and stared hard at Sam.

"You're a third-year student of Criminology at City College," he said, "with a focus on data science."

It was not a question.

Sam had told the others as much in the billiard room before dinner. That could easily have gotten back to Nestrom via the staff. In the movies, staff were always gossiping. Maybe that was true in real life.

But Sam wondered how Nestrom knew Sam was a junior. He hadn't mentioned that detail to the others.

"Yes, si—"

"Your grades are exemplary, as is the quality of your work. You're top of your class by a wide margin, but your professors claim you show little interest in pursuing a career in the subject."

Nestrom had to have done some kind of background check. A thorough one. And he had to have done it in the two hours between Sam entering the house and Nestrom sitting down to dinner.

Nestrom was a tech billionaire, and had been for a long time. Sam wasn't surprised he had the resources to pull up dirt on someone. He could probably find the personal cell number of the president's third-favorite prostitute within three minutes.

But still. This shit was creepy.

Sam said nothing. He merely stared back at Nestrom.

Nestrom hadn't asked a question, after all. And from the way he'd cut Sam off a moment ago, it was clear he wasn't looking for conversation. If Nestrom was going to play internet stalker, Sam would let him have his fun.

"Your history prior to matriculation is equally interesting. A number of different grade schools and high schools over the years. Top of your class in each. Again, though, you showed great aptitude but little passion for your subjects."

Sam smiled slightly at that. How many high school kids showed passion for their subjects?

"A great deal of displacement as a child, with some gaps in your school enrollment record. You only graduated with other children your age because of your remarkable ability to complete the coursework you had missed, even when you had enrolled just a few months before the end of term."

"Daddy, do we really have to do this inquisition every time?" said Kat softly, with a smile. She seemed to be trying to charm her father into easing off on Sam.

It didn't work.

"Yes, Katerina. We do," said Nestrom sharply, his eyes boring into Kat's. His mouth worked strangely, jerking and spasming, like Nestrom had something he wanted to say, but could barely keep himself from saying it. He pressed his lips into a flat line, let out a huff through his nose, and the spasming stopped.

"Even more so this time," Nestrom continued, his voice now calm, but still menacing. "Your usual friends"—he said the word with a sneer—"are bad enough. But if you're going to bring a stranger off the train to spend the night under my roof, I have the right to know who he is."

His eyes slid back to Sam, one corner of his mouth perked. "If that requires an inquisition, so be it."

Nestrom continued. "Your parents have an even more colorful past," he said, watching Sam closely. "Both career criminals, escaping arrest seemingly through a mix of cleverness and dumb luck." His slight smile did not reach his cold eyes. "This explains your frequent moves during your childhood."

*Dumb luck.* Sam clenched his fists under the table. He could feel the blood draining from his face, but didn't allow himself to look away from Nestrom. He noticed for the first time that Nestrom's eyes were pale, almost colorless.

Nestrom seemed to sense Sam's unease. Those pale eyes

narrowed slightly and the smile at one corner of his mouth spread to the other.

"Your parents escaped arrest until one day, about fifteen years ago, when your father was shot and killed during a bank robbery." He paused, tilting his head at Sam as if observing a lab rat after administering an experimental drug. "Killed in your mother's arms."

Sam tore his eyes away then, staring down at the ridiculous bite of blood-red sorbet in the frost-cold earthenware cup before him.

"Tragic," Nestrom continued. "Unlucky, really. The robbery was someone else's. Your father got caught in a crossfire as the thieves made their escape. Your mother was recognized by the police on the scene as she was trying to resuscitate him. When the ambulance arrived, your father was already dead." His smile widened. "And your mother was already in custody."

Sam felt Kat's hand on his fist. After a moment, he opened it to grip her hand in his, grateful for her warmth.

"And she has been incarcerated ever since, serving four consecutive ten-year sentences for robbery. In a federal prison just north of here, actually." Nestrom brought his champagne flute to his lips, his eyes sliding to Kat. "Just a few stops farther on the train." He drank deeply, draining his glass, then bent forward to his sorbet.

As if it were a signal, the others, who had been sitting dead silent and perfectly still, bent to their own desserts.

Robotic, mechanical, his mind spinning in place like a race car on ice, Sam did the same.

Nothing Nestrom had said was a surprise to Sam, of course, aside from the fact that Nestrom knew it at all. The unfeeling delivery was irritating, naturally, and probably done intentionally to antagonize Sam. Why Nestrom would bother antagonizing Sam, a nobody that Nestrom had just met, Sam had no idea. But who knew what went on in the minds of these reclusive billionaires? They were practically a different species.

Besides, the antagonism didn't work. Sam didn't usually divulge his life story to a table full of people he'd just met, but he wasn't ashamed of anything Nestrom had said. He just didn't like being reminded of it during dessert.

As far as any criminal implications, Sam had been a minor during his parents' criminal careers. Any record of Sam's criminal involvement would have been expunged when he became an adult.

If his parents had ever been caught.

Which they hadn't.

His parents had been too smart for that. Too careful. Too gifted. As far as the authorities knew, Sam had no involvement in the robberies over the years.

Sam didn't mind that Nestrom had exposed his history, and he didn't really mind that he'd done it so coldly. He didn't even mind the casual way Nestrom had mentioned Sam's father's death.

What he minded was that Nestrom seemed to enjoy it. He seemed to enjoy knowing that Sam was surprised at how much information Nestrom had gathered in such a short time.

Sam was guessing at Nestrom's feelings, of course, but Sam had studied people for a long time. His whole life, really. It was one of the many things his parents had taught him. Nestrom seemed like the type of person who, above all else, wanted to feel like the smartest person in the room.

At all times.

At all costs.

And just like Brandon at the pool table, Sam was happy to let him believe it.

The sorbet was a tart black raspberry, a deep red, with a tang that puckered Sam's tongue. It was a single scoop, barely two mouthfuls, served in a hard earthenware cup that was as cold as the sorbet itself.

"Your interest in criminology is obvious," said Nestrom after he'd swallowed his last bite of sorbet and the staff had cleared the earthenware cups and champagne flutes and replaced them with tiny glasses of port wine and plates of chocolate cake, "as is the source of the funds to pay for your education. Though I do wonder how those funds escaped reclamation by the authorities." He smiled at Sam, this time with a shine in his eyes. "I'm sure I'll have that answer by morning."

Sam looked at the cake on his plate. A sharp slice of dense, rich chocolate, dusted with powdered sugar. Three raspberries nestled beside it. An odd three-tined fork balanced on the plate next to that. Sam had never seen a fork like it before. Short and narrow, rounded on one side.

A fork made specifically for dessert? For chocolate cake?

The wealthy were insane.

Nestrom tipped his glass of port up to his lips. When he pulled it away, his lips were stained as dark red as the sorbet had been.

"What I wonder," Nestrom continued, "is what you intend to do when you graduate. Do you think you can get your mother released from prison? Do you intend to go on to study law and appeal her convictions? Curry favor with Attorney General Jenkins by graduating as valedictorian from his beloved alma mater? Is all of this the attempt of a naive and misguided child to rescue his sole surviving parent from living the rest of her life in jail?"

He set down his glass and forked a bite of cake into his mouth, the powdered sugar covering the port wine stain on his lips like the snow outside would cover a blood stain on the decking. He chewed thoughtfully, patiently, then raised his eyebrows to Sam.

"Are you waiting for an answer?" said Sam.

Nestrom swallowed. "If you wouldn't mind."

"And if I would?"

Nestrom gave a toothy grin, and a shiver ran down Sam's spine. "You're a handsome young man. I'm sure there are any number of homes that would take in a needy stranger like yourself on a frigid, wintery night. It is Christmas Eve, after all. People like to pretend they're good on Christmas Eve." He took another bite, spoke while he chewed. "Although I will warn you, it'll be tough to get an Uber in this weather, and the nearest home is at least seven miles away."

Sam smiled softly and took a bite of his own cake. It was delicious, rich and smooth and heavy, almost like fudge. He chewed slowly, looking around the table. Brandon's head was bent so low he was practically eating directly from his plate. Christa and Thomas looked only at their plates and at each other, eating their desserts mechanically, one bite after another, jaws working up and down, up and down. Cress had seemed half-drunk by the fish course. She seemed fully gone now, lolled back in her chair, ignoring the cake, but clutching her empty port glass to her breast like it was the photo of a lost lover.

Only Kat, beside Sam, seemed like she'd been listening at all. Her brow was furrowed, her jaw clenched as she stared at her plate. She cut a bite from her cake, the side of her fork clinking hard against the china. She put it slowly in her mouth, but did not chew. When she noticed Sam looking at her, she slid her hand into his once more and gave it a single, firm squeeze.

Sam sipped his port and savored the way the sweet, silky liquid accented the chocolate and even brought back hints of the raspberry sorbet.

The wealthy might be insane, but they had good taste in food.

"Education is its own reward," Sam said at last. "My parents"—he lingered on the word—"taught me that. Thanks to them, I don't need money, so I don't need to work." He shrugged and took another bite of cake. "I'm just using my good fortune to better myself as best I can."

Nestrom stared at him for a long moment, hard and intense.

Sam stared back, relaxed and politely curious.

He no longer felt the impact of Nestrom's intense stare. He had nothing to prove to Nestrom, and nothing to hide. Tomorrow morning, Sam would be gone and would never see Nestrom or his family again.

Nestrom was an egomaniac, through and through, and a bully. But if the man needed to play some kind of mind game with Sam, so be it. That was his problem.

After a long moment, Nestrom grinned, threw back the rest of his port, and signaled to Phillip. The staff scurried to clear away the plates.

"I'll take my coffee in my office, Phillip," he said.

"Very good, sir," Phillip bowed.

"Enjoy your evening, everyone," he muttered as he stood, wiping his mouth on his napkin. "And Mr. Davis," he said. "Don't run off in the morning." He dipped his head and grinned knowingly. Sam felt a chill come over him. "There's something I would like to discuss with you before you go."

With that, he left the room. The only sound was the sound of the staff going about their work. And the stunned silence of the others.

# 9



After a second of silence, the room burst into a cacophony of sound, the chatter of voices rushing to fill the silence like air rushes to fill a vacuum, everyone talking over each other.

"Jesus, I thought he'd never leave," said Christa.

"What the fuck was that all about?" said Brandon.

"He's even worse than I remember," said Cress, "and I remember a lot."

"Can you fucking believe the way he grilled Sam?" said Kat.

Thomas said nothing, but shook his head angrily.

Only Sam was quiet, unperturbed.

The staff had set pots of coffee in the center of the table, along with plates of macarons and madeleines. They wheeled in a cart with more port wine, and decanters of what looked like brandy and Scotch. Brandon immediately got up to pour himself three fingers of Scotch, tossing back the first pour while standing at the cart, then refilling his glass before slumping back down in his chair.

The shift in attitude was dramatic and immediate. The

instant the door had closed behind Nestrom, the demeanor of every person in the room had changed markedly. From reticent to opinionated. From deferential to irreverent. From demure to angry.

And no one had a kind word for their father.

"I'm sorry, Sam," said Kat, laying her hand on his arm. "You didn't deserve to be spoken to like that. He was way out of line."

"He did the same thing to me the first time I met him," said Thomas. "Don't take it personally."

"Do take it personally," said Christa. "Unlike my husband, maybe you've got the balls to do something about it."

Sam could feel Thomas tense beside him, but Thomas didn't say anything, just stood to pour himself a brandy.

"I'll have a brandy, too, dear," called Christa sweetly across the table.

"My brother is an asshole," said Cress, her words slurring just a touch. "Always has been, always will be, until the day he dies."

"May that day be as soon as possible," said Brandon, holding up his glass.

All the others held up their glasses, too, as if on cue, then drank in a momentary silence. The silence continued for a few more moments, each person seemingly lost in their own thoughts.

"Anyway, you won't see him again," said Kat. "He's had his fun for the night, and now he's back in his workshop doing whatever the fuck he does."

"He's down there all day, all night, every day, every night," said Brandon to his glass. "Never comes up for meals, takes all of his meetings virtually, even sleeps down there half the time."

Thomas laughed ruefully. "He doesn't take meetings at all, virtually or otherwise."

"His next big invention," said Cress. "The famous Dr. Christopher Nestrom, unparalleled genius, gone to the mountaintop until he deigns to cast his pearls before the swine of humanity."

"Only the mountaintop is a Batcave," said Christa.

"Like Tony Stark," sneered Brandon. "He thinks he's a super-hero. Saving humanity one glitchy smartphone at a time."

"What is he working on these days?" asked Sam.

Kat snorted. "You think he tells us? We're not even allowed in there. It's all sealed tight with biometric locks. He's got cameras, motion detectors, lockdown doors. Fucking place has more security than the Mona Lisa at the Louvre."

"Even his supposed CEO over here has no clue what he's doing," said Christa, gesturing across the table at her husband. "His Number 2 man. Might as well be number two million."

Thomas didn't look up at his wife, but he turned his head when Sam looked at him.

"It's true," Thomas nodded. "I approve the R&D budget each fiscal year, and there's a line item that's all for him. A big one. But I have no idea how it's spent. I'm just rubber-stamping it as a tax deduction for him."

"You don't approve shit, darling," scoffed Christa. "You just do what you're told, like a good little doggie."

"And what does that make you, then?" said Brandon.

"A good little dog sitter," said Christa.

She smiled over her glass at Thomas as she sipped her brandy. Thomas smiled back, seemingly unperturbed by his wife's insults. There was a glint of conspiracy in his smile, the kind you see between a couple that has been together for a long time.

It was the first time Sam had seen the slightest hint of intimacy between them.

"He doesn't spend any time with you at all?" said Sam.

"Never has before," said Brandon. "Why would he start now?"

"Even when you were little kids?"

"The only person my dear brother loves is himself," said Cress.

"The only *living* person," Kat corrected.

They all fell eerily silent, staring into their glasses or up at the ceiling.

"He loved my mother," Kat explained to Sam. "Or so I'm told."

"You can believe it," said Cress, standing to pour herself a brandy. "Your mother made Dear Richard almost human."

"Why do you call him Richard?" asked Sam.

"You would too if he'd called you Trucky your whole life," Cress said over her shoulder. She took a long pull from the brandy, then refilled her glass.

"Big as a truck," said Thomas in response to Sam's confused expression.

"Aunty Cress wasn't always the svelte goddess you see before you," said Christa.

"I haven't been overweight since I hit puberty and got my growth spurt," said Cress, "but he still calls me the same damn thing he did when he was seven years old."

"And that's why she calls him Richard," smiled Kat.

Cress knocked back another swallow of brandy. "Because he's a fucking dick."

Everyone nodded in agreement.

Everyone.

A loving family Christmas indeed.

# 10



They had moved from the dining room into yet another huge room. It was larger than the billiard room and had no pool table, but this room was also lined with bookshelves, with an enormous stone fireplace set in the far wall, a fire crackling happily inside.

Several leather couches were arranged around the fireplace, and cushy leather armchairs were distributed in pairs along the book-lined walls. A large table with chairs stood in the center of the room, some distance behind the couches.

Above the fireplace, a flat-screen television filled the wall. It was the biggest television Sam had ever seen, but no one bothered to turn it on or even look in its direction. Despite the television's size, the scale of the room made it easy to ignore.

The TV was the first piece of actual technology Sam had found in the house since he'd arrived, aside from everyone's cellphones. Seemed odd for a tech entrepreneur, but Sam had always heard stories about tech leaders pushing their products on the masses, but refusing to allow their own children to use them. The modern, capitalist version of a good, old-fashioned drug trade.

"Are we going to talk about the elephant in the room?" asked Brandon. At the blank stares from the others, he said, pointing to Sam, "This guy, and his criminal past."

Cress blew a raspberry. "Who gives a fuck? If we talked about all the illegal shit I've done in my life, we'd be here for a week." She made a dismissive wave with her hands. "Let's drink Scotch and smoke Cubans."

She filled three tumblers of Scotch from a wet bar between two bookcases, so well integrated into the wall that that Sam hadn't even noticed it. She, Thomas, and Brandon nestled themselves into the couches before the fire, lit cigars as fat as sausages, and smoked them with unadulterated relish, blowing plumes of thick smoke up into the air.

Thomas offered one to Sam, but he politely declined. It was all he could do to keep from vomiting at the smell of the pungent smoke billowing from their mouths. From behind, it looked like their heads were ablaze. The grey smoke formed a lazy cloud over their heads.

Fortunately, whether by accident or by design, the air flow in the room kept the cloud centered on the smokers, slowly pulling it upward into vents tastefully hidden in the ceiling above them.

The room was carpeted from wall to wall. The thick, luxurious carpet mushed under Sam's shoes, rocking his feet, making each step slightly unsteady. If he were at home, Sam would have had his shoes and socks off in a heartbeat, sinking his bare feet into the velvety pile, maybe even laying on his stomach before the fire like a contented kitten, sleeping off the meal and the alcohol.

As it was, he settled into one of the overstuffed leather armchairs. Kat brought a pot of coffee in from the dining room, poured it into several cups from the wet bar. She laced each cup of coffee with a healthy splash of Baileys and passed one to Sam and another to Christa.

They talked Sam into joining them around the large table for a game of Hearts. Sam hadn't played in years, not since his parents had caught the bug one summer. The three of them had done nothing but play Hearts that year when they weren't working.

That was a long time ago, but Sam quickly picked it up again. Before long, he and Kat and Christa were shit-talking and laughing and playing as fast and as dirty as they could.

When their cigars burned away, the others filtered over and joined in until all six of them were playing as raucous and foul-mouthed a game of Hearts as Sam had ever played.

The coffee and Baileys kept flowing. When the coffee ran out, they switched to straight Baileys. When the Baileys ran out, they switched to Scotch, neat.

Sam had no idea if that ran out or not. By that point, his elbow was bending of its own accord and he'd lost himself to the warm, pleasant embrace of the fine liquor.

He thought either Cress or Brandon would be the first to bow out, given the prodigious amounts of alcohol both had consumed that night, but was surprised when Christa stood from the table first, stretched tall toward the ceiling like a Siamese cat, and called to her husband.

"Come on, Thomas," she said. "Time for me to unwrap my Christmas present."

Thomas dropped his cards without hesitation and jumped up from the table so fast his chair rocked back on two legs and nearly tumbled over. Sam heard his voice, low and intimate, as the two exited the room, then Christa's laughter pealing through the air, bright and shimmering, as the door swung shut behind them.

Cress was the next to retire. At the end of a hand a short while later, she pushed her chair back from the table.

"Time for me to go to bed," she said as she stood. She walked around the table to Sam's chair, dragged one finger along his arm. "Not time for me to go to sleep, though."

"Aunty," growled Kat.

Cress leaned down, put her mouth to Sam's ear. "Help an old woman to bed, child?" she said.

Her hot breath sent warm shivers all through Sam's body. She flicked Sam's earlobe into her mouth with her tongue and sucked it hard.

"Good night, Aunt Cress," said Kat, her voice rising in volume. And deepening with warning.

Cress bit down hard on Sam's earlobe. Sam jumped. "You know where to find me," she whispered.

She stood up. "Good night, children," she called, waving over her shoulder as she left the room. She walked slowly, swinging her hips seductively, relishing in the knowledge that every pair of eyes was watching her go.

Sam had no idea where to find her. No idea where her bedroom might have been in the enormous house. And he was okay with that. To be honest, even if he'd wanted to, Sam wasn't sure he could handle Cress.

He wasn't sure he could handle Kat, either.

He wasn't even sure he could handle all the Scotch he'd been drinking.

With Cress gone, only Brandon, Kat, and Sam remained in the room. None of them moved to gather the cards scattered on the table and deal another hand. They all sat slumped back in their chairs, fatigue finally settling over them, staring ahead, eyes unfocused, lost in their own thoughts.

Kat threw her hand lazily over the back of Sam's chair, letting her fingers absent-mindedly stroke his neck. Tingles shot through Sam's body with each soft touch of Kat's skin.

A clock chimed the hour somewhere in the house.

Midnight.

"Another Christmas," said Brandon. He drained the last swallow of Scotch from his glass. For once, he didn't move to refill it. "Merry fucking Christmas."

"What happens tomorrow?" asked Sam. He hadn't seen any decorations anywhere in the house. No Christmas tree. Not even a wreath. "Do you all open gifts in the morning?"

Brandon snorted. "Tomorrow," he said, "our father will take his breakfast in his workshop. Then, he'll take his lunch in his workshop. After that, he'll most likely take his dinner in his workshop. And then, at some point, I assume he'll sleep."

"We can only assume he sleeps," said Kat. "I've never seen it myself. He might have cured the need for sleep by now and just not bothered to share it with anyone."

There was silence for a long moment.

"Well, he sure as shit hasn't shared it with me," said Brandon with a sigh, dragging himself up from his chair. "Good night." He kissed his sister sweetly on the top of her head. "Merry Christmas."

"Merry Christmas," Kat replied.

Brandon bent down to give Kat a hug. They shared a long look after, one that Sam didn't understand. Something between them, some agreement or mutual understanding.

They were twins, twins that had grown up together in this very dysfunctional family. Shared trauma of a sort, Sam figured. Things were always harder during the holidays.

Brandon stared hard at Sam, then dragged his eyes away as if he were working very hard not to roll them. He mumbled something that might have been "good night" or "Merry Christmas", then stumbled from the room.

"Well," said Sam when the door snicked shut behind Brandon. "What should we do now—"

Kat's mouth was on his, soft and insistent. She straddled him on the chair, bunched Sam's shirt in her fist, pulled him toward her even as she pushed herself hard against him.

Sam's body responded in an instant. All fatigue gone. All drunkenness replaced by a different, much headier intoxication.

Kat pulled him off the chair onto his feet, stripped him down to his waist, slid one soft, warm hand down his chest, then pushed him back, then back again.

Backwards toward the fireplace.

He stepped backward. She stalked forward.

She speared him with her stare, her eyes flashing with mischievous desire, and turned on her megawatt smile.

Sam had been wrong before.

Kat wasn't just gorgeous.

She was heart-stoppingly, world-endingly gorgeous.

She unbuttoned her top.

One.

Button.

At.

A.

Time.

Kat took off her shirt and Sam lost his mind. All the blood flowed away from his brain and down to the parts that needed it most.

The fire was still roaring after all this time.

The carpet was lush, warm and soft against Sam's back.

It was going to be a very, very merry Christmas after all.

# 11



Sam woke in grey semi-darkness.

Silence.

Cool air stood goosebumps on his skin.

He was naked, on top of the rumpled sheets of a very large bed.

He stared at a coffered ceiling, dim outlines in the dark high above him.

As his mind slowly pieced itself back together, he stared at the coffers. Little grey postage stamps. Picture frames. Square windows set within larger windows. Windows within windows, like a view into infinity.

His mouth was dry and fuzzy. His head was just as fuzzy. It throbbed behind his left eye.

He closed his eyes and rubbed at his temple, trying to massage the throb away.

It didn't work.

He let his hand flop back down on the bed.

It flopped against something.

Against someone.

Sam looked over and saw Kat, lying on her stomach. Sam was naked, but Kat was dressed in a t-shirt and underwear.

Memories of the night before came back to him.

Good memories.

Very, very good memories.

Memories in front of the fireplace. Memories on the landing in the stairwell. Memories in the bed.

More memories in the bed.

Even more memories in the bed.

There were a lot of memories, all of them good.

Last time he saw Kat, she wasn't wearing anything at all.

That was another good memory.

His mind wasn't the only part of his body that remembered.

He rolled onto his side and ran a hand down Kat's back, over the curve of her behind, and along the soft, warm skin of one long leg.

Kat murmured softly. Her eyes flickered open and she smiled sleepily, her sultry, half-lidded eyes igniting.

She remembered, too.

**12**

When Sam opened his eyes again, harsh white light streamed through a tall window, stabbing deep into his brain.

The long, dark curtains had been thrown back. Through the window, Sam could see snow hammering down, a wall of white static. When he stood and stepped to the cold glass, he could barely see ten feet outside through the driving storm.

So much for catching the train today.

He turned back to the bed.

Kat was gone.

Must have gotten up early and left to let Sam sleep. He gathered his clothes from the floor and pulled on his pants, then walked, barefoot and bleary, into the adjoining bathroom to wash up.

He emerged into the hallway a short time later, showered and dressed, and worked his way through the labyrinth of the house to the main staircase. As he descended, he found staff darting around, hard expressions on their faces. They ignored Sam completely.

Phillip stood off to one side near a small doorway, speaking in soft tones to a tall, older woman. He noticed Sam from the corner of his eye, dismissed the woman, and strode to meet Sam at the foot of the stairs.

"Miss Katerina and the others are in the morning room," said Phillip. His tone was as smooth and regal as ever, but his face lacked its usual composure. He looked pale and worn. "Please follow me."

Phillip led him through another labyrinth of hallways, turn after turn, until they came to a doorway. He opened the door inward, stepped inside, and held his arm out, inviting Sam to enter.

The room was bathed in white, snowy, early-morning light. It streamed in through windows that covered one full wall, looking out onto what was probably the backyard.

Backyard was too mundane a word. It was more like a football field outside the breakfast nook.

That day, it was a featureless expanse of white behind a curtain of driving snow.

Much smaller than the other rooms Sam had seen, the morning room held only a table and chairs and a glass-fronted hutch on one wall that held plates and glasses.

Kat was already seated at the table, as were all the others except for Brandon. They were each in various states of disarray. Thomas's face was drawn, his eyes underscored with dark circles. Christa's eyes and nose were pink and inflamed, her cheeks wet. She clutched a tattered tissue in her hand. In the hard light, Cress finally looked her age. No makeup, hair tousled. Her eyes sunk deep and her skin looked crêpey and translucent. She cradled a steaming mug and stared out the window, her eyes far away.

Kat wore soft, fuzzy pants and socks and a baggy sweater. She sat with one foot tucked under her on the chair, her knee by her cheek. When she looked over and saw Sam, she reached her hand out to him. Her eyes were dark, serious. Gone was the hungry fire Sam had seen that morning, the mischievous glow he'd seen the night before. Her face—no less gorgeous for the pale light, no less beautiful for her grave expression—bore witness to some heavy burden weighing on Kat's mind.

Sam took her hand and sat on the chair beside her. Staff members materialized with a small silver French press and a mug, set a sugar dish and a small pourer filled with cream beside it. They pressed the coffee, filled the mug, and departed. Sam poured the cream and spooned the sugar, stirring his coffee mechanically.

No one said a word. The only sound was the scraping of Sam's spoon against the bottom of his mug, the occasional hitch of Christa's breath as she wept softly.

The door banged open and Brandon stumbled in, clearly having just woken. He was barefoot and wore a thin robe over a t-shirt and boxer shorts. The strap of the robe swung back and forth as he worked his way to a chair, rubbing his face and groaning. His eyes were bloodshot, his hair spiked every which way. He had a shadow of stubble across his sallow face.

He looked like hell.

Again, staff appeared with coffee and sugar. No cream. They must have known how Brandon liked his coffee in the morning.

Brandon fixed his coffee, took a long swallow, fell back hard in his chair, then scowled and said, "What the fuck am I doing awake right now? There better be a goddamn emergency, and it better be a fucking good one."

No one spoke.

Finally, Thomas leaned forward on the table and folded his hands together, studying them. He bit his lower lip and looked up at Brandon.

"Your father is dead," he said.

Christa sobbed once, then covered her mouth with her

tissue. Thomas flicked his eyes toward her, then back down to study his hands on the table once more.

Brandon stared at Thomas for a long moment, the same dark scowl on his face. He glanced around at the others in turn, then back to Thomas. He opened his mouth and drew a breath, flicked his eyes toward Sam, then closed his mouth again, his brow furrowing.

Sam's mind reeled. He wanted to think he hadn't heard Thomas right, but he knew he had.

Dr. Nestrom was dead?

He had that ridiculous thought, the one that everyone seemed to have when someone died unexpectedly: How could Nestrom be dead? Sam had just seen him last night.

It was the first coherent thought that went through Sam's mind. Ridiculous, of course. As if death isolated its victims before taking them and waited an appropriate amount of time, just so the living wouldn't be quite so shocked at their absence.

Ridiculous as it was, it was a natural thought, since humans always believed—sometimes deep down, sometimes more obviously—that they were the center of the universe.

But the news was no less shocking for it.

Just last night, Nestrom had seemed in perfect health. He wasn't particularly old. Not at all sickly. But maybe he'd had a medical condition. A heart problem or epilepsy or some other condition that wasn't obvious to the eye.

"How?" said Sam, the question escaping his lips before he could think to hold it back.

Thomas shook his head slowly and released a long breath. "We don't know. All we know is that Phillip found him in his workshop when he delivered breakfast this morning."

Sam nodded, more because he didn't know what else to do than from any real insight that Thomas's statement had provided.

In reality, Thomas's statement raised more questions in

Sam's mind. Old questions ingrained by a lifetime of helping his parents plan robberies and cover their tracks. And newer questions learned from several years of studying criminology. Questions about the body, the scene of discovery, the means of discovery, whether the authorities had been notified, and a thousand others.

Questions about foul play.

Sam's mind naturally went to foul play. Call it a criminal's intuition. Or maybe just inherent skepticism.

He looked around the table.

Motive. Means. Opportunity. The detective's triumvirate.

He didn't learn that in school. He learned that from watching too many cop shows on television. Most of them were bullshit, but that nugget was pure wisdom.

If this were a murder, who had a motive to kill Dr. Nestrom?

Thomas, the undervalued employee.

Christa, the unappreciated eldest daughter.

Kat and Brandon, the ignored and abandoned children.

Cress, the verbally abused elder sister.

Just normal family problems.

Normal for a totally dysfunctional family, that is, but surely not enough motive for murder. Right?

Something niggled in the back of Sam's mind. A nagging question, one that he knew would not go away.

"Have the police been called yet?" he asked quietly.

Kat nodded. "Phillip called them right away, but they can't get anyone out here till the storm blows over and the roads are cleared."

"What did he tell them?"

"Only that someone had died," said Thomas. "He didn't give any more details than that."

Sam looked through the huge windows at the blizzard raging outside. The police wouldn't be coming any time soon. And Sam wouldn't be leaving any time soon, either. And that meant he could be trapped in a house in the middle of nowhere with a killer.

Or not. Maybe Nestrom had a heart attack. Or choked on his own ambition.

But Sam wasn't going to take any chances. He'd known a few murderers in his day. His parents had worked with them from time to time. Nasty bunch, murderers. Once a person has killed another person, once they've crossed that line, the bar for killing again gets a lot lower.

Sam looked around the table once more. He didn't relish the idea of sleeping under the same roof as a killer. That meant he had to take it upon himself to find the answers to all those questions in his mind.

Everyone at that table had a motive, however thin or hard to believe.

But who'd had the means?

And who'd had the opportunity?

**13**

"Can we go down and see the workshop?" asked Sam.

It was an indelicate question, way out of line for a guy who had known the family for less than twenty-four hours.

The looks on the faces of the others around the table showed that they thought so, too. But there was no other way around it. Sam wanted to know how Nestrom's death had happened, as much for his own safety and peace of mind as for anything else.

And the most obvious place to start was in the workshop.

"You fucking asshole," said Brandon, rising from his chair.

"Brandon," said Kat, "calm down."

Though she seemed to be trying to defuse the tension, Kat's voice was hard-edged, too.

"Why the hell do you want to see the workshop?" asked Cress.

"Criminology student," mumbled Thomas.

"So, what, you're going to write a thesis about this?" said Cress. "You're going to play Columbo, are you? That's my brother down there. Dead."

Her voice hitched on the last word. Christa tried to hold Cress' hand, but Cress shook it off and turned her shoulder to the table, staring out the window and cradling her coffee mug more closely.

Sam hadn't seen her take a single sip, and the steam had stopped rising from it. It was probably cold by now.

Brandon sat back down in a huff. No one said a word for a time.

Then Thomas asked, softly, "Why do you want to go down there?"

"I mean no disrespect," said Sam, leaning forward in his chair, "and it's not from some kind of academic curiosity. It's just that the snowstorm doesn't seem to be letting up. The police aren't going to be able to get here, and we should record the scene somehow. Capture it so that, when they do come, they'll have a record of everything as it was."

"If we just leave it alone," growled Brandon, "they'll have a perfect record of how it was."

"No, they won't," Sam replied. "The storm is still in full swing. I don't know what the weather report says, but let's just be optimistic and say it stops this afternoon. The road crews will start cleaning up, but they'll start with the main roads in town. That'll take all night. They won't get to the side roads until tomorrow, and they probably won't get way out here until the next day."

"So what?" said Cress, bitterly. "Three days from now, my brother will still be dead. What difference does it make?"

For someone who just last night had been the first to call her brother an asshole, Cress was taking things awfully hard.

Still, families were weird, and brothers and sisters were especially weird. Sam was an only child, so he didn't know from experience, but he'd seen a lot of fucked up sibling relationships among his friends over the years.

"The difference is... and I apologize, but this is going to be a little graphic... a body will start to... change... even in just three days."

"Change?" sneered Brandon. "How the fuck could it change? He's dead."

"Decompose, Brandon," said Kat quietly. "The body will start to decompose."

Christa's quiet sobbing started again. Thomas put a distracted arm around her shoulder, his brow furrowed in thought.

"Fucking hell." Brandon shook his head. "That's disgusting." He leaned his elbows on the table, put his head in his hands, and rubbed his temples in circles.

The sat in silence for a moment.

"I want to see it, too," said Kat quietly.

"Kat," said Brandon, disbelief on his face.

"I want to see it." She stared hard at her brother, steel in her eyes. "I want to see how my father died."

Where Sam's suggestion had been met with stiff, instinctive resistance, from Kat's lips the idea sunk in. Around the table, Sam could see wheels turning as they each considered it.

"Okay," said Thomas.

Brandon and Cress snapped their heads toward him.

"*If* we go down there," he said, "what would we do?"

"Take pictures of everything," said Sam. "Everything. From every angle. Don't touch anything, but photograph it all."

"And what about the body?" Thomas said.

Sam sighed. "We will have to move it. Hopefully before rigor mortis sets in, if it hasn't already."

"Where the fuck are we going to put a dead body?" said Brandon.

Sam shrugged. "Somewhere cold. Like a freezer. Or a refrigerator, at least."

"Oh my God," said Cress in disgust.

"I don't think we have anything like that here," said Kat.

"Nothing big enough for a body." She looked around at the others. "Do we?"

Everyone either shrugged or shook their heads noncommittally.

"To be honest, we're the last people who would know something like that," said Thomas.

"I don't even remember where the fucking kitchen is," said Brandon.

"Phillip would know, wouldn't he?" asked Sam.

They summoned Phillip. He came in with somber elegance and stood patiently beside the table.

"Phillip," asked Kat, "do we have any large refrigerators or freezers here?"

"Yes, miss," Phillip replied. "We have several walk-in refrigerators and a walk-in freezer."

"Are they large enough to hold a body?"

For the first time since he'd arrived, Sam saw Phillip lose his carefully arranged composure. His face paled and his eyes opened wide in horror, but only for a moment. He quickly regained his poise. Sam could see his mind working as he realized what Kat's question suggested.

"Nothing large enough for that, I'm afraid," he said slowly, thinking things through. "And we restocked our food supplies in preparation for both the holiday and the storm, so I don't believe we would be able to move our stores to make room enough for... a person to rest inside."

Kat sighed. "Thank you, Phillip," she said.

Phillip bowed his head and turned to leave, then stopped.

"However," he said.

Everyone turned their heads back toward him.

Phillip looked out the window at the blinding snow, which had only intensified. "I believe we could store a body outside for a time," he said. "If absolutely necessary."

**14**

After winding through another maze of hallways—the layout of the house was so non-sensical it had to have been deliberate— Phillip led them through a wide, heavy door. The size and the heft of the door gave Sam the impression that it might be a fire door, one that would stay standing, unharmed, even if the house burned to the ground around it.

He wondered if Dr. Nestrom had fireproofed his entire workshop, like one giant fireproof safe. If so, that showed where Nestrom's priorities lay. He fireproofed the workshop and left his family to fend for themselves in the rest of the house.

If Sam were part of that family, he might have had a motive to kill Nestrom, too.

They descended a long, wide, twisting staircase that curled down for at least two flights. Both the stairs and the walls were made of smooth concrete. Small dents the size of a fingertip pocked the walls at random, tiny imperfections that were probably put there intentionally, to add texture or to break up visually the endless expanse of concrete that surrounded them.

The stairs seemed to wind down forever. Nestrom's workshop was not only fireproof, it was underground, as well. Better protection from temperature fluctuations, maybe? Easier to secure it from snooping or hacking, if the ground somehow blocked any incoming electronic signals?

At last they came to a glass vestibule the size of a large shower. One glass door blocked them from entering the vestibule. Inside, another door guarded entrance to the workshop visible beyond.

"Why two doors?" asked Sam.

"The doors are both soundproof," explained Phillip. "But from the inner vestibule, one can—" He grimaced. "One *could* converse with Dr. Nestrom through a speaker before entering the workshop."

Nestrom was secretive, then. So secretive that he built a soundproof room outside of his soundproof workshop, just so others who might be nearby couldn't hear a conversation he was having with someone who wanted to come in.

I guess when you've got all the money in the world, you can afford to indulge your crazy.

Sam wondered why, though, if Nestrom was so secretive, he would build the workshop entrance entirely from glass. No one could hear him, but anyone could see him.

Through the two layers of glass, Sam could see the workshop, a large room made mostly of concrete. Lights set into the ceiling cast a dim blue glow over the room, making it seem colder than it was. In fact, counter-intuitively, the air had grown warmer as they descended the staircase. Outside the door, Sam was warm enough that he felt a droplet of sweat crawl down his side under his t-shirt and sweater.

It was either from the temperature or the situation.

Despite a childhood full of crime and the fact that he was now a criminology major, Sam had never seen a dead body before. His parents were entirely opposed to the use of violence in anything, robberies or daily life. They never even raised their voices in anger, even in the heat of a job when their plans inevitably crumbled. They were pleasant, happy people. Loving spouses and loving parents.

They couldn't have been more different from the family Sam had met last night, the remnants of which clustered around him as they waited for Phillip to unlock the doors.

Beyond those doors was the body of Dr. Christopher Nestrom.

Phillip lay his thumb against a fingerprint sensor in the wall beside the outer door. The door clicked open. Thomas held the it open while Phillip stepped inside the vestibule, then straightened his back to align his eye with a retinal scanner beside the inner door.

Sam heard a knocking sound, like a recording of someone knocking on a wooden front door, coming from a speaker set into the wall. A woman's voice coyly called, "Who is it?"

Christa and Cress both gasped.

"What?" said Brandon, confused by their reactions.

"That's Mom's voice," whispered Christa.

"Phillip Winston," said Phillip, his enunciation clear and precise.

"It's good to see you again, Phillip," the voice said warmly as the inner door lock clicked. "Come on in."

Phillip held the door open as everyone filed into the workshop. As in the stairwell, the air was warm. But it felt fresher inside the workshop. There was a movement to it that made it feel less claustrophobic, less stifling than Sam had expected. There must be a good ventilation system somewhere. Maybe an air purifier, as well.

They all gathered by the doorway, fanning out to the sides as if afraid to enter the space where their father had worked all day, every day. The space where so many world-changing inventions had been conceived and developed. The space they had never been allowed to enter while their father was alive.

Directly in front of them, four large rectangular tables stood in the center of the wide, deep room. Each table held an array of components and machines, all meticulously ordered on the tabletops. One held a variety of computer parts, circuit boards, wires, and so on. Another held what looked like lenses for eyeglasses, in all shapes, sizes, and colors, along with some kind of device that resembled a huge, high-tech microscope. A third table held a bunch of blueprints and printouts and papers of all kinds.

On one side of the fourth table were several plastic trays. One was filled with tiny eyeglass hinges, another with even tinier screws. A third tray held a handful of miniature screwdrivers, and in a fourth tray were what looked like scaled-down glue guns. The whole setup looked like the back room of a eyeglass store.

On the other side of the table sat a variety of electrical testing equipment. Long metal leads connected to red and black wires which led to black metal boxes with windows behind which a thin red sweep hand rested idle on one side of a pale yellow dial.

Between the two, a row of eyeglasses lay neatly folded in a tray in the center of the table.

It was all a bunch of stuff that Sam knew nothing about. Technical stuff. Computer stuff. World-changing tech billionaire stuff.

The thing that Sam did understand was behind the tables. Along the floor there, Sam could see a pair of black sneakers pointed straight up in the air.

He shouldered past Phillip and strode to the spot. Nestrom lay on the floor, his eyes wide, staring sightlessly up at the ceiling. He was wearing the same thing he'd worn at dinner: black jeans and a black t-shirt. His mouth hung casually open like he was about to comment on the storm outside or ask Sam if he would like some tea.

Sam squatted beside the corpse. Nestrom lay prone on his back on the floor, his arms by his sides. That would help with moving the body, since it was clear to Sam that rigor mortis had already set in. The arms and legs looked unnaturally stiff.

When he heard Christa cry out, Sam turned to see the others standing behind him, looking down at the scene. When she saw her brother's body, Cress sucked in a sharp breath of air and turned away. Thomas, Kat, and Brandon looked grimly down as Sam circled Nestrom.

He didn't touch anything. He didn't want his fingerprints anywhere near the scene. But he wanted to see what could be seen before they moved Nestrom. He wanted to see any clues before they were accidentally obscured.

Or deliberately removed.

"Didn't you say we were supposed to take pictures, or something?" said Brandon, his arms folded across his chest.

"Yes," murmured Sam. He looked up at them. "Each of you take a section of the room and photograph everything you can with your phones. Don't touch anything without gloves on." He looked around the room. In a workshop like this, with all of this delicate equipment, there had to be a box of disposable medical gloves somewhere.

There. Against the wall.

He pointed toward the gloves. "Grab a pair of gloves before you do anything," he said. "Then photograph everything you can, from every angle you can. Get it all on camera."

"I'll supervise from over here," said Cress, pointing toward the door. "Technology gives me herpes."

"As if you don't already have it," said Christa.

"I'm clean where it counts, honey," replied Cress with a dismissive wave.

"What are you going to do while we're doing all of your grunt work for you?" Brandon asked Sam.

Sam sighed, looking down at Nestrom as he pulled on the gloves Kat had given him. "I'm going to photograph this corpse."

**15**

Sam had taken one class in forensic science and one class in crime scene investigation. Neither one prepared him to be the lead in the first stage of an investigation with an actual dead body.

But he had to figure it out. No one else there would do it.

Thankfully, he'd gotten no complaints from the others when he assigned them their tasks. Even Brandon diligently photographed the area he'd been given, the table with all of the eyeglasses. The others were spread throughout the workshop, their phones clicking away as they catalogued the room.

Sam didn't really care about their photos, though the police might. Sam just wanted to keep them busy. And keep them out of his way.

He photographed the corpse and the area around it. He didn't see any rips in Nestrom's clothing, no cuts on the arms from defensive maneuvers, no broken fingernails or scratches on his hands that might indicate a struggle. There were no obvious bruises or marks on his face or neck. The only odd marks Sam could see were a faint dark circle above Nestrom's right ear and an indentation above his left.

With all of the eyeglasses in the room, it wasn't hard to make the leap. The marks could easily have been from a pair of glasses that were too tight. If he'd worn them for a while, removed them and set them back on the table, then died of a heart attack or something, that might explain those marks.

It would explain the indentation, anyway. It was shaped like a section of the arm of a pair of eyeglasses. It didn't explain the dark circle, though. Maybe the glasses were dirty? Maybe Nestrom had had some dirt on his fingers when he removed the glasses?

Sam checked the sides of Nestrom's nose looking for more indentations, like you'd get from the nose piece of a pair of glasses. He didn't see any, but that didn't ruin his hypothesis. It just didn't add any evidence to it.

At any rate, there were no obvious signs of break-in in the workshop. Nothing was in disarray and there was nothing about the body or the clothing that would indicate any struggle with an intruder or a potential murderer.

That didn't mean Nestrom wasn't murdered. Just that there was no struggle. The murderer could have snuck up on Nestrom. Or it could have been someone he already knew, someone Nestrom himself had let in to the workshop.

But even the way Nestrom was laying on the ground seemed benign. He was flat on his back, limbs by his side, legs straight. If he had fallen backward, chances were that he would have hit something, a table or a chair, and his body would have twisted before it hit the ground. Or, if he were still conscious as he fell, he would have thrown his arms out or twisted his body to try to catch himself. None of that was the case here.

Sam carefully photographed everything. Then, with Thomas's help, he rolled Nestrom's body onto its stomach so he could examine the backside.

If Nestrom had been unconscious and had somehow fallen straight back without hitting anything, he would at the very least have hit the back of his head on the concrete floor. Hard. Hard enough to cause bleeding, certainly. Maybe hard enough to crack the skull open.

But there wasn't anything there. No blood on the floor or on Nestrom's head, no signs of bruising, no soft spots where the bones may have broken. Nestrom's thick hair wasn't even mussed at the back. Either Nestrom had lowered himself to the ground, like he might have done if he'd had a heart attack, or he was lowered to the ground by someone else.

Like his murderer. Someone he knew. Someone who surprised him, killed him suddenly, from close range, then caught his body and lowered it to the ground and situated it into the neat, tidy position in which Sam had found it.

But why would a killer bother with arranging the body?

And how would they even get in? The workshop security was tight.

Too many questions. Not nearly enough answers.

"You're just going to leave him like that?" said Christa. "Face down on the floor?"

"I don't think he'll complain," said Cress, who had wandered over to watch the proceedings. Her dry humor was coming back. So much for her period of mourning.

"I just mean, won't it hurt the body somehow?" said Christa. "Squish his nose and tamper with the evidence or something?"

Sam moved on from the head and examined the rest of the backside of the body, but didn't see anything unusual there, either. He photographed everything, then he and Thomas rolled the corpse back over.

"That's why we photograph everything," Sam said. "Just so there's a record. But we're going to move the body, anyway." He called to the butler, who was still standing by the door as if afraid to step further into the room, "Phillip, did you have somewhere in mind where we could store the body outside?"

"There is an unheated outbuilding just outside on the grounds, a storage shed for the gardener's tools. It has a large table that can be used, er, for the purpose." Phillip couldn't hide the squeamish look on his face.

Sam and Thomas hoisted Nestrom's body off the floor, with Sam gripping under the shoulders and Thomas holding the feet. The body lay board-straight between them. That made it easier to carry than if it were flopping around loose, but it still weighed a ton. They groaned, struggling to lift the corpse high enough to clear the work tables as they made their way to the door.

"Help them, Brandon," said Cress.

"Fuck no. I don't want to touch it," said Brandon, cringing away.

Kat sighed and stepped in beside Sam. Sam shifted so they each held one shoulder.

"Fine," muttered Brandon. He joined Thomas, each man holding a leg.

The four of them lifted the body higher, up onto their shoulders, like four pallbearers with a coffin.

Except there was no coffin, just a stiff corpse. Sam tried not to think too much it, about the way the coldness seeped from the corpse into his own body, sending a chill through him that came from more than the temperature difference. He tried not to think about how close his face was to Nestrom's skin. Nestrom was wearing only a t-shirt, and his bare arm brushed against Sam's cheek as they walked, sending shivers to chase the chill through his body.

They worked their way through the glass doors and started up the stairs. Phillip went ahead to hold the door at the top. Kat was shorter than the three men, so the corpse tended to lean toward her corner. With her and Sam on the downstairs side, that made it difficult to negotiate the winding staircase. They backed slowly down the stairs again and turned in a small circle inside the workshop so that Sam and Kat were leading the way. It wasn't much easier, but at least Kat's height difference didn't combine with the force of gravity to add to the problem.

"I don't know why..."—Brandon grunted halfway up the stairs—"...I have to be..."—another grunt—"...on the heavy side..."—more grunting as they twisted around a tight corner—"...this wasn't even my idea..."

The stairs were twisting, but wide. Moving Nestrom's stiff body was like moving a couch up four flights of stairs. Sam had moved much heavier couches up much smaller staircases in his time.

Still, Nestrom's body was heavy. A hundred fifty pounds, at least. Maybe closer to two hundred. By the time they reached the top, all four of them were out of breath and sweating. Phillip pitched in, reaching down from the doorway to help pull the body up, while Christa and even Cress helped push from the bottom.

"Can we take a break, please?" groaned Brandon once they reached the top of the stairs.

"And what, just leave him here?" said Cress. "On the floor?"

"I don't give a fuck where we put him," said Brandon, "as long as we put him down. Prop him in the corner, for all I care."

"I could use a break," said Kat, panting softly.

"Okay, let's set him down on his feet," said Sam. "That way we won't have to lift him all the way up again."

Brandon and Thomas carefully set Nestrom's feet down on the smooth stone floor, then helped Sam and Kat twist and lever the body to a standing position against the wall. The body was so stiff, the feet so flat, that it stood on its own without the need for anyone to hold it upright. Nestrom's corpse stood there, eyes staring, mouth open, as if the man himself were having a conversation with the group.

"He looks like an animatronic doll," said Christa. "Like at Disney World."

"I hate those things," muttered Brandon. He shivered, shaking out his arms and legs. "Fucking hell. Even dead, the guy haunts me."

"I thought being dead was a prerequisite for haunting," said Cress.

"Yeah, well, as far as I'm concerned, being drunk is a prerequisite for being haunted." Brandon disappeared down the hallway.

"Hey, don't run off," called Thomas. "We'll need you to help carry again."

Brandon muttered something unintelligible before disappearing around a corner.

"We won't see him again anytime soon," said Cress. "And I'm not lifting that thing, so I guess it's up to you, Christa."

"'That thing' is your brother," said Christa.

"Didn't like touching him when he was alive, don't like touching him when he's dead."

Christa didn't seem like she cared to touch him, either.

Sam looked around the group. Brandon wasn't the only one missing.

"Where did Phillip go?" he asked.

As if on cue, they heard a soft rushing sound, like wind, growing louder. Phillip appeared in the hallway rolling a long serving cart draped in a tablecloth. The wheels rolling along the smooth floor made the wind-like sound.

"As there are no more stairs to negotiate," said Phillip, "I thought this might be of use."

"Phillip, you're a fucking lifesaver," said Cress. "Christa was about to have to carry that corpse all the way outside." She pulled up the tablecloth and peered under the cart. "I don't suppose you have any vodka under here, do you?"

"It's ten o'clock in the morning," said Christa.

"Gin, then."

"I'm afraid not, ma'am," said Phillip.

"Let's just get this over with," Kat said quietly.

While Phillip held the cart steady, Sam and Thomas tilted Nestrom's body onto the cart and covered it with the tablecloth. Nestrom's legs and feet stuck straight off the end of the cart, and the wheels squeaked under the weight, but otherwise the rig served well enough as a makeshift gurney.

"To the morgue, Phillip," called Cress, pointing straight ahead like a calvary general. "Lead on."

Sam pushed the cart as Phillip led them through the hallways and down a ramp into the staff section of the house.

"I've never been down here before," said Thomas.

"I didn't even know it was here," Cress replied. "And I grew up in this house."

Phillip said nothing, his face impassive as he led them down a long hallway. No winding labyrinth down here. Just long, straight hallways. The layout was utilitarian, meant for a purpose.

Sam saw no one along the path. He wondered if Phillip had warned everyone they would be coming, that they would be intruding on the personal space of the staff, so that the staff could all disperse and avoid having to smile and offer to help.

"This way," said Phillip as they came to a door on the left, a heavy door with a window set into it. Phillip held the door open as Sam worked the gurney around the tight turn.

As soon as he stepped through the door, the temperature immediately dropped. The hallway was short and narrow, with another door at the far end that must have led directly outside.

The far door had a glass window set into it. Sam assumed that you could normally see the grounds outside through that window, but with the blizzard, it was just a glowing rectangle of white. He shivered in the chill air. His thin sweater was not enough to keep him warm in the great outdoors. Not in the middle of a blizzard.

Phillip squeezed past the cart in the narrow hallway, apologizing profusely for making Kat and Cress move to let him pass.

"It will be very cold outside," he warned. "Perhaps I can accompany Mr. Davis to the gardener's shed alone, and we can meet the rest of you back inside?"

"Sounds good to me," said Cress, immediately heading back through the door into the warmer hallway. "Which way to the vodka?"

Thomas and Christa followed behind her.

"I'll come with you two," said Kat, smiling faintly and squeezing Sam's arm.

"Very well, miss," replied Phillip.

When Phillip pushed open the outside door, an icy wind whipped into the hall, bringing with it a flurry of drifting snow. It swirled around Sam and Kat as they instinctively turned away. The wind was like a slap, like Mother Nature was smacking them in the face.

And maybe Sam deserved to be slapped. Not for the first time that morning, certainly not for the first time since the previous evening, as Sam wheeled Nestrom's corpse toward the blinding white light of the outdoors, he wondered what the hell he'd gotten himself into.

# 16

DECEMBER 25, 11:01AM

The word "shed" was a dramatic understatement. The gardener's tool shed was at least as big as a three-car garage.

Three large cars. Like Cadillac SUVs. With room left over for a full workbench. And maybe even a small coffee shop.

"Will this be sufficient, Mr. Davis?" asked Phillip.

Sam eyed the butler carefully, keeping his own face as impassive as Phillip's. Either this butler was a total automaton or he was fucking with Sam.

Honestly, it could have gone either way, but Sam didn't like to underestimate people. In his experience, you tended to get burned when you underestimated people.

"Yeah, Phillip," Sam replied, allowing himself a wry smile. "I think this will do just fine."

Phillip nodded his head in return. Sam thought he saw a small smile touching the corners of Phillip's eyes.

So he had a sense of humor after all.

The tool shed was one long, rectangular room with a peaked

ceiling. Windows lined one long wall, diffusing the bright white light from the snowglare throughout the room, giving it an ethereal glow, like being inside a cloud.

True to the building's name, tools lined the length of the other wall, an endless array of tools of all kinds, all hung neatly on a pale brown pegboard above a long wooden workbench. Five different kinds of hammers, at least two dozen screwdrivers, shovels and diggers and sprayers and trimmers. All clean, neat, and orderly. It looked more like a hardware store than a storage shed.

On the far side, perpendicular to the wall with the tools, Sam saw a garage door that filled the entire wall. Parked in front of it in neat rows were three riding lawnmowers of varying sizes, some kind of tilling machine with a sharp-looking augur set on its side under a metal cover, and several other large machines whose purposes Sam didn't know, but which looked vaguely landscaping-related.

Despite the fact that everything in it was clean and practically gleaming, as if everything was brand new, the shed smelled faintly of gasoline and soil and cut grass. Musty and fecund.

And cold. The walls blocked the wind, but the temperature inside the shed wasn't much higher than it was outside. Phillip hadn't been joking when he said the building was unheated. The floor was concrete, and the chill seeped up through Sam's shoes.

In the center of the room was a wide table half as long as the building itself. The frame of the table was metal, but the top was two-inch-thick wood, pocked and scarred and scratched from years of use. At the moment, there was nothing on top of it. And it was plenty big enough to hold a corpse for a few days.

Sam ran his hands over the uneven surface. Despite the scarring, the wood was perfectly smooth. Any imperfections must have been sanded as soon as they were made.

Phillip reached under the gurney and removed a thin yellow blanket, which he laid carefully on the table. He then pulled on some white cloth gloves he'd taken from his pocket. White Mickey Mouse gloves. Like butlers in the movies always wore, posh English butlers who never touched anything with their bare hands, so as not to smudge the serving silver.

Gloves on, Phillip helped Sam and Kat to shift Nestrom's body from the cart to the table. Carefully, they set the body down. Phillip then covered it with the white sheet from the cart.

With the frigid air, the white glow from the windows, and the shape of the body under the sheet, it really did look like a morgue. Sam shivered from more than just the cold. He smoothed the sheet over the body, as much to give himself something to do as for any other reason, some movement to shake out the shivers. As he did so, his hand brushed over the front pocket of Nestrom's jeans.

Sam stopped short.

He'd felt something there. Something in Nestrom's pocket.

"Hang on," said Sam, pushing the sheet back to reveal Nestrom's jeans. "I forgot to go through the pockets."

"Isn't that a little disrespectful?" said Kat.

"Maybe so," said Sam, "but it might give us some clue as to how he died."

"A clue?" Kat frowned. "Are we investigating something? I thought we were just documenting things and waiting for the police to get here."

"No, we are," said Sam quickly, "we are. It's just, while we're here, we might as well..."

Sam waved his hands toward Nestrom's body in a vague gesture.

Kat arched an eyebrow. Sam leaned in toward her.

"Don't you want to know how he died? Aren't you curious?"

Kat's frown deepened. Seconds ticked by as she stared at Nestrom's corpse, her eyes unfocused.

As she stared at her father's dead body.

Laying under a sheet.

On a table in a gardener's shed.

What was Sam doing? What kind of an asshole was he, forcing Kat to treat this like some kind of cop show when her father had just died? It was bad enough she'd had to move the body. Now Sam was making her think about clues and investigations and, by association, foul play?

He shook his head slowly. "Kat, I'm so sorry. Forget I said—"

"What's in his pocket?" she said.

"I... don't know."

Kat looked up sharply, her eyes flashing. "I want to know what's in his pocket." Her stare was as stiff as the wind outside, and twice as cold. "I want to know how my father died."

Sam folded the sheet down off of Nestrom's body from head to toe, setting it on the end of the table by Nestrom's feet. Kat watched, her arms crossed over her chest, her thumb tapping against her lips.

From the right front pocket of Nestrom's jeans, Sam retrieved a small piece of paper, folded in half, and a tiny metal thumb drive. That's what he'd felt earlier. He set them both down on the folded sheet, then gestured to Kat, suggesting she search the other pocket, since she was closer. Her eyes widened and she shook her head quickly.

Understandable. Sam didn't know if Kat was the type who would want to stay busy, just to keep herself distracted, or if she would prefer to keep her distance. Apparently, she was the latter.

In fact, Sam had to remind himself that he barely knew Kat at all. He'd only met her less than a day ago. It seemed like a lifetime. A crazy, eventful lifetime. But still, less than a day.

He walked around behind her, giving her a comforting squeeze on the arm as he passed. In Nestrom's left front pocket, Sam found what seemed to be a tiny screwdriver, the kind that would be used for eyeglasses. Like those he'd seen in the workshop, it was made of hard plastic instead of metal, and the tip was tiny, so needle-fine it was almost an awl. He set it beside the thumb drive and the folded paper.

Sam glanced at Nestrom's black t-shirt, but it had no front pocket. With some effort, he rolled the body onto its left side and checked the right back pocket.

Empty.

He walked back around to the other side of the table and did the same with the left back pocket.

This time, Sam found a small photograph, about three inches by five inches, well-creased. The colors were fading, but the resolution was high.

It was a picture of a blonde-haired woman sitting cross-legged in front of a huge Christmas tree, the white tree lights glowing behind her, silver and gold ornaments gleaming, white ribbons winding through the branches. She wore comfortable pants and a thick, baggy sweater. Her face was open and kind. It radiated joy and love, even from the photograph. Just looking at her image brought a wash of warmth through Sam's body. She reminded him of his own mother.

Around the woman, the floor was covered with Christmas presents in a riot of bright colors. Some of the gifts were still wrapped. Others had been reduced to bare boxes and torn wrapping paper in piles by her side.

In the background on one side were two children, a young boy in blue footie pajamas and an older girl in a yellow nightdress. The boy couldn't have been more than three years old, his brown hair short, a white plastic pacifier jutting from his mouth. He knelt on the floor, only his shoulders and head visible above the chaos of presents and wrapping paper.

The girl, her back toward the camera, had blonde hair like the woman. It fell in a tidy bundle down to the center of her back. Her head was turned to look over one shoulder, surveying the gifts on the floor as if searching for something. Sam guessed she was maybe nine years old.

On the other side of the woman stood a third child, a girl the same age as the little boy, dressed in a blue t-shirt and grey pajama pants. She held a small square package in front of her, still wrapped, arms outstretched as she offered it to the woman with a smile.

Sam recognized that smile.

Even as a small child, Kat had that heart-stopping smile.

He held out the image to her. She furrowed her eyebrows and shook her head slowly as she examined it.

"Is that you?" asked Sam.

"I don't know," Kat replied. "I guess it must be. Me, Brandon, Christa." She paused for a moment, her brow wrinkling in puzzlement. "And my mother."

"You've never seen this picture before?"

Kat shook her head.

Phillip stepped forward, held out his hand. "If I may?"

Kat seemed as surprised by Phillip's forwardness as Sam, but she gave him the photo. His face lit up as soon as he saw it.

"Ah, yes," he smiled. "That's Mrs. Nestrom." The words came out in a whisper, almost reverent. "And, yes, that would be you, Miss Katerina." He looked warmly at Kat. "And Master Brandon and Mrs. Crowell."

Kat peered over Phillip's shoulder. "How old are we there?"

They examined the photo together.

"This must have been taken in 1996, if I were to hazard a guess," said Phillip.

"Awfully specific for a guess," said Sam.

"The Christmas before that, the twins would still have been

in training pants." His voice fell quiet. "And Mrs. Nestrom passed early the next year."

Phillip's face fell into a somber frown as his eyes stared unseeing at the photo. A long, quiet moment passed. He shook himself back to the present, glancing apologetically at Kat and Sam.

"You would have been three years old," he said, handing the photo back to Kat.

What a strange life Phillip must have led. To spend your entire life serving a family, living with them, treating them like your own, but always having to hide your emotions. Never able to show joy or despair or anger or fear. Sam couldn't do it. Wouldn't want to. But he admired Phillip's self-control.

"Why would Nestrom carry that photo in his back pocket?" asked Sam.

Phillip took a quick breath and held it for a moment, seeming to consider his next words carefully.

"I can't answer that question directly, as I never heard Dr. Nestrom discuss it openly." He tilted his head thoughtfully. "But from time to time, when he seemed not yet to be aware of my presence, I did see him looking at that photo. Or at *a* photo, anyway. I assume it would have been that one."

He smiled sadly.

"In fact," Phillip said, "now that I think of it, I saw Dr. Nestrom print out a photo more than once. A photo about that size. I suspect he may have looked at it so often that he wore the paper out and had to print a fresh copy from time to time."

"But it's just a random picture," said Kat. "We're not even looking at the camera."

"Your father loved Christmas," said Phillip. "When your mother was still alive," he added quickly. "He loved to watch your faces when you saw the gifts under the tree, when you opened your presents. He would photograph and record the scene every year." Phillip smiled. "And he did it himself. Insisted on it. Wouldn't let me or any of the other staff do it for him."

"My dad? Loved Christmas?" Kat scoffed. "He's the original Scrooge. I haven't seen him on Christmas morning... ever. Not once in my whole life."

"Your mother died when you were very young," said Phillip softly, his voice thick. "Your father changed quite a bit after her death." He cleared his throat and stared at the floor. When he looked up again, his professional stoicism had returned. "Mrs. Crowell may be old enough remember what Dr. Nestrom was like. Perhaps she can share more with you."

He folded his white-gloved hands in front of him and stepped back from the table.

Sam looked over the body once more, slowly, from head to toe. He noticed a wedding ring on Nestrom's left hand, a simple, plain gold band.

"He still wore his wedding ring?"

"Mr. Nestrom never removed it," said Phillip.

Sam glanced across the table at the other hand. There was a ring on that one, too. He walked around to examine it more closely.

That ring was also made of gold, but it was far more elaborate. As the band curled toward the top of Nestrom's finger, it doubled in thickness and widened into a flat bezel on the top. Set into the bezel was a brilliant diamond cut in a triangular shape.

"That is the diamond from Mrs. Nestrom's wedding ring," Phillip said. "Mr. Nestrom had it put into a custom setting so that he could wear it himself. In her memory."

Sam lifted Nestrom's hand to get a better look at the ring, ignoring the unnerving feeling of the corpse's cold, hard skin.

"It's a trillion cut," said Phillip. "Triangular on top and pyramidal on the bottom. A beautiful and unusual cut." His voice softened. "For a beautiful and unusual woman." He looked up and cleared his throat. "As Dr. Nestrom would often say."

The ring was fascinating. Sam had never seen that shape before. He ran his finger over the profile, then tugged at the ring, trying to pull it off of Nestrom's finger.

"What are you doing?" said Kat.

"Might be important," said Sam. The ring wouldn't budge. He pulled on it, pushed up on the bottom and tried to slide it. Nothing.

"Sam, come on. Please."

He hooked one finger around the top, bracing it against the diamond setting. With his thumb braced underneath, he pulled again.

The diamond popped off the setting. Luckily, it popped straight into Sam's cupped palm.

"Nice going," said Kat. "You managed to desecrate my father's corpse and my mother's memory in one fell swoop."

Sam neck and cheeks flushed hot. What had he been thinking? As he fumbled with the diamond, trying to put it back in place, his mind raced with self-admonishment. Removing jewelry from a corpse in front of witnesses? He wasn't robbing the dead man. He was just looking for clues. Stupid.

Sam's fumbling wasn't getting him anywhere until he took a deep breath and looked closely at what he was doing. The diamond was cut into a triangular shape, but it came to a point at the bottom, almost like an upside-down pyramid. The bezel of the ring had a pyramidal depression set into it. Sam flipped the diamond over, point down, and pushed it carefully into the depression. With a slight adjustment to find just the right angle, the diamond popped back into place with a satisfying click.

Kind of a weird ring. A little unstable for a diamond setting. But, Nestrom was a little unstable himself. Sam was just glad he got the ring reassembled without any lasting damage. None that he could tell, anyway.

Whether or not there was lasting damage to his reputation, especially in Kat's eyes, remained to be seen.

"Okay," said Sam, after giving Kat a sheepish, apologetic look. "We've got a photograph, a screwdriver, a thumb drive, and a piece of paper." Kat set the photo beside the other items. Sam picked up the folded paper. "Let's start with this."

"Aren't you worried about fingerprints or something?" asked Kat.

"Shit," said Sam. He patted his pockets. "I don't have any gloves."

"Here," said Kat, pulling two pair from her back pocket and handing one pair to Sam. "I took extras from the workshop."

Properly gloved, Sam unfolded the paper. There were two words scratched in black ink in the center. The handwriting was thick and sure, the strokes sharp.

"That's my father's handwriting," said Kat.

The note was upside down. Sam turned it upright so he could read what was written there.

*For Sam*, it said.

Sam balked.

He read it again.

*For Sam.*

What the fuck?

"What the fuck?" said Kat. "Why would my father have a note in his pocket addressed to you?"

"It's not addressed to me," said Sam. "It just says 'For Sam'. There's nothing else there."

Kat looked down at the row of objects on the sheet.

"It was in the pocket with the thumb drive," she said. "Maybe the note means that the thumb drive is for you."

Sam picked up the drive. There didn't seem to be anything special about it. It was a brushed metal stick not much longer than the tip of his finger with a slim silver connector sticking out from one end.

"I only brought my phone," he said. "I can't read this. I don't have a computer with me."

"Me, neither," Kat replied, "but I know where we can find one."

## 17

It seemed odd to Sam to be back in Nestrom's workshop again. When Nestrom's body had been there, it had felt like a rescue or a crime scene investigation. An official act. Like Sam had the right to be there. Plus, he'd been there with all of the others.

Now, Nestrom's body was gone. The room was dark and quiet, and it was just him, Kat, and Phillip in the workshop. The others didn't even know they were down there. Sam felt like they were intruding, doing something sneaky or illicit.

"His computer is over here," said Kat.

Phillip waited by the entrance as Kat led Sam past the four worktables to a space in the back of the workshop. A well-used couch lay against one wall, with a blanket piled on one end and a stack of pillows on the other. A desk and a rolling office chair stood beside it. The desk was empty except for a silver laptop and a small atomic clock showing the date and time.

Kat opened the laptop. The screen sprung immediately to life as Kat began to type.

"He didn't have a password on his computer?" asked Sam.

Kat shrugged without looking away from the screen. "Maybe he figured the room was secure enough that he didn't need one."

She opened some windows on the computer, then held her hand over her shoulder. Sam gave her the thumb drive and waited as she inserted it into the port on the side of the laptop.

One of the windows updated with a list of files. Sam bent down to read the filenames more closely. Every name was a string of numbers, followed by an underscore and another string of numbers.

And they were all video files.

Why would Nestrom have a thumb drive full of video files in his pocket? And why would he want Sam to have them? Were they surveillance recordings? Would they show how he died? If so, how on earth would Nestrom have put a video of his own death on the thumb drive?

Kat scrolled through the list, scrolling and scrolling until she found a file at the very bottom named "README.mp4". She looked over her shoulder at Sam, who shrugged in response and nodded. Kat double-clicked the file.

A video player filled the screen and began to play. In the video, Nestrom was seated in his office, in the very chair Kat was sitting in.

"Documenting the time," said Nestrom as he held up a clock, the same atomic clock that stood on the desk in front of Sam. The date on the clock was December 25. The time was 1:02AM.

Early on Christmas morning.

Earlier that very day.

Nestrom leaned forward to set the clock back on the desk, then settled in front of the camera again. His face and torso filled the frame.

"It's possible that many people will see this video. For all I know, the whole world will see it. At the very least, I expect one person to see it, a man going by the name Sam Davis." Sam glanced at Kat, but she didn't take her eyes from the screen. "And I expect Sam Davis to bring it to the authorities."

Sam looked around for another chair. Finding none, he squatted beside Kat, his face level with the laptop screen.

"In fact," Nestrom continued, "I insist that Sam bring it to the authorities as soon as he is able." He cleared his throat. "And just so I don't have to dance around with the language, I'll assume I'm speaking directly to Sam from now on."

Sam scooted closer to the camera and stared straight at the lens, shivering at Nestrom's gaze.

"Sam," Nestrom continued, "you've found this video and the thumb drive it's stored on, one way or another. I won't put any protections on it. No passwords or administrator restrictions. Should you see fit to copy and distribute this video, that's your call. I won't stop you. I'm sure it will interest plenty of people. You might even make some money from it."

What the hell was this? It had the air of a confession video. Sam was sure Nestrom had plenty of skeletons in his closet. No one became as rich and powerful as Nestrom without collecting a few along the way. But why would he feel the need to confess them? And why would he want Sam to have it?

"Hell, you'd probably make a lot of money from it," Nestrom chuckled, "though you'd make a lot more from the other videos on the thumb drive." He leaned forward. "Not that you need the money," he said with a wink and a knowing smile.

Kat turned her head toward Sam.

Sam didn't look at her, just kept his eyes on the laptop screen.

"But please," Nestrom went on, "whatever you do, make sure a copy gets to the proper authorities. Because if you're watching this, it means I'm dead."

Nestrom leaned even closer to the camera. His face filled the screen. He stared straight into the lens, his pale eyes staring into Sam's soul with the same intensity they had at the dinner table the night before.

"I'm dead," Nestrom said with a heavy sigh, "and someone in my own household killed me."

**18**

The video stopped abruptly.

Sam and Kat stared silently at the black screen, their reflections staring back at them, astonished looks on their faces.

"Do you really think he was murdered?" said Kat, her voice soft. She leaned back in her chair, craning her neck back toward the door.

Sam glanced over. Phillip waited patiently, his demeanor showing no hint that he'd heard the video.

But then, Phillip's demeanor rarely showed any hint of anything beyond polite deference and a professional eagerness to serve.

"I have no idea," replied Sam.

He considered sharing his suspicions with Kat, but he had no evidence to back them up. All he had was a hunch, a feeling. And that might have been caused by an overactive imagination and too many movies when he was a kid.

And whether or not Nestrom had been murdered wasn't the

most pressing question in Sam's mind at that moment. Sam was wondering why Nestrom had felt like he *would* be murdered. And who he thought might want to kill him.

Someone in his own household.

And why would he compile a thumb drive full of videos? What was in those videos? And why would he want Sam to have them? There was no way Nestrom could have known Sam was coming that night, so the decision to make the video and write the note had to have been made on Christmas Eve, probably after dinner.

"You're the criminology student," said Kat. "What do we do now?"

Sam shrugged. "I guess we send the video to the authorities. That's what Nestrom wanted, right?"

"The police won't be here for days. You said that yourself."

"We can just email it to them,"

"To who? The chief of police? I don't even know who that is."

"I'm sure we can look that up on the internet."

Kat peered at the list of filenames, then shook her head. "Even if we could find out who it was, and find out their email address, and write a message that didn't make us sound totally crazy," she gestured toward the computer screen, "the video file is too big. It won't go through on email."

Sam sighed. "We'll just have to show it to them when they get here, then."

Kat nodded slowly, an uneasy disquiet falling over them both.

"But do you really think he was murdered?" asked Kat, her voice low, eyes flicking toward Phillip in the distance.

"Nestrom seemed to think so," Sam replied.

"But what if he wasn't?" She turned on the chair, swiveling to face Sam. "My father was a recluse. Brilliant, but a little nuts. Had all kinds of theories about artificial intelligence and the surveillance state. He thought he was constantly being watched by the Chinese government, the Russian government, the American government. That kind of thing."

Sam nodded. Typical tech person delusions. Every tech person Sam had ever met who had found any success at all thought the whole world was snooping on them, as if they were the most important person in the world and everyone was dying to find out their secrets. For most of them, of course, these were just delusions of grandeur.

For Nestrom, though, he might have been right.

"If this was just more paranoia," Kat continued, "and he died of natural causes, this would just stir up trouble, lead the police down a blind alley, and waste everyone's time and energy, wouldn't it?"

"What if he was?" said Sam.

"Was what? Paranoid?"

"What if he was murdered."

Kat's eyes widened. "So you *do* think he was murdered."

Sam shook his head. "I have no idea," he said. "We found him down here, dead. No signs of struggle. No scratches, bruises. Nothing in the office was broken or seemed out of place." He looked over his shoulder at the workshop. "It doesn't look like a murder scene. But we can't know for sure. That's why we need the authorities."

"But we can't let them down here."

That caught Sam by surprise.

"Why not? We have to let them down here. We found a dead body down here."

"We can show them the body, but we can't let them into the workshop."

"We have to. They'll need to investigate the place where the body was found."

"But they don't know where the body was found."

Sam tilted his head. He didn't expect this kind of thing from Kat. Brandon, maybe. Cress, for sure. But, from Kat, it was surprising.

He'd known her less than a day, Sam reminded himself. Why should he be surprised?

"And you don't think we should tell them?" he said.

Kat blew out a heavy breath, clearly struggling in her mind with how to handle the situation. "This is my father's workshop. He never let anyone down here." She stared hard at Sam. "No one. He'd be angry to know we had all been in here. But he'd be furious if we let the police traipse through here like a herd of elephants, messing with all of his research." She shook her head. "I mean, it makes sense. It's probably the right thing to do. But, my father wouldn't have wanted it. And Thomas will never allow it."

"Thomas?" That was a real shocker. Friendly, get-along-with-everyone Thomas seemed like the last person who would impede a police investigation. "Why would Thomas lie to the police?"

She waved her hands at the room. "All of this stuff belongs to the company. It's proprietary research."

"Proprietary research," said Sam. He couldn't believe what he was hearing.

"It's valuable intellectual property, potentially worth hundreds of billions of dollars to whoever can use it. Cops or no cops, the company won't give this up. Not unless they have to."

She might have a point. Whatever Nestrom was working on —and the press said he was always working on something—the company would not want to let it get out to the public.

"What would you want to do, then?" Sam said. "We can't just leave Nestrom in the shed and shrug our shoulders when they ask where we found him."

"But we already moved him. We have to tell the cops that,

anyway. And there's nothing out of place in here. You said that yourself."

"So you want to tell the cops he died somewhere else?"

"What's the harm?"

"What's the harm?" Sam shrugged nonchalantly. "Not much. Lying to the police. Impeding an investigation. Covering up the circumstances of a man's death. Maybe accessory to murder. Pretty sure those are all illegal."

"Only if they catch us."

"No, they're illegal even if they don't catch us. We only go to prison if they catch us. You ever been inside a prison, Kat?"

Kat rolled her eyes.

"I'm guessing that's a no." Sam smiled at her. "Look, I don't have a problem breaking the law. I just don't want to do it unless it's for a good reason."

"Making billions of dollars isn't a good enough reason?"

"Making billions of dollars for someone else?" Sam arched an eyebrow. "No."

He saw anger flash behind Kat's eyes. It quickly faded, masked by a slow smile. The smile spread, larger and larger. Kat licked her lips.

"Maybe I can think of another reason?"

She swiveled the chair toward Sam, spread her legs to straddle him where he squatted beside her.

"That's a good reason," Sam replied, "but not to lie to the police."

"That's okay," said Kat, glancing again to make sure Phillip couldn't see. "It'll be good for something else."

She grabbed Sam's shirt in both hands and pulled him to her.

"What the fuck are you two doing down here?" came a rough voice from behind Sam.

He and Kat immediately broke apart. It certainly wasn't Phillip's voice.

Sam craned his neck to see who was standing behind him.
He sighed.

It was Brandon.

# 19



Brandon scowled at Sam and Kat, a drink sweating in his hand.

"What we're doing," said Kat sweetly, pushing off of Sam and swiveling back toward the desk, "is none of your fucking business."

Sam stood. He'd been squatting too long. His knees ached as the blood rushed into them.

And away from other parts of him.

"Fucking business is right," sneered Brandon. He pinned Sam with the kind of stare that only a brother can give to the guy who's sleeping with his sister. "The old man hasn't even been dead one day. Can't you keep it in your pants?"

Kat came up beside Sam, her hands shoved in her pockets. She pulled one hand out and slid it around Sam's arm. "Why should he? Dear old daddy's not gonna care anymore."

Sam stole a glance over Kat's shoulder at the laptop on the desk. The thumb drive was gone and all the windows on the screen were closed. The only thing left on screen was a message about the thumb drive being improperly ejected.

Brandon followed Sam's eyes. He pushed past the two of them, pushing them apart in the process, and stood before the desk.

"Snooping around his computer?" He took a swig of his drink. "Why didn't I think of that?" He bent over the screen. "How'd you get through all the passwords and shit?"

"He didn't have any," said Kat.

Brandon frowned at her.

"Bullshit," he said, his eyes narrowed.

Kat shrugged.

Brandon stared hard at her, then at Sam.

"Huh," he said, finally. "Never could figure out that asshole." He straightened. "Did you find anything?"

"Nothing interesting," said Kat quickly. She walked away from the laptop and around the corner to the workbench with all of the papers strewn across it, Sam and Brandon following. "Guess he kept everything out here somewhere." She picked up a huge piece of paper, some kind of schematic drawing, and perused it.

"On paper?" Brandon peered over her shoulder. "What is it?" he asked.

"It's top-secret proprietary intellectual property," said Thomas.

Sam looked up. Thomas strode toward them between the workbenches, his face stern.

"And it's the property of Nestech, Incorporated."

Thomas's voice was louder and firmer than Sam had heard it before.

"Jesus, it's a fucking reunion down here," muttered Brandon. "Funeral's not until later," he said, louder, to Thomas. "If we even have one."

"I'm going to ask you all to leave now," Thomas said. "As Sam said earlier, we need to preserve this area for the authorities."

Kat snorted. "For the company, you mean."

"That, too." Thomas smiled. His smile was friendly, but Sam could see the corporate gears turning behind his eyes. Unlike the prior evening, when Thomas had been relaxed and sociable, and this morning, when he'd been in pure shock, now he was all business. This was the CEO of one of the largest companies in the world. For the first time since Sam had arrived, he acted like it. Finally out from under Nestrom's shadow, maybe?

Brandon tossed back the last of his drink, waggled the empty tumbler back and forth.

"I need a refill, anyway," he said, moving toward the door.

Kat followed. Thomas held his arm out, inviting Sam to exit ahead of him, that same corporate smile on his face.

Flicking off the lights and locking the room, Phillip followed Thomas out the door.

Phillip was the last to leave.

As he trudged up the stairs, Sam noted that fact.

Phillip was always the last to leave.

**20**

DECEMBER 25, 1:37PM


Sam hung back as they climbed up the long, winding staircase from Nestrom's workshop, waiting until Thomas had caught up to him.

"What do you plan to do, Thomas?" he said. "When the authorities arrive, I mean?"

"We'll cooperate fully with their investigation," Thomas replied. "Whatever they need."

"What about all that 'top-secret IP' stuff?"

Thomas set his mouth in a tight line. "There will be corporate representatives present at all times when the authorities are in that workshop. We will make sure no company property is tampered with or removed."

"You're gonna hang around down there while the cops are crawling all over it?"

Thomas laughed. "Not me," he said. "We've got people who know a lot more than me who will keep an eye on things."

"Oh yeah? Like who?"

"Our lead counsel, for one."

"A lawyer?"

"And our head of information security, for another."

They wound around the corner, climbing the seemingly endless staircase. No wonder Nestrom never left his workshop. Too many damn stairs to climb.

"A lawyer and an InfoSec guy."

"And their teams and whoever else they appoint to join them. At least one Nestech employee for every non-employee on the premises."

"Okay, but what can they do? If the cops want something, they can just take it, can't they?"

"Absolutely not," said Thomas, seemingly offended by the suggestion. "This is a private residence, and that"—he pointed down the stairs toward the workshop—"is corporate property. The police won't set foot in that room without my permission. Believe me."

"What if they get here before your guys?"

"I won't even let them in until my people are here. At this point, a few minutes' delay won't matter."

They finally reached the top of the stairs. Sam saw Kat and Brandon discussing something down the hallway. The discussion seemed heated, but their voices were too low for Sam to hear. They looked over. Brandon's gaze was withering, his expression dark. He practically spat venom when he saw Sam. He muttered something to Kat and stalked off down the hallway.

Probably in search of that refill he wanted.

Kat waited for Sam and Thomas to come to her.

"What's wrong with him?" Sam said, jerking his chin down the hallway toward Brandon.

"It'd be summer before I finished answering that question," said Kat with a sigh.

She didn't seem willing to elaborate, so Sam didn't push. "Your brother-in-law seems to be on the same page as you, Kat," he said, nodding toward Thomas. "More or less."

"That's nice to hear. What about?"

"He won't let the cops in the workshop, either. Not without his corporate goons on scene first."

"We have corporate goons? That's even nicer to hear."

"We don't have goons," said Thomas. "What we have is even more dangerous."

"Oh?" said Kat. "What's that?"

"Lawyers," said Thomas with a curt smile.

Kat smiled back. "You should get your lawyers to keep the cops out of the workshop altogether."

"Kat wants to lie about where we found your father-in-law's body," Sam said to Thomas. "Tell the police we found him in the kitchen or something."

Thomas looked aghast. "Absolutely not," he said.

"Why not?" said Kat. "The cops won't know any better, and it keeps them from snooping through all of my father's stuff."

"They may or may not know any better," said Thomas, "but if they figured it out—and they probably would. The police aren't idiots—the blowback on the company would be horrendous. Can you imagine the headlines? 'Cover-up at Nestech'. 'Conspiracy around death of founder'." Thomas shook his head. "No, it's not worth the PR risk. We'll let them look, but we'll NDA them as best we can when they arrive and make sure they never look at anything confidential without Nestech personnel on scene. And if anything leaks to the press, even the color of the paint on the walls, *we'll* be the ones investigating *them*."

Thomas's eyes were alight. When Sam had first met Thomas and found out what he did for the company, Sam couldn't understand why Nestrom would have picked someone like him as CEO. Thomas had seemed happy-go-lucky and amiable. A good communicator, but not someone that seemed to be particularly strong-willed or opinionated. Sam had assumed Nestrom had given Thomas the job just to keep it in the family, and because Thomas could easily be controlled.

But now he was starting to see another side of Thomas. Thomas the businessman. And it was kind of impressive.

"That sounds like a better plan," said Sam to Kat.

Thomas pushed past them down the hallway. "I hope so," he said, "because it's the plan we're going with."

"Maybe it is better," grumbled Kat as she and Sam followed Thomas, "but I still like my plan the best."

# 21



Sam followed Thomas and Kat through the maze of hallways to a room he hadn't seen before, one with windows that covered the entire wall from floor to ceiling. Massive panes of glass with no shutters or drapes.

The windows looked out over the front of the house. The blizzard had eased. The snow was less driving, the clouds still thick, but brighter. Sam could see the entryway, the circular drive, the fountain in the center of the circle, now covered with snow. The driveway snaked away past a featureless expanse that ended in an icy pond. Beyond that, a stand of trees grew into a wide forest as Sam let his eye trace back to the horizon. Somewhere in the distance, he thought he could see the indentation of the main road, covered with snow.

Still impassable.

The light from the windows suffused the space with a white glow. But where the light at breakfast that morning had been ethereal and restful, the afternoon light was crisp and hard. Where the morning light softened edges, like a dream, this light accentuated them, brought fine details into stark relief. Everything he saw looked so clear and sharp, Sam felt like he was on some kind of drug.

The wall of windows was on Sam's left as he entered. A fireplace roared in the wall to his right. The blast of heat and the red glow battled with the cool, blue-tinted light from the windows, with Sam caught between. And before him, on the front line in the war between ice and fire, sat a long leather couch.

"This is where my father liked to come when he wasn't in his workshop," said Kat. "He called it his liminal space".

"Was this room off-limits to you, too?"

"No, actually." Kat smiled softly. "He wasn't in here often, but he let us come in with him, if we found him here. We could read a book or even chat with him, if he was in a good mood."

"Was he ever?"

"In a good mood?" Kat shrugged. "Sometimes." She waggled her head from side to side. "Maybe not a lot, but sometimes." She looked around the room. "I have some good memories in here," she said softly.

Paintings covered every inch of the wall opposite Sam. The colors and styles of the artwork varied as wildly as the size and types of the frames. Small squares in rough-hewn wood frames depicted pastoral scenes of barns and meadows in a realistic style, the bright yellows and greens of spring vibrant on the canvases. Mid-sized rectangles in gilt, ornate frames showed lakes and rivers overhung with trees and branches, leaves dipping down into the water, dirt and fallen leaves and other debris all around, all in an impressionistic style, like Monet.

And one or two larger paintings, metal frames gleaming in the light. Wild abstract paintings, like those splatter paintings from the artist whose name Sam could never remember. Jack something. Like the artist had flicked a brush full of paint at the canvas and worked with whatever came out. Only instead of colorful splatters, the paintings on the wall in front of Sam were different shades of black and white. One painting had white and grey and black splatters. Another was nothing but white, in subtly varying shades.

Sam leaned in close to that canvas and found even more variation, even more hues of white. And the paint strokes varied, too. Some were splattered, some were brushed across the scene. Others looked like they may have been carefully etched into the canvas with a knife or a paint scraper. The image rewarded close inspection, revealing a whole world of detail that wasn't visible from even a foot or two away.

"My mother was an artist," said Kat, stepping to Sam's side. "Or so I'm told. She had a studio on the other side of the house, but my father liked to hang her work all over. When she died, he pulled some of her work into this room."

"Did he sell the rest?"

Kat shook her head. "It's in a storage room. Under the house, like the workshop. It's all climate-controlled and things like that, but all of the paintings are in crates and boxes. Hidden away."

"That's a shame. These are beautiful."

"I think he came in here to feel closer to her," said Kat. "That's my story, anyway. He never said so." After a moment, she added, "That's why I came in here."

"To be closer to your mother?"

"To be closer to both of them."

Sam turned to look at the other wall. Like the wall of paintings, this one was covered floor to ceiling with framed art. But instead of paintings, these were photographs.

"Your mom was a photographer, too?"

Kat nodded. "Painting, drawing, photography, even a little sculpting."

"Did she sell her work or just make it for herself?"

"No, she was very popular. Had a few gallery shows in the city. Sold out every time. Her career was starting to take off when she died." She gave Sam a weak smile that faded as quickly as it had come. "Again, so I'm told."

The photographs had a much different character from the paintings. The paintings were vivid, alive, and exciting, but they all held a kind of optimism. They seemed—to Sam, at least—to depict landscapes, even the abstract splatter paintings. And those landscapes had a tranquility that complemented the optimism. Even the wild splatters of the black-and-white paintings carried a hopefulness in the abandon of the strokes.

The photographs, on the other hand, were dark. Many were abstract, objects with blurred edges or streaks of color from a moving lens. Others were nudes, but in close-up. Some black-and-white, others in color, all had a graininess to their texture. Close-ups of sharp angles in harsh light. A portrait of a face, filling the frame from a close, frontal angle.

One large photo was a striking shot of a nude woman staring out a tall window, her back toward the camera. The image was taken from a long distance, so that the woman appeared as only a small figure in the lower corner, the window towering above her tiny form.

The images were aggressive, opinionated. While the paintings filled Sam with hope and joy and wonder, the photographs invoked anger, loneliness, and a bitter divisiveness.

"Did your mother make these photos, too?"

Kat nodded.

"They're very... powerful."

"Bleak, you mean," smiled Kat. "I've seen other photos of hers, in a book I found on a shelf in my father's library. They're not nearly so dark. For some reason, my father chose these photos to hang in here, opposite those paintings."

"Georgie was a complicated woman," said Cress. She had come up behind them, admiring the photos, too. "And a wonderful artist. She would have taken the art world by the balls if she'd lived. She would have out-Anseled Ansel Adams, out-Warholed Andy Warhol, out-Pollacked Jackson Pollack. Shown all those arrogant dick-holders what a woman could really do. She was that good."

Jackson Pollack. That was the splatter artist Sam had been trying to remember.

"She would have made your father's genius look silly by comparison," said Cress, leaning in conspiratorially. "He needed someone like that. Someone he could look up to. They were perfect for each other."

"How did she—" asked Sam, but the question was cut off by the sound of voices coming from the hallway.

Arguing voices.

Growing louder.

"—fucking cares about any of that shit?"

"I do. It's important."

"Important to you. Not to anyone else."

"It should be important to you. If you knew what was good for you. If you would stop drinking for one day."

Brandon banged into the room, his drink sloshing wildly in the tumbler in his hand. Christa came in close behind.

"Fuck off," said Brandon over his shoulder. He took a belt from his glass and looked around the room. "Great. Another family reunion. We should really start doing this less often."

He flopped down on one side of the couch, his drink cradled in his lap.

Thomas had been staring out the window, arms folded, pinching his chin between his thumb and forefinger. He turned and surveyed the room.

"Good," he said. "Everyone's here."

"What do you want, Thomas?" said Brandon. "This alcohol isn't going to drink itself." As if to demonstrate, he drained his glass in one large gulp.

How on earth the man could still walk after all the alcohol

he consumed was a mystery to Sam. And there was a time when Sam could hold his own with anyone in a drinking contest.

"What I want," said Thomas, "is to discuss our plan."

"I plan to get another drink," said Brandon, "as soon as humanly possible." He moved to get up from the couch, but Christa pushed him back with two straight fingers jabbed into his collarbone.

"What plan, Thomas?" said Christa, spitting the words through clenched teeth as she glared at Brandon.

Thomas looked at each of them in turn, letting his eyes rest last upon Sam. "Our plan to deal with the police," he said.

# 22



If Thomas thought that coming up with a plan would have been easy, the edge in his normally cheerful, professional voice showed that he wasn't feeling that way anymore.

Still, Sam had to hand it to him. That edge hadn't crept into Thomas's voice until after a solid forty-five minutes of bickering among his family members. Sam would have lost his cool a lot sooner.

Everyone seemed to have a different idea of how to handle the police. Thomas wanted to have company people on site monitoring the police at all times. He made clear that he was unwilling to negotiate on that point. Aside from that, he was happy to allow the police free access to the house and the grounds.

Others, including Kat, disagreed. Though she didn't use the words, Kat essentially wanted to falsify evidence and claim to the police that they'd discovered Nestrom in his bedroom.

Cress wanted to bury Nestrom in the snow and be done with it.

Christa wanted to go through the workshop, take pout anything important, then set it all back up again, putting Nestrom's body where they'd found it. In other words, she wanted to falsify evidence, too.

Brandon wanted everyone to just leave the house altogether and let the cops do what they would.

Thomas's idea was the only one with even a shred of rationality. All of the other ideas were the fantasies of a family too rich and too coddled to understand how the real world worked. Two people wanted to try to fool the police, two wanted to run away.

None of those ideas were likely to work.

Then again, maybe things really were different for the wealthy.

After nearly an hour of bickering, of tearing down one idea after another, Thomas held up his hands. The room quieted immediately, like an elementary school teacher quieting a classroom of unruly seven-year-olds.

"Nestech staff will be on site the entire time," Thomas said. "They will observe while the police examine the body and the workshop."

"What about us?" said Brandon.

"I'm sure we'll all be asked to give statements," Thomas replied. "Just tell the truth and answer their questions and everything will be over as soon as possible, I'm sure."

"You're sure," scoffed Cress. "You don't know the police like I do, Tommy."

"This isn't like showing your tits in Vegas, Cress," said Christa. "The police take deaths a little more seriously."

"My tits were serious back then," said Cress. She threw a leering glance at Sam. "Still are."

"Ew," said Brandon from the couch.

Cress swung a heavily-jeweled hand at the back of Brandon's head. Sam heard a loud crack, then Brandon howled with pain and indignation. Cress must have caught him in the skull with one of the many rings adorning her fingers. With as much jewelry as she wore on her fingers, she might as well have been wearing brass knuckles.

"What do you think, Sam?" asked Thomas. "You're the only one who hasn't said anything."

"I think your plan is a good one," said Sam, eliciting a groan from Brandon. "We're all going to have to stay here until the police are done investigating. They will definitely want to speak to us. The staff, as well."

"Yeah, why isn't Phillip up here?" said Cress. "He's always skulking around. He probably knows more than any of us."

"I'll inform Phillip," said Thomas, "but I'm sure he won't be going anywhere."

"It's an inconvenience, for sure," Sam continued, "but it could be worse. This house is hardly a prison cell."

"Easy for you to say."

Sam would have expected that kind of comment from Brandon, or maybe from Cress. He was surprised to hear it come from Kat.

"Just answer the questions the police have," said Sam. "We're all suspects. That's just the way it goes."

"Suspects?" said Christa. "Suspects for what?"

"Any time there's an unexpected death, the police will always consider foul play." Sam shrugged. "The first people to be considered are always family, close friends, and anyone who was with the victim when they died. It's just procedure. If you answer their questions honestly, they'll work it out and we can all go back to our lives." Sam grinned. "Unless one of us actually did murder Nestrom."

He intentionally made his voice sound light-hearted, like he were making a crude joke. But Sam watched the faces of the others very carefully as he said the words.

None of them laughed. None of them smiled. None of them made eye contact with Sam.

Kat and Brandon looked at each other, then down at the floor. Christa and Thomas looked at each other, then down at the floor or out the window. And Cress just swallowed hard and stared down at the rings on her fingers.

That's when Sam knew for sure that he was in a room full of murder suspects.

And he couldn't deny it. The realization gave him a thrill.

## 23

DECEMBER 25, 4:53PM

They were all back in the billiard room again. At almost the exact same time they'd been in there the night before.

Creatures of habit.

The blizzard had picked up again as darkness had fallen, the snow now driving as hard as ever. It was a good thing they'd moved Nestrom's body into the gardener's shed. The resurgence of the storm would push out the arrival of the police by at least another day. If they hadn't moved it, Nestrom's body would be looking pretty gross by the time the cops finally showed.

Brandon was drinking on the couch, his head nodding backward again and again. Finally showing some effect from the copious amounts of alcohol he'd been drinking all day.

Thomas, seated at a round table in the corner, was typing furiously on his cell phone, his face set in a focused frown, thumbs twitching like mad as he sent text after text and email after email. If it were up to him, Sam wasn't so sure he'd be using anything as easily traceable as email or text to summon the Nestech troops, but Thomas seemed to want to play this as above-board as possible.

Christa sat beside Thomas, idly paging through a book she'd pulled off the shelf behind her. She already looked more bored than distraught, and it hadn't even been a day since her father had died.

Kat sat on the couch beside Sam. She'd kicked off her shoes and pulled her feet up. She leaned against Sam's shoulder and stared blankly into the cracking, popping fire that Phillip had started for them.

The only one who showed any liveliness was Cress. She sat opposite Sam, on the couch beside Brandon, regaling the room with a sordid tale about her escapades with some long-dead entertainer, someone who had been a big deal back in the day but whose name Sam couldn't quite place. He'd heard the name before. A singer of some kind. A crooner. But there was no way Sam could have named any of the man's songs off the top of his head.

Still, Cress prattled on. Sex and booze and drugs and more sex and more booze. Scandal and subterfuge. Running from paparazzi and ex-wives and current wives, winding through narrow tunnels in the back of hotel kitchens and underground parking lots. The kind of thing that Cress probably thought would impress everyone, make her seem hot and exciting and vivacious, but which really made her seem like a relic from times long past when that sort of behavior seemed exotic, instead of just self-destructive.

Sam didn't mind, though. Cress didn't expect any interaction from her audience. Didn't want it, even. When Sam had asked a question, she'd answered it sharply, as if annoyed at the interruption. So, he stopped interrupting. Just listened to the drone of her voice—part cackling witch, part game show announcer— and let his mind wander as he looked around the room.

He still couldn't get a bead on these odd people he'd fallen in with. They were all über-wealthy brats with far too high a sense of entitlement. Thomas was the only possible exception, since he'd come from outside the family, but after enough time with Christa, not to mention his time as CEO of Nestrom's corporation, the entitlement may have wormed itself into his psyche.

And some of them were better than others at hiding the entitlement. Brandon made no effort at all. Neither did Cress. Christa seemed to want to earn her way into it by fawning over her father, even though it was obvious to Sam, even in just the brief interactions he'd witnessed over dinner, that fawning was the last thing Nestrom valued.

Thomas tried to earn it through his position at the company. Of all of them, he might have the most claim to entitlement, especially if he was as effective every day as he seemed now, working diligently to rally the mighty forces of Nestrom, Inc. to protect whatever intellectual property there might be in the workshop below them. And to protect the mighty legacy of Dr. Christopher Nestrom himself.

And then there was Kat.

Mysterious, irresistible, devastatingly attractive Kat.

Sam had to admit that his initial assessment of Kat's beauty had been off by orders of magnitude. Maybe it was the wealth. Maybe it was the sex. Maybe it was just the intrigue, but the woman sent warm shivers up and down Sam's spine every time he looked at her. Even when she wasn't flashing him that megawatt smile.

She craned her head back toward him, gave him a soft squeeze on his calf and a sleepy, smoky, half-lidded look that got him hard in an instant.

Shit.

Sam was falling for Kat.

That was not a good thing under any circumstance, but especially not now, when she was a potential murder suspect. The last thing Sam wanted was to attract the attention of the police as anything but the straight-laced son of criminal parents who had seen the error of his parents' ways and was doing his best to make good. And as someone who showed real promise as a data analyst for the good guys.

Sam had a cover to maintain, after all.

**24**

Brandon had been complaining for over an hour when Phillip finally summoned them to dinner. The arrangement was similar to the previous night, except that the chair at the head of the table was conspicuously empty. The emptiness hung like a hangman's noose over the table.

Brandon had tried to sit in Nestrom's chair, to make light of Nestrom's absence, but no one had acknowledged him in any way. Even the staff had served his food to his usual place, so he'd been forced to skulk back to his chair to eat.

Unlike the previous night, where everything was timed to Nestrom's movements, the staff waited patiently for everyone to finish each course before clearing and serving the next. Even that simple courtesy was enough to loosen the noose's knot and give the dinner a more relaxed feeling. Soon, after what had started as an oddly reverent meal, almost as if they were all paying forced respects to Nestrom through the oppressive silence, the conversation began to flow more naturally.

"God, I feel like I could eat a horse. An elephant, even," said

Brandon as he lifted his bowl to slurp down the last of his beef consommé. "Hell, I could even eat—"

"Don't say it," warned Kat, not even bothering to look up.

Brandon grinned across the table at her.

"Maybe we could convince Phillip to serve dinner a little earlier," said Thomas, "now that... well..."

"Now that the old dictator is out of office?" cackled Cress.

"Who's the new dictator?" asked Kat softly.

"The king is dead. Long live the king?" said Christa.

Kat nodded. "Who's the new king?" She looked around the table, but suddenly everyone's soup bowls had become incredibly interesting to them. No one met her eye.

"Did Nestrom have a will?" asked Sam.

All eyes turned to Thomas, who gave a quick glance to Cress. She stared daggers at her bowl, the muscles in her jaw flexing as she clenched her teeth.

Thomas shrugged. "If he has one, I've never seen it."

"What about succession planning?" Sam asked him. "For the company?"

"We talked to him about it for years," Thomas sighed, "but Nestrom always brushed us off. Said there was time to figure that out later."

"No shit?" Brandon said. He gave a low whistle. "Time to short some Nestech stock."

Thomas's face hardened. "You'll be in jail for insider trading if you do. I'll call the SEC myself."

"Really, Thomas? We're family." The sarcasm dripped from Brandon's lips as he lifted his tumbler and took a long pull on his drink.

The staff came to clear out the soup bowls and bring the next course.

"Phillip, do you know if Dr. Nestrom had a will or a trust of any kind?" asked Sam. It was a long shot, but sometimes staff knew more than family. Even down to surprisingly intimate details.

"I was not privy to Dr. Nestrom's personal arrangements," said Phillip, "but after Mrs. Nestrom's passing, he did retain an estate planner, whom he met at regular intervals."

"There you go," said Sam. "The new dictator is in the will. Or the trust. Or whatever Nestrom set up with the estate planner."

"Well, we won't need to meet with that person for some time," said Christa. "Until after the funeral, at least."

"Fuck that," said Brandon. "I say we call the asshole after dinner."

"Fuck the will," said Cress, lifting her glass in a mock toast, draining it, and holding it up to the staff for a refill. Brandon fell silent. Christa reached over to hold Cress' hand, but Cress jerked it away in anger.

"He won't read the will to you over the phone, Brandon," said Kat, once Cress' glass had been refilled.

"He won't if we don't call him."

"No one is calling anyone," said Thomas. His voice was quiet, but authoritative. It drew everyone's eyes back to him. Sam had a feeling he knew who the new dictator was, will or no will.

"The founder and director of the largest company in the world has just died," Thomas continued. "This news will rattle markets around the world." He glared at Brandon, who grinned and tipped his glass at Thomas. "We have to control this information very carefully."

Cress snorted. "Control it? The cops will broadcast it as soon as they get it. They probably already have."

"No, they haven't," said Thomas. "I've been watching the news, monitoring the usual sources. The police can't release any information without the consent of the family."

"As long as there's no evidence of foul play." Sam could practically hear the sound as all eyes swiveled from Thomas to him. He smiled innocently back at them all. "I'm just saying. If it becomes a criminal investigation, they can say whatever they want."

Silence.

Long silence.

Sam kept smiling back at everyone.

"Well," said Thomas, finally, "I'm sure it won't come to that."

From the looks on some of their faces, Sam wasn't so sure at all.

# 25



After dinner, the others made various excuses and disappeared, leaving Kat and Sam alone on the couch in the parlor. The heat from the fire brought a sleepy haze over Sam. He leaned his head back against the warm leather and watched the orange and yellow fireglow play over the long, smooth line of Kat's neck and across her cheeks. It danced in her dark eyes as she stared into the flames. She seemed unusually distracted, almost moody.

Sam had to pull his gaze away before he fell into those eyes. He stared into the fire instead.

He did not want to be swept away again. Every time, he wound up hurt. Disillusioned, at best. Heartbroken, at worst. And yet, every time, even when he swore he would never look at another woman for the rest of his life, someone would come along and Sam would fall all over again.

And fall hard.

He fell so hard, he was amazed his heart was the only thing broken. He should have been in a wheelchair by now.

As the flames ducked and dodged in the fireplace, the sound of them like a crackling wind in his ears, Sam imagined himself drifting, floating on that wind, floating down, down, down into a soft bed of pillows. Kat was there, waiting, that arresting smile in full force.

Sam floated down onto the pillows, into Kat's arms.

And kept going, down through the pillows, incorporeal as clouds. Kat's smile never wavered as Sam slipped through her arms, slipped through the pillows.

Onto the sharp spikes hidden beneath.

Sam's head snapped up, his eyes shot wide.

The flames were low, the air cold.

Mesmerized by the fire, lulled from without by the heat of the flames and lulled from within by the port wine from dinner, he must have nodded off.

And when he woke, Kat was nowhere to be found.

Sam rolled his neck, stretching muscles grown stiff from his awkward position on the couch. What was comfortable for a minute was not necessarily comfortable for an hour.

Or longer. How long had he been asleep anyway?

He pulled his phone from his pocket as he wandered slowly into the hallway. It was after eleven. He'd been out for over an hour. He rubbed both hands over his face, trying to rub the sleep out.

Then he stopped cold.

He heard voices.

He ducked against the wall, wedged in the corner of a doorway where the hall from the parlor met the larger cross-corridor.

Two voices, a man and a woman.

Whispering.

He couldn't quite make out the words, but the sounds were sharp and quick, as if the two were arguing about something.

"It doesn't fucking matter." The man's voice rose in volume before the other person shushed him down again.

Brandon's voice.

But who was he talking to?

Sam edged closer, straining to hear.

The whispers grew sharper and more rapid, but no louder.

Sam wasn't close enough. He decided to risk a peek to see who was with Brandon. Late-night whispers in dark hallways in a house where a man had died not twenty-four hours earlier were not innocent things. Sam had to see who was speaking with Brandon.

He took a long slow breath, and edged around the corner.

And nearly ran into Kat.

They both yelped and jumped back from each other.

"Fuck," said Kat, putting her hand to her heart. "You scared the shit out of me."

Sam's heart was hammering in his ears, but he put on a crooked grin. "Me, too," he said, trying to peer over Kat's shoulder without being too obvious about it. "I just woke up. Wondered where you'd gotten to."

He couldn't make out anything in the gloomy darkness of the hallway behind Kat.

"I just got up to use the bathroom," she said. "You were sleeping so soundly, I didn't want to wake you."

"Who were you talking to?" he asked.

She looked puzzled. "What do you mean?"

"I heard voices. Just now. Were you talking to someone?"

She smiled softly, prettily. "No," she said, stepping toward him again and sliding her arms along his sides. "Just me."

She slid closer to him. In the chill of the hallway, Sam could feel her warmth, like sitting in front of the fire again. The pretty softness of her smile took on another quality, a mischievous one that set Sam's chest to fluttering.

Kat pulled him close, slid one hand behind his neck, pulled his head down and put her mouth against his ear. Her breath was hot, her voice sultry and low.

Now Sam was feeling things in more than just his chest.

"Now that you're awake," Kat purred, the hand that wasn't on Sam's neck running along his back, exploring the skin beneath his shirt, exploring lower, lower, "why don't we go to bed?"

**26**

DECEMBER 26, 1:19AM

Sam woke, naked, in Kat's bed.

There were worse places to be.

The room was pitch black, and Sam was wide awake.

He'd dozed after their lovemaking, but his earlier nap had been enough that he was no longer sleepy, once the languid post-sex haze had worn off.

He reached his arm out to his side to find Kat, but he found only empty sheets.

Cold, empty sheets.

Kat was gone.

Maybe she was in the bathroom.

But the sheets were cold. She'd been gone a long time. Maybe she had gone down to the kitchen to fix a late-night snack.

Sam lay in the dark for a moment, gathering his thoughts. At this point, Sam was fairly certain that Nestrom had not died of natural causes. Given the weather and the timing of his death, it was most likely that someone in the house had killed him. Sam couldn't rule out a slow-acting poison, and he had to confirm that Nestrom hadn't touched or opened any mail that could have been laced, but those were long shots. Most deaths—most murders—were not complicated. The killers were usually the most likely suspects.

And in this case, the most likely suspects were the family members. Nestrom himself had suspected as much, Sherlocking his own murder from beyond the grave.

Sam needed to find out who the killer was.

Motive, means, opportunity.

The motives were there, for every one of them. He couldn't tell the means yet. His examination of the body hadn't yielded any obvious clues.

But what about opportunity? Nestrom's body had been found in his workshop. Either he'd been killed there, or he'd been killed somewhere else and his body had been left there.

Either way, the killer had to have had access to the workshop. To Sam's knowledge, the only one who had access, other than Nestrom himself, was Phillip.

That made Phillip a suspect, too.

Could someone else have had access to the workshop? Someone in the family, perhaps, or one of the other staff members?

Nestrom didn't seem like the type to share that kind of access on a whim. What was the point of locking a door if you gave everyone the key? And there was little love lost with his family members, so he doubted he'd share access with them out of the goodness of his heart.

Maybe Thomas had it, as an officer of Nestech? Some kind of corporate redundancy thing? But Thomas had shown no hint of being familiar with the workshop when they'd gone down there originally. From the way he looked around, all wide-eyed and awestruck, it seemed like he'd never been in there before. Didn't mean he didn't have access, but it made it seem less likely.

Sam thought back to the security measures themselves. A biometric scan and a voice recognition scan. Could those be fooled? Could the killer have used Nestrom's corpse to bypass the biometrics? Could they have used a recording to bypass the voice reco?

Seems like Nestrom would have thought of that, would have had a security algorithm sophisticated enough to distinguish a recording from a real voice.

But algorithms were just code, and computers were just dumb boxes running the code. If someone knew enough about the algorithm, they could find a way to fool it. Voice recognition was about fuzzy frequency matching. If you knew what to do and you got the right frequencies in the right way, any algorithm could be fooled, no matter how sophisticated. Sam's criminology training had taught him that much.

And his criminal training had proved it.

Sam had to check out the workshop again. He was wide awake now, and Kat was gone. Sam wasn't going to fall back asleep for a while. He figured he might as well get out of bed and start looking for answers to some of these nagging questions.

**27**

DECEMBER 26, 1:42AM

Sam's bare feet made no sound as he padded down the stairs to the workshop. The concrete was ice cold against his skin, sending an involuntary shiver through his body. He had gone barefoot so he could make as little noise as possible as he crept through the house. He didn't know who might still be awake, and he didn't want to be seen or heard.

But he'd encountered no one at all as he picked his way through the labyrinthine halls, peeking around corners and moving on barefoot tiptoe. He made it all the way to the door down to the workshop without seeing or hearing anyone. He could have worn his shoes all along. And with the frigid cold seeping into the soles of his feet as he started down the stairs, he wished he had.

There were no lights in the stairwell. There was probably a switch at the top that he should have thrown, but he wasn't about to go back up now. Sam kept his hand along the inner wall, feeling the smooth-worn pocks and chips of the stamped concrete beneath his fingers. Why was concrete always the building material of choice for these tech magnates? Concrete and glass. It was beautiful, but so cold. So mechanical. So inhuman.

Maybe that was why they liked it. Sam didn't know a whole lot of tech billionaires, but the stereotype was that they were all antisocial nerds who'd been bullied in high school and were now taking their revenge on society by getting rich and running the place, imposing their ideals on the jocks and the cheer-leaders who'd been their tormentors so long ago. And getting rich by charging them an annual arm and a leg in the process.

If you're antisocial *(and you know it, clap your hands)*, you'd be drawn to inhuman things. Safer things. Things that you can control. Things that won't judge you. Cold metal and heavy concrete. Beeps and bloops and blinking cursors. Deep, dark underground lairs with three layers of security.

Sam saw a subtle blue glow up ahead in the darkness. It grew wider and brighter as he curled down the stairs.

He knew he would find nothing but locked doors when he got down there, but he figured it was worth a shot to have a look. Maybe he could figure out how to get the doors open. Maybe he could see something through the glass that would be useful. Or maybe he would just waste time until he felt sleepy again.

It didn't matter. He wasn't tired, and he had to do something. He took the last step with a wide stride toward the glass vestibule outside the workshop door.

And pulled himself up short.

Kat was standing right in front of him.

On the other side of the glass.

Kat's eyes were as wide with shock as Sam's must have been, but she had the presence of mind to reach behind her before the inner door swung shut, keeping it open with her hand.

"What are you doing here?" said Sam.

Kat's mouth moved, but Sam heard nothing.

Soundproof glass, Sam remembered.

Sam gestured to his ears and shook his head. Kat nodded and opened the outer door, still holding the inner door open.

"Fancy meeting you here," she said as Sam stepped inside the vestibule.

"Yeah, no kidding. What are you doing?"

"Same as you, I guess," she said. "Couldn't sleep. Thought I'd poke around and see what I could see down here."

"How did you get in?"

Kat ducked her head, a sheepish look on her face. "I woke up Phillip. He wasn't too happy about it, I'm sure, but he didn't complain."

He wouldn't have. Not Phillip. He was too professional for that. Once again, Sam admired the man for his self-control. Sam could never keep a job like that, where he meekly did the bidding of his employers, never showing any hint of emotion. Even when they rousted him from a sound sleep just to open a door.

"Did you find anything?" asked Sam.

"Not really." Kat pushed open the inner door. Sam followed her into the workshop. "Just all of my father's things. Trying to figure out what he was up to when he died. Maybe get a clue into who would have killed him—if that's really what happened—and why."

"I never asked you," said Sam. "Do you think he was murdered?"

Kat winced at the word. "I don't want to think so," she said. "I don't want to believe that someone in my family would do such a thing." She sighed heavily and shrugged. "But I can't rule it out." A rueful smile twisted her beautiful mouth. "I guess that's why I'm down here at one in the morning. Trying to find some answers."

The room was dark, the only glow coming from a series of blue lights set at intervals into the wall near the ceiling. Safety lights or night lights or something like that. Seemed an odd thing to install in a workshop, but Nestrom had been an odd man.

"Is there a light switch somewhere?" asked Sam.

Kat used the glow of her phone screen to find the switch. The room burst into light. Sam winced and shielded his eyes with his hand, momentarily blind after so long creeping through the darkness.

Once his eyes had acclimated, Sam surveyed the scene. It was much as it had been the day before, of course. Nothing appeared to be missing. Nothing appeared to have been moved. If Kat had been poking around, as she had said, she'd been very careful not to leave any trace.

They again grabbed medical gloves from the box along the wall. As Sam pulled his gloves on, he catalogued the room in his mind, separating it into zones to aid his search for information. The workbenches in front he labeled the work zone. The section in back with the couch and the desk was the living zone.

In the work zone were four workbenches, arranged in a square. Sam stepped slowly through them. The one on his left, closest to the door, held a mess of computer parts. In his mind, Sam labeled that the computer station. Across from that, on his right, the bench held a microscope and several piles of lenses in varying shapes and sizes. That was the optical station.

Sam stepped past those two benches toward the two on the far side of the square. On his right was the workbench covered with papers and blueprints. Sam labeled it the library station. And across from that, on his left, was the table that had the eyeglass frames and electrical testing equipment. Sam labeled that one the assembly station.

Computer parts, optical components, notes and papers, and eyeglass assembly.

Clearly, Nestrom was building some kind of wearable tech, some kind of glasses. Augmented reality and virtual reality were two of the hot topics du jour in the tech world, but no one had cracked them yet. Google Glass had been fantastic, but people had widely criticized it for its seeming privacy violations. Brilliant, but ahead of its time. The fastest soldier catches the most arrows, after all.

Other attempts were clunky, ugly devices that made their users look like eyeless cyborgs, with massive plastic boxes hanging off of their faces. No one had yet found the ideal combination of features, software, technology, privacy, and all-important fashion.

But, judging from the prototypes on the assembly station, Nestrom had come close. Very, very close, if the tech actually worked. And whoever cracked the AR/VR nut first would stand to make a fortune.

The kind of fortune people would kill for.

"What was your father working on?"

"No one knew," Kat said, coming to stand beside Sam. "He never spoke about his works in progress. Just dropped them on the world when they were done."

On the table was a row of eyeglasses, folded and set neatly into a felt tray. They all had dark frames and clear lenses. Each one looked like a normal pair of eyeglasses, one that a stylish tech bro would wear. Slightly nerdy, but expensive looking. Something that said *I'm smart and I'm rich and you can't bully me anymore because I can find out everything about you and pay to have you destroyed, quietly and completely.*

"What about manufacturing? His company had to have some lead time to produce whatever he invented, right?"

"My father built his company from scratch. He knew all the contacts, all the suppliers and producers. According to Thomas, he had a tendency to inform everyone all at once, putting in production orders and specs at the same time that he informed the board of the new products. It was a bit of a sore spot for Thomas."

Sam nodded. Thomas wouldn't have liked to seem unaware.

Most executives—most people, especially wealthy ones—liked to seem omniscient. And being caught off-guard would not be good for Thomas's image with the board.

"Your dad didn't lack for confidence, did he?" Sam was sure the board of directors would also have resented being merely informed about the company's new direction, rather than being given an active say in it. Those kinds of people tended to have egos that were even bigger than their net worth. They wouldn't like being out of the loop.

But would one of them have wanted to kill Nestrom over a slight like that? Sam doubted it. They might not like having their egos bruised, but Nestrom was a genius, geniuses made products people wanted to buy, and bruised egos rested very easy on deep beds of fresh money.

But what about Thomas? Would he have killed Nestrom just so he could be the one to deliver a new breakthrough?

Sam turned to look through the papers at the library station, looking first for any mail items. Boxes or envelopes that could have been laced with poison. But he found nothing. If Nestrom had been poisoned, it seemed unlikely it came from someone outside the house.

Instead of mail, Sam found dozens of scholarly articles at the library station. The papers were heavily annotated with high-lighted passages, underlined sections, and notes in the margins, scrawled in that same sure, sharp script that Sam had seen on the note he'd found in Nestrom's pocket.

Nestrom's handwriting.

Sam scanned quickly through the papers. They were all highly technical scientific papers, with complex diagrams and table after table of statistics. Sam was a smart guy and more computer-savvy than most, but he lacked the expertise to know exactly what he was looking at. However, from the diagrams and the context, it was pretty clear that Nestrom had been closely following the latest research in the fields of optics, artificial intelligence, and augmented reality.

So he was probably working on AR glasses, after all. And, if someone was willing to kill him for his research, he'd either built a working prototype or he was about to.

Sam turned back to the table behind him, the assembly station. He counted five pairs of glasses. Five prototypes. They looked identical, but may have had subtle differences in their lenses or their software or something not visible to Sam's eye.

He picked up one pair and unfolded it, turning it around in his gloved hands, examining it closely from every angle. It was light, made of some kind of black resin or composite. Sam noticed a number, 1237.5, etched on the outside of one earpiece, near the temple. It was barely visible, the number carved into the material of the frame.

In fact, the frames looked almost like they were 3-D printed. Sam looked around the workshop and spied a small 3-D printer in one corner, an unassuming glass box with a metal platform in the bottom and a nozzle hanging above it.

Aside from the materials and the number, the glasses looked exactly like a normal pair of eyeglasses, only there was no prescription on the clear lenses. When Sam held them up and looked through them, he could see what was on the other side, without any optical distortion at all. Just clear glass.

Sam wanted to put the glasses on, to see what they did. But he was aware that something had killed Nestrom, maybe in the very spot where Sam was standing. What if Nestrom's death had something to do with the glasses? What if there had been some electrical short, some flaw in the design or error in the construction that had killed him while he wore the glasses? The same thing could happen to Sam.

And yet, Nestrom hadn't been wearing any glasses when Sam found his body. And the glasses on the workbench had all been neatly folded. Not the kind of thing that someone would do as they were dying.

No, it was unlikely that the glasses had killed Nestrom.

Unlikely, but not impossible.

Sam took a deep breath and put the glasses on.

**28**

As soon as Sam put the glasses on, all the sound around him went silent. There must have been some kind of noise cancellation hardware at work in the earpieces. The ambient room noise, the sound of Kat moving beside him, everything fell into a soft hush.

"What are you doing?" asked Kat. Her voice cut through the hush, crystal clear, even more clear than usual. Something in the glasses was enhancing sound, as well, but in an intelligent way. Somehow identifying and enhancing the sounds that were important while keeping the unimportant background noise quiet.

"Only one way to see what these do," said Sam.

"You're not going to turn them on, are you? Isn't that, like, evidence tampering or proprietary information or something?"

"I won't tell if you won't."

It was odd that somehow the glasses were already working, even though Sam hadn't touched a power button. Just by putting them on, the glasses enhanced his hearing. But there must be more that they could do. And there had to be a switch to turn them on.

With both hands at once, Sam felt along the earpieces for a button.

"But you don't know what might happen—" said Kat.

Sam didn't find a button, but he must have touched something, because the glasses suddenly transformed. All outside sound faded to a low hiss, and instead of seeing the room in front of him, the lenses went opaque, then lit up with the Nestrom logo, a capital letter N in vibrant, pale blue font. It pulsed subtly. Sam noticed with a start that it was pulsing in time with his heartbeat.

After a few seconds, the logo went away, the sound came back, and Sam saw the room in front of him just as he had a moment ago. Only now, everything in the room was outlined in thin chalk-white lines on a background the same pale blue color as the Nestrom logo. It was as if the world around him had transformed into an architect's blueprint.

He could see the computer station, with Kat standing beside it, outlined in white. The detail was amazing, like one of those movies where they took real actors and transformed them into cartoons. Kat's hair, the lines of her face and her lips, her neck, all were hyper-realistic, but abstracted to chalk lines.

He turned to his right to see the workbench in front of him and the wall ten feet behind it, turned further to see the living area, the couch and the desk outlined in white in the distance.

And then the view transformed again. The blue background slowly faded. The chalk outlines disappeared. And Sam was looking at the world, as normal, just as if he were looking through clear lenses once more.

Only it was different. Subtly different, but different. The colors were just a touch brighter. The light above the desk was slightly more crisp. There was more definition in the dark shadows, more detail in the brightly lit areas. Sam could make out the edges of the bulb in the lamp, even though it was normally too bright to look at directly. It was as if Sam were seeing the world as a high dynamic range photograph.

And the sharpness was increased, too. Sam looked at the wall above the desk. Everything was in normal perspective, normal size, but Sam found that somehow he could read the tiny print on a piece of paper that hung on the other side of the room. It was at least thirty feet away, printed in small font, taped to the wall. There was no way he should have been able to make it out, but there it was in front of him, the letters still tiny, but somehow as legible from thirty feet away as they would have been if he were standing right in front of it.

Sam laughed out loud.

The note said, *Amazing, isn't it? You're not dreaming. These glasses really are that incredible.*

Nestrom had an odd sense of humor.

When he turned back to Kat to tell her what he was seeing, Sam nearly fell over backwards.

Her face was practically glowing. He could see every detail of her skin, her hair, her clothing. Her eyes, beautiful and dark before, now showed a depth and complexity that he hadn't previously noticed. Hadn't noticed or hadn't been able to perceive.

He didn't know if the glasses were inventing reality or just enhancing it, but Sam knew that after a short time wearing the device, he would never want to take it off again. Life was just too much better with the glasses on. Clearer and sharper. More vivid and engaging.

That was Nestrom's genius, after all. He gave people products they didn't know they wanted, then made them so good they couldn't live without them. He'd done it first with the phone, then again with the ecosystem around it. And now he'd done it once more with these AR glasses.

They really were incredible. And they would sell like crazy, no matter what they cost. Whoever brought these to market would soon be the richest person or the largest company in the world by a wide margin.

Sam's amazement didn't stop. As he wore the glasses, his awareness expanded, bit by bit. His ability to see and hear the room more clearly was just the start. Soon, his hearing extended even further. He felt like he could hear the mice in the walls. But the sound didn't overwhelm him. It wasn't a cacophony of sound crashing in on him from all around. He could isolate specific sounds just by thinking about them. Anything he wasn't focused on faded into the background.

Then his awareness somehow expanded outside the room. He could see Kat in front of him, but he could simultaneously see the stairwell behind her and the hallway above them both.

No, *see* wasn't the right word. He could *sense* them somehow. Like seeing, but without having the visual in front of him. Like the sound, the awareness was unobtrusive, but undeniably present.

He had no idea how the tech was doing it, how it was tapping into his brain like that, but Sam felt powerful, all-knowing. He felt like a superhero. The feeling was euphoric, like the best drug in the world.

And that's why Sam took the glasses off.

He had no idea what they were doing to him, but he knew he liked it and wanted more. In fact, he never wanted it to stop.

The glasses were amazing.

And dangerous.

That kind of power would not become just another piece of overpriced tech hardware. That kind of power would be guarded jealously. Wars would be fought with and for those capabilities.

That kind of breakthrough went far beyond simple supply and demand. It was a leap forward in the way humans could exist in the world. Whoever wore those glasses would have a clear and undeniable advantage over those who didn't have their own pair.

Was that the final prototype? Was that what Nestrom intended to release? Or did he recognize the danger inherent in the kinds of sensory enhancements the glasses gave to the wearer? Was he working to somehow temper that effect and bring it down to a more tenable level?

Or was he planning on selling it to the highest bidder? To the US government? Or, perhaps, to a less savory buyer, a terrorist or a rogue regime?

No, Nestrom didn't seem the type for those kinds of games. And it certainly didn't seem like he needed the money.

But some rich people never had enough. And even if Nestrom wasn't that way, there were lots of other people who did want the money. If they knew what Nestrom had here, they would have plenty of reason to kill him for it.

But who knew about it?

Who might have been able to find out what Nestrom had created?

It had to have been someone in the family. Someone in the house.

Someone that Sam now saw every day.

**29**

DECEMBER 26, 2:32AM

Sam took the glasses off, held them in his hands. Such power in such a simple device. Just a pair of glasses.

Only these glasses would change the world forever.

He looked up at Kat. Her arms were folded across her chest. Her foot tapped impatiently against the concrete floor. The expression on her face was one Sam hadn't seen before. But it didn't look good.

"Finished playing yet?" she said.

Sam smiled sheepishly. He looked around the room. Everything was the same, but everything looked different. And he didn't just mean the appearance. Yes, without the glasses, the whole room seemed darker, fuzzier. But what really struck him was the way he felt a pang in his chest, a sense of loss, of depression, without the extra-sensory awareness the glasses had afforded.

And that was part of the danger of the glasses. Like any sense-enhancing drug, the come-down was just as bad as the high had been good.

Fortunately, Sam had expected that. And he hadn't worn the glasses long enough to be too hooked.

Beyond just the physical appearance, though, everything in the room took on new meaning in light of what Sam had discovered. Nestrom was no fool. And Sam didn't know for sure, but he didn't get the sense in his short time with Nestrom that the man would do anything for money or power. He already had enough of both, and he felt like Nestrom knew that.

That means that Nestrom would probably have been acutely aware of the power and potential danger of the device he'd built.

So what would he have done about it?

He wouldn't have destroyed it. Nestrom may have been smart enough to fear the power of the glasses, but he was still too arrogant not to look for a way to bring them to market. Like so many tech geniuses, he probably thought he could solve all of the world's problems himself, if only he bestowed upon the world some time from his busy schedule to work on them.

No, Nestrom would have looked for a way to pare back the power of the glasses. Like a speed limiter on a super-fast car, he would have found a way to control the extent to which the glasses enhanced the senses and awareness of the wearer.

The version Sam had just taken off was too powerful. Either Nestrom had still been tinkering or there was another, newer prototype out there somewhere. If it wasn't in the workshop, where could it be?

"Did your father ever work anywhere else? In an office upstairs, maybe, or in another building when he traveled?"

"Traveled?" Kat blew a raspberry. "My father hadn't left this house for ten years. And no, as far as I know, he only worked down here. Everything he did was under lock and key. Even the computers in here are isolated, disconnected from the internet and from the house network except for that terminal." She pointed toward a small monitor that Sam hadn't even noticed in the far corner. "Other than that, this whole workshop is completely self-contained."

Sam nodded slowly. If his hunch was correct, then there was a prototype missing. Maybe it was somewhere in the room, undiscovered in a drawer or under a pile of papers. Didn't seem like Nestrom's style to be that messy with such an important piece of hardware, but Sam couldn't rule it out.

But he had a hunch they wouldn't find the prototype, no matter how many drawers or closets they opened.

"Why do you ask?" said Kat, frowning.

Sam debated on sharing his thoughts with Kat, but decided against it. They were still too speculative, too unformed to be worth sharing.

He smiled at her. "Just trying to get the full picture."

He wandered into the living area, scanning the couch and the desk. They looked the same as they had the day before. Same rumpled blanket and pillow on the couch. Same spare desk, with just the lamp, the clock, and the laptop. Sam smiled at the paper taped to the wall above the desk as he sat down in front of the laptop. He realized he was still holding the prototype in his hands. He folded it neatly and set it on the desk, then opened the laptop.

"Do you still have the thumb drive?" he asked Kat.

Kat's eyes widened, then she looked away from Sam, down at the floor. She tapped both front pockets of her pants at once, the fingers of both hands curling slightly, feeling for something inside. She hesitated, only for a second, then dug into one pocket and pulled out the thumb drive.

Sam put the drive into the port. It was so small his thumb practically obscured the brushed metal enclosure of the tiny device. He clicked into the file system of the computer and scanned through the endless list of files on the drive.

He went back to the top of the list and tapped to preview the first video. Nestrom's face filled the screen, setting up the camera for the recording. As he pulled back, Sam could see that Nestrom was standing at the assembly station. He checked the connection of a small wire that ran from the laptop to a small box on the workbench. Satisfied, he faced the camera and spoke in a clear, slow voice.

"Dr. Christopher Nestrom. March twenty-third, 2009. Six seventeen PM." To document the time visually, Nestrom held up the same tiny clock he'd shown in the video Sam had watched earlier, the clock from the desk. "Nestrom 3 version fifty-four point two. Test number one."

Nestrom clicked a few buttons and the screen shifted to a three-window view. One-third of the screen was split into two, top and bottom, showing two live camera feeds of Nestrom. One feed was a front view focused on his face. The other feed showed Nestrom sidelong from further away, a shot that showed Nestrom's full body standing in front of the workbench.

The other two-thirds of the screen was dark. In the camera feeds, Sam watched as Nestrom put on a pair of glasses. They were quite a bit different from the glasses Sam had just worn. These were twice as large, boxy and ugly, with wires coming off of both sides and lenses that looked like they'd been wrapped onto the frame with electrical tape.

Nestrom pushed something on the side of the glasses and the black screen came to life, showing the blue Nestrom logo that Sam had seen when he'd turned on the glasses himself.

They were watching a feed from straight off of the glasses. In the recording, Sam was seeing what Nestrom himself had seen through his glasses.

The logo faded and the screen filled with a wireframe view of the room, similar to the one presented to Sam, but with green lines on a black background instead of the white-on-blue view Sam's glasses had provided.

"Boot successful," said Nestrom, his lips moving in the

camera feed, the only thing visible beneath the monstrosity he wore over his eyes. "Wireframe loaded."

Sam watched Nestrom turn his head in the camera feed. The view in the feed from the glasses lagged, then glitched, then went completely black.

"Fail on spatial reprocessing," said Nestrom. Instead of sounding frustrated or defeated, he almost sounded cheerful, like he was glad his test had failed.

In the camera feed, Nestrom took off the glasses and switched off the video. The screen went black and the recording ended.

Sam sat back in his chair, Kat standing beside him. They both looked at the dark laptop screen in silence for a moment.

"2009?" said Sam. "That was over twelve years ago."

"How many of those videos are there?" asked Kat.

Sam scrolled through the file list. It went on and on. There seemed to be hundreds, maybe even thousands of video files there.

Every one was titled with a series of numbers, underscores, and dots. Sam squinted at the one they'd just watched. "20090323_1817_54.2_1.mp4".

Date, time, hardware version, test number, all separated by underscores.

Sam scrolled to the end of the file list. The README.mp4 file they'd watched the night before was at the very bottom. Just above that was a file named "20221225_0235_1237.6_3.mp4".

Christmas morning at two AM.

That had to have been filmed just before Nestrom died.

"Version 1237?" said Kat, incredulous. She'd figured out the file naming convention, too. "He made more than twelve hundred versions of those glasses?" She looked behind her at the workshop. "Where the hell does he keep them all?"

"Good question," said Sam. He closed the laptop and stood. It was a good question, and one he wanted to find the answer to, but he was a little surprised Kat hadn't noticed the date and time on the last video. He would have thought that would have caught her attention more than the hardware version.

But he was relieved that she hadn't. Truth was, he didn't want to watch the videos with Kat. Not all of them.

Especially not the last one.

There was a chance that the last video showed some clue as to who killed Nestrom. Sam didn't want Kat to see it and warn her family about the evidence.

It would be a perfectly natural thing to do. Protecting her family. But Sam didn't want her to be in that position.

And he didn't want the killer to know they'd found any evidence.

"Let's see if we can find the prototypes," Sam said. They'd photographed everything around Nestrom on the first day, but they hadn't taken the time to really explore the workshop. There were doors Sam hadn't yet opened, drawers he hadn't looked through.

And every time he dug a little deeper, it seemed that Sam found something new.

**30**

DECEMBER 26, 4:12AM


Sam and Kat had searched the workshop thoroughly, opening every door and every drawer, turning over every stack of papers, feeling through every box of wires or components.

By the end of it, Sam was dead tired. It was past four in the morning, after all.

They'd found the prototypes, all neatly labeled with version numbers and dates, set in a series of roll-out drawers in a tall cabinet in a deep room, a kind of giant-sized walk-in closet in one corner of the workshop. The drawers held the glasses in felt trays similar to the one that held the glasses at the assembly station.

Sam scanned the version numbers and dates, looking for any gaps. He found none. Every prototype was there in its proper place, all in order. From version 1.0 all the way up to version 1236.6.

He went back out to the assembly station, looked more closely at the felt tray that held the glasses there. Each slot was labeled, from version 1237.0 all the way up to the one Sam had worn, version 1237.5. Every slot was full.

Except one.

And the hardware version in the last video on the thumb drive was not 1237.5. It was 1237.6.

That prototype was missing.

"I don't know about you," said Kat from behind Sam, "but I'm beat."

He turned to see her standing at the desk. She pulled the thumb drive from its port, snapped shut the laptop, and handed the drive to Sam.

Then she ran her hands down his arms, slid them around to the small of his back, and pulled him close. Sam could feel her heat through his clothes, could feel her hip bones against his thighs.

Could feel other things, too.

Even at four in the morning, dead tired, the woman could get Sam's heart thumping.

And who was he to resist?

**31**

When Sam woke, Kat was lying beside him in bed, her back turned toward him.

They were both naked. The moonlight slanted through the curtain, ran its silvery fingertip along the curve of Kat's bare shoulder, down the side of her torso, into the swale of her waist and back up to the curve of her hip, then feathered along her long leg.

Sam couldn't resist. He slid quietly out of bed and took his sketchbook and pencils from his bag, sat on the floor, his back pressed against the wall, sketching the woman lying before him.

After a while, she rolled over in her sleep, rolled toward Sam. He sketched in a trance, a frenzy, his pencil moving of its own accord, desperate to record Kat's ethereal beauty, to bear witness to the heart-stopping perfection of the scene. The light, the tousled bedsheets, the gorgeous form.

He sketched her body, her face. Scene and detail, his pencils filling page after page.

When he was spent, when sleep caught up to him once

more, the passion of creation exorcised from his mind and body, Sam slid back into bed.

Kat rolled over again, again put her back to Sam. He smiled lazily, put his arm along her hip, and snugged up against her, feeling the heat of her body along the full length of his.

He kissed her shoulder softly once, then again. Kat moaned softly and rolled in his embrace. Her eyes opened, lids heavy with sleep, and Sam's heart stopped at the ravishing look in them.

Hungry. Passionate.

He wanted to draw that hunger, that passion, to capture it in his sketchbook.

But he wanted something else even more.

He kissed her, deep and long, and let himself go, under Kat's spell once again.

Oh yeah. Sam was falling for her.

How could he not?

**32**

Even Brandon was awake by the time Sam and Kat made it down to breakfast. He sat at the table with Thomas and Christa, his head in his hands over a steaming mug.

The snow was still falling outside the windows, but the light was clear and bright, and the wind seemed to have died down somewhat. Instead of a driving wall of grey snow, Sam saw a drifting blanket of white snow.

An improvement.

Brandon lifted his head when Sam and Kat entered. He looked terrible. His eyes were red-rimmed and bloodshot, with deep, dark circles underneath. His hair was a rat's nest of tangles, his chin blotched with a patchwork of stubble.

"Someone opened the rabbit hutch, I guess," he muttered in a gravelly voice, then pulled a long, greedy sip from the mug in front of him.

"Whiskey for breakfast again?" said Kat. She stepped behind Brandon's chair and gave him a kiss on the top of his head.

"Black coffee," said Brandon. He set his head back in his

hands. "I'm starting to think that drinking isn't very good for my health."

"What a breakthrough," said Christa. "Thomas and I will alert the medical community. I'm sure they'll want to know."

Thomas didn't look up from his phone, where he was tapping away with both thumbs.

Sam and Kat sat down beside each other at the end of the table. The staff immediately brought Kat a toasted English muffin with butter and jam. They served cups of hot coffee to both of them, with cream and sugar.

Phillip appeared beside Sam.

"Would you care for breakfast, Mr. Davis?" he asked.

"Um..." Sam looked around. Everyone else had finished eating. "I'll just have what she's having," he said, gesturing to Kat's plate.

Phillip nodded and disappeared again. Moments later, Sam had an English muffin of his own, with bowls of butter, jam, and various other spreads on the table before him.

"You can ask for anything you want, you know," said Kat. "We've got pretty much everything in the kitchen."

"I'm not used to people waiting on me."

"Give it a chance," said Cress, strolling into the room. "It grows on you."

"We don't want to hear about anything that might be growing on you, Auntie," said Christa.

Everyone seemed to be back to their normal spirits again. Cress was dressed in elegantly casual clothes, the kind Sam imagined a sheik's wife might wear while she was watching Netflix, if sheik's wives did such a thing.

Thomas set his phone down on the table with a clatter and leaned forward in his chair.

"Any progress on the investigation, Sam?" he asked.

Sam sucked in a surprised breath, then coughed out the bite

of English muffin he'd been eating. Kat patted him on the back softly.

"Investigation?" Sam said.

"You're the crime expert," said Christa. "Aren't you investigating the scene to make sure there was no foul play or whatever?"

"I wouldn't say that," said Sam.

"You two were sneaking around in the workshop last night," said Brandon. At the surprised looks on Sam's and Kat's faces, Brandon nodded. "Oh yeah, I can hear fucking everything."

"And everything fucking," said Cress with a cackle. Her clothes may have been elegant, but she had one of the raunchiest mouths Sam had ever heard.

"What did you find?" asked Thomas.

Sam shook his head slowly. "We looked around, just seeing if anything jumped out. But we didn't really find anything useful." He glanced at Kat, but she chewed her English muffin, her face neutral.

Thomas speared Sam with a hard stare. Sam returned it calmly. He would have thought such a stare to be out of character for Thomas, but after the last day or so, he was beginning to think that the friendly, easy-going manner he'd encountered on Christmas Eve was the real anomaly.

"You know everything down there is Nestech property," he said. "If anything were to go missing, it would be prosecuted as theft."

Sam raised his eyebrows.

"I'm not accusing anyone," said Thomas, holding up his hands, palms out, looking around the table. "I'm just making sure everyone is clear. Nestech will pursue any evidence of property theft. And there's nothing I'll be able to do to stop it."

Sam highly doubted that, but found it interesting that Thomas would feel the need to make the threat, all the same.

"So, I'll ask you again," said Thomas. "What did you find down there?"

Sam glanced again at Kat. She lifted an eyebrow, waiting for Sam's response.

"We found prototypes," Sam said. "Lots and lots of prototypes."

"Prototypes of what?" asked Christa.

"Augmented-reality glasses."

"I knew it," said Brandon. He pounded the table with his fist, then winced in pain at the heavy thud and pressed on his temples. "I knew he was doing AR shit," he said more softly.

"Brilliant," said Christa. "You knew the tech billionaire was working on the hottest future market in the tech world. You're a real visionary."

Brandon shot her a withering look. Christa didn't wither in the slightest.

"Did you try any of the prototypes on?" asked Thomas.

"I did," nodded Sam.

The muscles in Thomas's jaw flexed over and over. "And?" he said, teeth gritted.

"It was amazing," Sam said. "Truly amazing. But not quite ready. I don't think Nestrom was finished working on them yet."

"Not ready?" scoffed Brandon. "Now you're a tech critic?"

"What makes you say they weren't ready, Sam?" asked Thomas. "Was the prototype glitchy?"

"No glitches. It ran very well. It just seemed like some of the features weren't quite finished."

"Not quite finished," Brandon said, his voice muffled with his head still in his hands. "That's so helpful."

Sam shrugged. "Like you said, I'm no tech critic." He grinned at Brandon. "I'm just a consumer."

Brandon glared at Sam, then glanced at Kat before burying his head in his hands again.

Sam followed Brandon's glance and caught Kat's eye. She just squeezed his hand and gave him a lukewarm smile.

"Since you brought it up, though," said Sam. "The whole investigation thing. I would like to speak with each of you. Individually."

The response was predictably unenthusiastic. Thomas picked up his phone and started typing away again. Brandon let his head fall back into his hands. Christa just stared out the window.

"Think of it as practice," said Sam. "For when the police arrive."

Only Cress even bothered to look at him. "I'll meet you one-on-one, darling," she said. "You just tell me when and where."

Sam suppressed a sigh. "No time like the present," he said.

**33**

Sam led Cress to the billiard room, where a fire was already burning. He wondered if the staff kept fires lit in every fireplace in the house, on the off chance that someone might come in, or if Phillip had somehow known that Sam would come to this room at this time for his interviews. It didn't seem possible that Phillip would know such a thing, but then it didn't seem possible that Phillip could be everywhere at once, either. And yet he was.

Sam held the door open for Cress. She sat in the center of one couch and patted the leather cushion beside her, looking up at Sam in her most alluring way.

There was no doubt she was beautiful, and not just for a woman her age. By that measure, she was a knockout. But Cress was beautiful for a woman of any age. Objectively beautiful, a trait that definitely ran in this family.

Despite Cress' urging, Sam sat in the chair beside the couch. Undeterred, Cress slid to the end of the couch, as close to Sam as she could get, and draped herself over the arm, resting her chin in one palm. Sam could feel Cress undressing him with her eyes, devouring him in her mind. It was an odd, uncomfortable feeling, one that instantly made him sympathize with every pretty girl in the world, who probably had endured this very feeling every day of their adult lives.

"Tell me, Cress," Sam began.

"Anything, my dear."

"Where were you on Christmas Eve after you left the parlor?"

"You want to know what I wore to bed?"

"I just want to know where—"

"Nothing." She leered at Sam. "Nothing at all."

"Okay," Sam smiled patiently. "And where were you before you got into bed?"

"Maybe it would be easier if we recreated the evening," said Cress. "We can go up to my room. I'll take my clothes off and get in bed. You can, too, if you like."

"I think we can just discuss it here."

"Might jog my memory."

"I'll take the risk."

"Humph," said Cress. "Not much of a detective, are you?" She leaned back against the couch and blew out a long breath. "I went straight to my room for the night."

"All night?"

"All night."

"And you were alone all night?"

"Unfortunately."

"Can anyone vouch for you?"

"Darling." Cress voice was a silky purr, but Sam could feel the sharp claws underneath. "How could anyone vouch for me if I was alone all night?"

Good point. "None of the staff helped you with anything? No late-night snacks?"

Cress unfurled herself from the couch until she stood, tall and lithe, hands on her hips before Sam, her eyes never leaving his.

"Do you think I got this body by eating late-night snacks?"

She strutted like a runway model to the sideboard, her heels clicking against the wood floor with each step.

"Drink?" she said over her shoulder, without looking.

Sam didn't bother to answer.

"When did you find out that your brother was dead?"

She turned, two fingers of whiskey in a tumbler in her hand, and leaned back against the sideboard.

"I was in the morning room drinking my coffee when Phillip told us."

"Us? Who was with you?"

"Thomas. Christa came in shortly afterward."

"What did Phillip say?"

Cress sipped her drink and shrugged.

"I have unfortunate news? Dr. Nestrom has passed? Blah blah blah? Something pompous sounding like that. You know Phillip."

"Try to think, Cress," urged Sam. "What words did Phillip use?"

"Is it really that important?"

"It could be."

Cress held up her glass. "You sure you don't want one?"

Sam shook his head.

She cradled the glass against her chest and stared into the fire. Her voice grew smaller, losing its usual bravado.

"He came in," she said, "looking even more somber than usual, if you can believe that. Thomas asked him what he wanted. Phillip said something like, I have terrible news for you both. I'm very sorry to be the bearer of bad tidings, but when I brought him his breakfast in the workshop this morning, as usual, I found Dr. Nestrom lying on the floor. He appeared to have passed on."

"That's what he said?" asked Sam.

"That's what I remember." Cress still stared into the fire. "I remember getting stuck on that phrase, *passed on*."

Cress stared silently into the fire for a long moment, then tossed back the rest of her whiskey and set the glass on the sideboard with a sharp rap.

"It's such a stupid phrase," she said, the bravado back in her voice as she strutted to the couch again. "I've always hated it. Dead is dead. Just say the goddamn word."

She sat down and crossed her long legs at the knee. Her foot dangled beside Sam's shin. Cress let it bob, rubbing softly against him as she propped her head against her hand, elbow resting on the arm of the couch, staring at Sam in a way that left little doubt about what was on her mind.

The woman was irrepressible.

But was it real, or just an act, a distraction?

"How did you feel when you heard the news?" Sam asked.

Cress laughed. "You mean, was I happy that my asshole brother was dead?" She fell back against the couch and turned away from Sam, folding her arms and staring into the fire again. "If you'd asked me how I thought I'd feel in that situation, I would have said I'd be happy. He was an asshole to me my whole life."

When she turned back to Sam, her eyes were soft and glistening.

"But I was sad." Her voice wavered and she swallowed hard. "I was." She pressed her finger beneath her eye, flicked off the tear that fell. "For a minute." She chuckled. "No one was more surprised than I was."

"And how do you feel now?"

Her chuckle became a sharp laugh.

"Now, I'm glad that fucker is dead." She leaned in toward Sam, put her hand on his knee and ran it slowly up his leg, her mouth twisted into a mischievous grin. "I wish I'd killed him myself."

**34**

"I loved my father," said Christa, eyes unfocused and distant. "He was a good father, especially after losing..." She shifted awkwardly on the couch. "After losing his wife."

"Your mother, you mean," said Sam.

"Yes, of course that's who I mean," Christa snapped. "What other wife did he have?" She pressed her lips together and looked away from Sam, toward the fire.

Sam had never heard anger from Christa before. Sadness, yes. Snarkiness, definitely. But she'd never snapped at anyone when he'd been around.

Of course, he hadn't been around for very long, and everyone got short-tempered from time to time. Especially under stressful circumstances.

"Where were you the night your father died?"

"In bed with my husband," said Christa. "If you're hoping for details, I'm afraid you'll be disappointed. I am not my aunt."

"Your aunt said she wished she'd killed Dr. Nestrom herself."

Christa laughed bitterly. "Are you surprised? My father wasn't exactly a loving brother, was he?"

"Was he a loving father?"

"I just said he was."

"You said he was a good father."

"What's the difference?"

Sam shrugged. "You can be a good father without being a loving one."

Christa let out a frustrated sigh and stared into the fire again.

Sam didn't try to fill the silence. He just let it build, the only sound the snap of the flames, the hiss of steam escaping from the burning wood.

"I came home from the science fair one year," Christa said at last. Her voice was small and quiet, and she faced the fire. Sam leaned forward in his chair to hear her better, the leather cushion protesting beneath him.

"I'd won first prize. The trophy was as tall as I was." That bitter laugh again. "Not that my father would have known. He didn't bother to leave his workshop to watch my presentation."

She stood and grabbed a metal poker from a brass holder beside the fireplace. The fire was roaring, but she jabbed at the wood anyway. Tiny orange specks floated up from the logs with each jab.

"I showed him the trophy and my project. I'd written a program that could listen to you ask a question and respond back. Simple answers, and you could only ask certain questions, but, still. Basic voice recognition. Simple AI. This was twenty-five years ago, remember. Not bad for a ten-year-old."

More jabs, harder this time. More orange specks floating in a tiny cloud around the growing wound in the wood.

"You know what my father said to me?" She tapped the sharp tip of the poker against the stone of the hearth. When she spoke, her voice was a whisper.

"He said it was useless." She jabbed again at the fire, hard.

The log split in two in an explosion of sparks. "Unrefined and useless."

The fire flared around the split log.

After a moment, the sparks settled and calmed again.

Christa looked over her shoulder as if remembering Sam were there. She set the poker carefully back into its holder, then sat back down on the couch. Perched on the edge of the leather cushion, she folded her legs demurely beneath her and smoothed her skirt over her knees.

"So no," she said, tilting her head and staring at Sam as if she were looking at an animal in a zoo exhibit, a pleasant, utterly false smile on her lips. "I wouldn't say he was a loving father at all."

**35**

Thomas sat in one of the leather armchairs facing the fire, the same chair Sam had been using. His focus was once again on his phone, his thumbs again tapping furiously.

As he moved to the chair beside Thomas and sat down, Sam peeked over Thomas's shoulder. Thomas was typing an email.

"You're working hard," Sam said.

"Lots to do," Thomas replied. "This whole death thing is kind of a big deal." He glanced at Sam drily, then focused back on his email.

"If you don't mind, I'd like to have your attention while we speak," said Sam. Thomas frowned down at his phone. "I promise I won't take any more of your time than I have to. I just have a few questions."

Thomas's thumbs flew for a few more seconds, then he tapped twice at the screen, hard, and set his phone face-down on the arm of the chair. He let out a deep breath, shifted in his chair to better face Sam, crossed his legs at the knee and folded his hands in his lap.

The very picture of the attentive CEO on stop fourteen of his latest listening tour, traveling through every department, every far-flung office in the company, listening tirelessly to all the petty, naive, and uninformed comments, complaints, and ideas from the company's many employees. Building good will and boosting morale, all so he could go back to his office and forget about the employees completely until the next listening tour.

Maybe that was too harsh. Thomas had struck Sam as a good man when they'd first met. His demeanor had been pleasant, and it had stayed that way, even when Christa had been openly mocking him. He'd even maintained that pleasantness at dinner, when Nestrom himself had emasculated Thomas with just a few cutting remarks.

And yet, since Nestrom's death, Sam had seen very little of that good nature. Since then, Thomas had seemed driven, commanding. Maybe even ruthless. Was that just the impact of the weight of responsibility that had fallen on Thomas's shoulders when Nestrom died? Or was this the real Thomas?

"You have my attention," Thomas said. His voice was smooth, his tone and his smile pleasant, but Sam could see the irritation in his eyes. Veiled. Well-hidden. To most people, it would be invisible. But to Sam it was unmistakable.

Thomas tapped the back of his phone repeatedly with one finger, like a timer telling Sam that his attention had a time limit.

"Please tell me where you were on Christmas Eve."

Thomas nodded slowly, looking down at his hands in his lap.

"After leaving you and the others in the parlor, Christa and I went to our bedroom. We spent the night together."

"You didn't leave your bedroom until morning?"

"We didn't leave the suite, no. I showered and I did some work in the sitting room for an hour or two, but I didn't leave the suite."

"And Christa? Was she with you the whole time?"

"She was in the bedroom asleep."

"The whole time?"

"Yes."

"You're sure?"

The muscles in Thomas's jaw flexed again. "Do you have reason to suspect my wife of something?"

"No, no," said Sam with a smile that he hoped would be soothing. "Just making sure I have the facts straight in my head."

Thomas's jaw muscles relaxed, but his finger went back to tapping on his phone. The clock was still ticking.

"You said you were working in the sitting room. What sort of work were you doing?"

Thomas shrugged. "Reviewing reports. Sending emails. Nothing unusual."

"And your email history would corroborate that?"

Thomas furrowed his brow in thought for a moment. "Yes, I believe so. I'm sure I sent at least a few emails that night." He sighed. "I usually do, despite the late hour. It's a bad habit. Bad for my direct reports, anyway."

"When did you learn of Nestrom's death?"

"Christmas Day, at breakfast. Phillip informed me."

"Did he tell anyone else?"

"No."

"You were the only one that Phillip told?"

"I was drinking my coffee in the breakfast room, reading the news on my phone, when he came in and told me what had happened."

"You were alone when he told you?"

Thomas's jaw flexed again. "Yes, I just said that."

Again, Sam wore the smile he hoped would be soothing. "Just making sure I heard you correctly. What did Phillip say to you? Please try to remember his exact words."

"His exact words?" Thomas frowned. "He said, I'm very sorry

to tell you, sir, that while serving his breakfast in the workshop this morning, per usual, I found Dr. Nestrom lying on the floor. He was not moving. He appeared to be dead."

"Those were his exact words?"

"Pretty much. You don't forget something like that."

"Did Phillip seem upset?"

Thomas shook his head slowly. "Maybe a little paler than usual, but you know Phillip. I'm not sure he'd seem upset if he were informing you of his own death."

"What did Phillip do then, after he told you the news?"

Thomas shrugged. "He left. Off to do whatever Phillip does.""

"And then?"

Thomas let out a heavy sigh, clearly irritated with the questioning. "Christa and Cress came in then. I told them both the news."

"How did they take it?"

"How do you think? Christa was devastated. First shock, then tears."

"What about Cress?"

Thomas looked to one side, trying to remember. "She didn't cry or anything. Not like Christa. But she seemed subdued. Unusual for her. I think she took it hard, in her own way."

"They both seemed surprised, then?"

Thomas sniffed in derision. "Sorry. Your job won't be quite that easy."

"What do you mean?"

"You're asking if they were surprised. I assume that if they weren't surprised, you'd think they had killed him. Right?"

Thomas raised his eyebrows as if he'd caught Sam red-handed.

"I was thinking they could have been told earlier."

Thomas's eyebrows fell, his face blank. "Oh."

It was a lie. Sam had been hoping the murderer might give themselves away like that. All of these people were amateurs.

Worse, they were arrogant amateurs. Whoever the killer was, they had to have made some kind of mistake.

But he didn't want Thomas to know that. He didn't want Thomas to know how Sam was approaching the investigation.

"What happened next?"

Thomas threw his hands up in exasperation. He rattled off a list in quick order. "Then Phillip brought breakfast. And then you and Kat came in, then Brandon. We told all of you. More surprise. More breakfast." He picked up his phone and waggled it at Sam. "Are we done, here, inspector? Can I get back to some real work?"

While Thomas tapped away on his phone once more, Sam stared into the fire. Between talking to Christa and talking to Thomas, more wood had been added. The fire was raging.

Phillip and his crack staff, at work again in his mysterious ways.

The house was full of mysteries.

**36**

DECEMBER 26, 12:51PM

Sam heard someone clear their throat behind him. Staring into the fire, he'd lost himself in his own thoughts for a while. He'd barely been aware of Thomas's tapping on his phone beside him, the sound fading into the crackling of the fire.

He turned to see Phillip standing in front of the doorway, both hands clasped calmly in front of him. In his dark suit, immaculate white shirt, and subtle, grey tie, Phillip was the very picture of professionalism. He seemed like he would have been as comfortable in a banquet hall as in a boardroom or an embassy or a palace. His air was calm and utterly unflappable.

"Begging your pardon, sirs," he said, his voice low and smooth as polished silver. "Lunch will be served in the west solar in ten minutes." He bowed his head slightly and turned to leave.

"Phillip," called Sam, standing. Phillip stopped in his tracks and turned slowly to face him. "Would you mind if I spoke to you for a few moments?" Sam looked at Thomas, who hadn't looked up from his phone. "Alone?"

Still staring at his phone, Thomas grunted and left the room.

Sam gestured to the chair Thomas had vacated. Phillip sat carefully, perched on the edge of the cushion as if he would be burned in sin if he allowed himself to enjoy a restful posture in front of a guest. His back was stiff, his hands laid on his thighs.

"How can I help you, Mr. Davis?"

"Would you please tell me how you found Dr. Nestrom's body?"

Phillip pulled in a long breath and nodded. After a pause, he said, "At precisely seven o'clock each morning, it was Dr. Nestrom's custom to take breakfast in his workshop. On Christmas morning, when I entered the workshop, Dr. Nestrom was nowhere in sight. This was not common, but not unusual. I brought his breakfast to the back of the workshop and set it on his desk."

"That's when you found the body?"

"No," said Phillip. "In fact, I must have walked right by it. I didn't notice the body until I was leaving."

Sam nodded. "What did you do then?"

"I called his name several times, as you can imagine, to see if I could rouse him. I bent down to him, thinking perhaps he was ill or had injured himself. That's when I noticed..."

"That he was dead."

A strange ripple of emotion crossed Phillip's face. It seemed to pinch in from all sides, as if he were warring with himself, trying to maintain his composure. His professionalism quickly regained control.

"I could see that his chest was not moving. I felt for his pulse in his neck and felt nothing. I held my silver serving tray to his nose. Dr. Nestrom was not breathing."

"Did you attempt to administer CPR?"

"That is not within my skill set, I'm afraid, Mr. Davis."

"Did you call 9-1-1?"

"Yes, from the telephone in the workshop."

Sam frowned. He didn't recall seeing a phone anywhere in the workshop.

"The computer terminal in the corner," explained Phillip. "It has an application on it that allows the user to make calls via the internet."

That made sense. Ridiculously over-engineered, but it made sense. But wouldn't it have been easier just to use a cellphone?

"I'm afraid there is no cellular connection in Dr. Nestrom's workshop," said Phillip when Sam asked the question. "A part of Dr. Nestrom's security measures."

"Speaking of security measures," said Sam, "do you know of anyone besides yourself who has can open the workshop doors?"

"To my knowledge, only Dr. Nestrom and myself have that ability."

Phillip's gaze was level and unwavering. He must have known how incriminating that single fact was. He wasn't stupid. But he offered the information without hesitation or pretext. That was a sign of an innocent man.

Or a very skilled liar.

"What did the police tell you?"

"As I mentioned to the others, once they had confirmed with me that the victim was, in fact, deceased, the police informed me that they would dispatch a team as soon as possible, but that they would be unable to do so until after the storm had stopped and the roads had been cleared."

"The victim?"

"I chose not identify the deceased over the phone," he said, "for the sake of propriety."

"Did they give you any instructions?"

"Just to leave the scene as untouched as possible until the authorities arrived."

"What did you do next?"

"I informed Mr. and Mrs. Crowell of the news."

"Thomas and Christa?"

"That's correct, sir."

"Just the two of them? No one else was present?"

"Not at that time, sir."

What the hell? Thomas said he'd been alone. Cress claimed it had been her and Thomas. Christa didn't mention it at all. And now Phillip was saying he'd told Christa and Thomas.

"What did you tell them? Can you recall your exact words?"

Phillip's eyebrows shot up in surprise for only a moment before he collected himself. "I'm not sure I can, Mr. Davis. You understand, I'm sure, that I was not fully myself at that moment."

"Of course, Phillip. Please, as best you can remember."

"I expressed my condolences and told them the news as gently as I could."

"What words do you remember using?"

Phillip bent his head in thought. "I regret to inform you that, early this morning, I discovered Mr. Nestrom prostrate on the floor in the workshop. He appears to be deceased."

"That's what you said?"

"Something along those lines, if I recall correctly, sir."

Four different accounts from four different people. Why the hell couldn't they remember such an important moment? One that had happened only one day before?

Or were they all lying?

"I'm very sorry, Mr. Davis," said Phillip, "but luncheon is about to begin. If there are no further questions..." His voice trailed off in a question.

"Of course, Phillip," said Sam. "Thank you for your time."

Phillip headed toward the door, then stopped halfway.

"Would you like me to escort you to the west solar, Mr. Davis? The way can be difficult to find."

Sam stood and followed Phillip through yet another maze of hallways. Still, the confusion of the hallways was nothing compared to the confusion in Sam's mind.

**37**

Lunch was served, and it was surprisingly well attended.

It was served in yet another room that Sam hadn't seen yet. The light was just as bright as the breakfast room, but this time it streamed through windows set high in one wall, almost like a clerestory. The orientation of the room allowed the light at that hour to fill the space, bouncing off the ornately-framed mirrors on the walls and making the silverware gleam and the crystal glasses sparkle.

The fare consisted of cold meats and cheeses. Chicken and roast beef and ham. Not deli slices like Sam would have eaten, but full chunks of breast meat, thick portions of roast, and ham off the bone. There were several varieties of cheese, each with its own board and knife, and several loaves of hot Italian bread cut into generous slices. A large bowl of salad served as a side.

Sam was a little surprised at the casual nature of the meal. He didn't think people as pampered as these would stoop so low as to build their own sandwiches and spoon their own salad, but everyone dug in without complaint.

And largely without comment. The meal was long and leisurely, but silent, save the sound of cutlery and wine pouring into glasses. Thomas and Christa stared at their phones. Cress read a newspaper. Brandon sulked at one end of the table. Even Kat was unusually quiet, reading a book with one hand while she ate.

Afterward, when Sam walked into the billiard room, Brandon lay prone on the couch before the fire, one hand draped over his eyes, the other tenting a tumbler of whiskey that sat on the floor beside the couch.

"Brandon," said Sam.

No response.

"Brandon?"

Again, no response. Was he sleeping? Passed out? Sam hadn't seen him drink anything but water at lunch. He must have poured himself the drink when he got to the room.

"Are you awake?"

"Of course I'm awake, you fucking asshole," Brandon said from under his arm.

"You weren't responding. I wasn't sure."

"You weren't saying anything for me to respond to."

The interview was off to a wonderful start.

"Right, okay." Sam sat in his usual armchair. "Tell me where you were on Christmas Eve, then."

"I think you should start a little further back than that."

"What do you mean?"

Brandon pulled in a deep sigh. With a groan, he swung his legs over the side of the couch and worked himself into a sitting position. He winced at the effort and took a pull from his whiskey.

"You think one of us killed our father."

"I'm trying to rule that out," Sam replied, keeping his face impassive.

"Right," Brandon said, drawing the word out in a sarcastic

drawl. Despite his behavior, Brandon was no dummy. "Don't you think you should be trying to figure out *why* one of us would kill him? Find a motive? Isn't that what they teach you detective types in school?"

"Do you have any theories?"

"Theories?" Brandon scoffed. "I have answers, not fucking theories."

"Let's hear them."

He held up one thumb. "Aunt Cress has hated my father for as long as I can remember. Probably her whole life. He treated her like shit. Even cut her out of his will."

"When did that happen? The part about the will?"

"Six months ago, maybe? They got into some big blow-up over the summer and he cut her out." Brandon snapped his fingers. "Just like that. His own sister." He shook his head. "Fucking dick."

Cress hadn't mentioned any of that to Sam, of course.

"You've seen the revised will?"

"Of course I haven't seen it. You were there earlier. No one even knows where it is. Or maybe that estate guy. But I have it on good authority."

"Who's authority?"

"A gentleman never tells."

Sam bit his tongue at that.

"Okay, that's Cress. Any other theories?"

Brandon held up his thumb again, then added two fingers. "Christa and my brother-in-law." He raised his eyebrows and nodded with slow importance. "Shit, I'm surprised they haven't killed him sooner."

"Why do you say that?"

"At least the rest of us stopped bothering to try to please him. But Christa and Thomas sucked up to my father every fucking day. 'Listen to this idea' or 'How can we help' or 'Look at this great thing I did for you and your company'. All that kind of bullshit."

"And did your father ever respond?"

"On a good day, he would ignore them. On a bad day, he would rip them apart, tell them they were idiots. Tell them to stop kissing his ass and do something useful. Tearing them both down. Disrespecting them."

"But he made Thomas CEO of his company. That's a big sign of respect, isn't it?"

"You'd think so. He did that right after the wedding. But all it did was give my father more reason and more opportunity to make Thomas feel small."

That fit with what Sam had witnessed at dinner. "How did Thomas respond?"

"When he came in, when he and Christa were dating, Thomas had his own company. Not a tech thing. Some kind of accounting startup or VC fund. Maybe a hedge fund. I don't know. Something boring like that."

Brandon slugged his drink. "Everyone assumed Kat would be CEO. She was already running her own tech startup. It made sense." He grinned. "The great Dr. Christopher Nestrom didn't get his way that time. So he bought Thomas's company and made Thomas CEO of Nestech, right? All smiles and slaps on the back. Not from my father, of course, but from the board and the press and whatnot."

Sam could imagine the scene. A younger Thomas, his beautiful new wife on his arm, his dreams coming true.

"And then the bullshit started. The abuse. Questioning Thomas's decisions, ripping into him about the numbers or the budget or whatever. It got so bad that Thomas tried to resign. Twice."

"Nestrom didn't let him?"

Brandon took another pull from his drink. "Eventually,

Thomas just got numb to it, I think. But that kind of thing doesn't just go away." He leaned toward Sam. "It festers."

"And Christa?"

Brandon sat back against the couch again. "Daddy's little girl. That's what she wanted to be, anyway. My whole life she's been trying to get a good word out of him, get him to show some sign of love. Of humanity, even."

"Didn't happen?"

Brandon shook his head slowly. "Not once. Not that I ever saw."

Sam stared into the fire, popping and crackling as if it had just been lit. The picture Brandon had painted of his father was horrible, but it jived with what Cress and Christa had said. It jived with what Sam himself had witnessed.

And yet, it didn't make sense. Why would Nestrom have been such an asshole to his family? What did he gain from it? Did he have any friends at all? Anyone he treated with kindness?

"That's Cress, Christa, and Thomas," Sam said to Brandon. "What about you?"

Brandon laughed, a quick, sharp bark. "I was the outcast from day one. The second twin. The only boy. With some fathers you might think that would be a good thing." He shook his head. "Not with mine." He drained his glass. "No point in trying to impress some asshole that obviously hated my guts."

"Was that reason enough to want to kill him?"

The look in Brandon's eyes sent a shiver of fear through Sam. "What do you think?"

He stood to refill his drink.

"Wanting to kill someone isn't a crime," Sam said as Brandon poured the whiskey. "If it were, everyone would be in jail."

Brandon leaned with his elbow on the mantle above the fireplace, rubbing his temples with that hand, his refreshed drink by his hip like a gunslinger waiting for the draw.

"I thought about it so many times over the years," he said

quietly. "Especially when I was younger. When I was a teenager, still living here in the summers and holidays. Imagined all the different ways I could do it." He kicked at the stone hearth with his boot, the tap of his toe a soft rhythm under the melody of the flames. He was silent for a long minute. Sam imagined he was ticking through all of those murder methods in his mind. "Lost interest after a while. Got used to it, maybe. Once I was old enough to leave, it didn't matter so much anymore."

"You don't still live here?"

Brandon scoffed. "God, no. Are you joking? None of us live here. That would be a fucking nightmare."

"Where do you all live?"

"Cress lives in the Hamptons year-round. One of the old money people out there, even though her money isn't that old. Isn't even hers. But most people don't know that. They probably just assume she's some wealthy heiress or widow or something."

Sam could imagine that. Cress wouldn't disabuse anyone of their preconceptions. She'd play them for all they were worth.

"Did Nestrom threaten to take away her house?"

"He can't," said Brandon. "It was my grandparents' house. They left it to Cress in their trust."

"So your family had money even then."

"Not like we do now, but yes."

"Where do Thomas and Christa live?"

"In California. Bay area. That's where Nestech HQ is."

Sam wondered what their lives were like out there, a continent away from Nestrom. Was that distance enough for them to feel free to be themselves? Were they happy out there, or were they still constantly trying to curry favor from Nestrom?

"And where—"

"I live where I want to live," said Brandon. "London. Paris. Venice. Barcelona for a while."

"Sounds expensive."

Brandon glared at him. "I pay my own way."

"How?"

Brandon squared his shoulders to Sam, took a menacing step toward him, then stopped. Sam could see the muscles in his face working, could see his mind spinning in his eyes. The waves of anger, of violence, coming off of Brandon were palpable. Subconsciously, Sam's muscles tensed, ready for a fight, if it came to that.

But some part of Brandon's mind won. His shoulders relaxed. He looked away from Sam, shaking his head slightly. When he looked back he wore a wry smile. He took a sip of his drink, staring at Sam over the rim of the glass.

"I'm very frugal," he grinned.

It was like Jekyll and Hyde. He'd been that way the first night, too, while playing pool in that very room. One moment he looked like he would rip Sam's head off. The next moment, he was calm and casual. Almost friendly, even.

Okay, maybe not friendly, but at least Sam didn't feel like Brandon would take a swing at him.

"What about Kat?"

"What about her?"

"Why would she want to kill your father?"

Brandon stared hard at Sam again. Again, Sam felt that tension in the air.

Mr. Hyde was near.

When Brandon spoke, his voice was low.

"Ask her yourself."

**38**

<br>

DECEMBER 26, 3:32PM

Sam wandered through the corridors. There were few windows in the interior of the house. The only light came from dim lights set deep in the ceilings, casting a faint blue-white glow over the stone floor, the concrete walls. The hall took on the feel of a hospital basement, the kind of hallway that led to a morgue.

He wasn't really going anywhere or looking for anyone. Sam had a vague notion in the back of his mind to find Kat. He wanted to talk things over with her, to tell her what he'd learned and see what she could make of it.

But the halls were empty. Sam saw no one, not even the staff.

He ducked through the door that led to the staff hallways, found his feet tracing the route they'd taken the day before.

Only one day before. It seemed like an eternity ago when they'd carried Nestrom's body into the gardener's shed.

Sam pushed open the door to the outside, shivered when a blast of cold air hit him. He hadn't planned on coming here, and so he hadn't brought his jacket.

But the sun was bright and warm against his face, the reflections off the snow blinding him. The sky was a heart-stopping, bottomless blue, not a cloud to be seen.

The storm had passed, finally.

That meant the police would be there soon.

Sam was running out of time.

**39**

Despite the bright sun outside, Sam had expected the shed to be cold, and it was. Each breath plumed out ahead of him.

What surprised him was the darkness. The last time he'd been in there, the natural light had been enough to brighten the room. But that had been before noon. Now it was late afternoon, and the sun would soon be down. The bright natural light had given way to a hazy gloom, the objects in the shed nothing but vague outlines in the encroaching dark.

He found a switch on the wall and flicked on the overhead lamps. In the fluorescent light that came on, the room took on a sterile, buzzing, unnatural glow. It seemed more like a morgue than ever.

The hallway, the lights. The dead body under a sheet on the table.

For all intents and purposes, this *was* a morgue now.

Sam pulled the sheet off of Nestrom's body. It lay there just as it had the last time Sam had seen it. He hadn't expected anything different, of course. It was a corpse, after all. An inanimate object. But the expression on Nestrom's face, the look of casual friendliness, still shocked Sam. No one had bothered to close his eyes. The juxtaposition of such a natural look with such an unnatural death jarred Sam's mind.

He didn't know why he'd come down here. He'd already searched the body, already found what clues it could offer. The thumb drive and the note to Sam. The weird screwdriver and the photograph.

Sam looked again at Nestrom's face, at the indentation above his left ear and the dark circle above his right. Sam had worn the prototype glasses, presumably very similar to the ones Nestrom had worn. But Sam didn't recall any indentations. And he certainly hadn't had any dark circles on his skin. He would have noticed that much.

But if the marks weren't from the glasses, what would have caused them?

And where was the last prototype? Sam had worn prototype 1237.5. But the final video had been the test for 1237.6. Where was version 6 now? Did the killer have it? Had they killed Nestrom to get it?

He pushed up onto his tiptoes, oriented his face to Nestrom's, trying to get a normal view, as if Nestrom were standing in front of him. Maybe looking at him in a normal way would help to highlight any abnormalities.

Sam craned his neck, leaning against the table, but couldn't quite get the view he wanted. He might have to find a ladder somewhere in the shed, or climb up on the table and straddle the corpse. He shuddered at the thought and pushed higher on his tiptoes, like a ballerina on point.

But Sam was no ballerina. He lost his balance and fell to the side, against the table. His arm came out to catch himself, his hand grabbing at the first purchase it could find.

On Nestrom's chest.

Sam caught his balance by leaning against a dead man's chest.

This wasn't the first dead body Sam had seen. Not by a long shot. And he wasn't a particularly squeamish man. But he still didn't like the feeling of pressing his hand against a dead man's cold, hard chest.

And yet, this time, when he did so, he felt something.

Something on Nestrom's chest.

Sam leaned close to Nestrom, peering at his neck. He pulled the collar of Nestrom's t-shirt to one side, gently.

There was a chain there. A chain around Nestrom's neck.

A necklace.

All discomfort forgotten, Sam felt around the back of Nestrom's neck, pushed his arm down through the collar of the t-shirt, searching for the clasp of the chain.

He found it, managed to pull it around where he could unclasp the chain and remove the necklace from Nestrom's body.

Dangling from the freed chain was a dull aluminum pendant. About as long as Sam's middle finger and only a quarter-inch thick, when viewed from the top it was shaped like a beer glass, wide and rectangular at the top, then tapering down until it flared out again at the bottom.

Set in the center of the top of the beer glass was a hole rimmed with a ruby-red inlay, oddly-shaped, like a triangle over-laid on a rectangle, with one point of the triangle sticking out the top of the rectangle and the other two points coming off the sides. It looked kind of like a spaceship viewed from overhead, or a Christmas tree on a wide stand. Positioned where it was at one end of the pendant, it made the pendant seem to Sam like an over-engineered bottle opener.

He held it in his palm. For its small size, the pendant was surprisingly heavy. Some kind of keepsake or trinket with sentimental value to Nestrom? He didn't strike Sam as the sentimental type. Certainly not enough to wear something like that around his neck. The photograph in the pocket had been surprising and sentimental, though. Maybe this pendant was an extension of that. Something his wife had made for him, perhaps?

On the chain beside the pendant, hanging from a keyring attached to one end, was another thumb drive. Unlike the other, this thumb drive was as thin as a razor blade, with bright brass strips on one side where it fit into a computer port.

A note and a thumb drive in Nestrom's pocket. A pendant and a thumb drive on a chain around his neck.

How many thumb drives did Nestrom need? And what the hell was on the new one?

**40**

When Sam opened the door and flicked off the lights in the shed, he found himself in near-total darkness. The horizon was a rapidly-darkening blue behind the trees.

Aside from a few startled staff members, who scurried away from him with quick nods of their heads and mumbled apologies, Sam found his way back into the main part of the house without seeing any of the others.

That was just the way he wanted it.

He needed to see what was on that new thumb drive, but he didn't want anyone else to know about it.

Including Kat.

It wasn't that he suspected Kat of anything. Far from it. But she was close with her family. Especially her brother.

And Sam did suspect Kat's family.

Especially her brother.

It was best if he could look at the drive alone, digest whatever information he found there, then bring it to Kat at the right time, in the right way.

He crept quietly through the hallways toward the door to the stairs leading down to the workshop. He'd walked that route enough times to remember the way, even if the rest of the house was still a confusing maze to him. He checked once more up and down the hallway to be sure he hadn't been seen, closed the door softly behind him, then jogged quickly and quietly down the curling staircase to the bottom.

Where he saw the outer door to the glass vestibule closing slowly behind Kat.

Sam pulled himself up short. Instinctively, he backed up the stairs into the shadows where he could watch Kat without danger of being seen.

But why? He was being silly. Why should he hide from Kat, watch her from the shadows like she was some kind of criminal? She must have thought of something, some clue, some inconsistency, some idea that might shed light on the murder. He should be helping her, not hiding from her. Sam shook his head, surprised at himself, and moved forward.

Sam cursed himself in his mind. He hadn't even thought about the locks on the workshop doors. He wouldn't have been able to get in once he got down there.

But Kat should have had the same problem, right? She'd said Phillip had let her in the previous night, but Phillip was nowhere to be found now. How had she gotten past the first door?

Kat stood inside the soundproof vestibule for a moment, her back toward Sam. To his astonishment, the inner door clicked open and Kat stepped inside.

Sam immediately stopped and slid further back into the shadows, his pulse suddenly pounding in his ears.

Kat had access to the workshop.

Phillip wasn't the only one with access.

Sam's mind reeled. That changed everything. At the very least, he'd assumed Phillip had to have been an accessory to the murder, either witting or unwitting. That's if he wasn't the murderer himself. No one could have gotten into the room without Phillip's help, unless they'd somehow tricked Nestrom himself into letting them in. And given Nestrom's relationships with his family, that seemed unlikely.

But if Kat had access, too, then...

Sam crept forward on the stairs, crouched in a dark corner, and watched Kat through the glass.

She pulled a pair of gloves from her pocket and put them on. Come to think of it, she seemed to have an unusually ready supply of medical gloves on her person at all times.

Sam watched as Kat searched the workshop, quickly and quietly, disturbing as little as possible. She opened doors and drawers, peering into them and feeling along their sides like she was looking for a hidden compartment. She went inside the prototype room, the small door closing automatically behind her, blending invisibly into the wall, but came out again after only a few minutes.

Sam couldn't recall seeing anything the other night. They'd searched the room thoroughly, found all the prototypes, save the one. Had Kat noticed the naming convention on the video files? Did she know there was a missing prototype?

He lost sight of her as she went around the corner to the living area in the back. The bright blue glow against the walls told him she'd opened the laptop. After only a few minutes, the glow went away again and Kat came back into Sam's view. She released a deep sigh and looked around the workshop again, seeming frustrated.

She made a move toward the door, and Sam got up to leave. He didn't want Kat to know he'd been there, hiding, watching. He didn't want her to have the slightest suspicion in her mind, to know that he might be considering her as a suspect.

Is that what she was now? Did Sam really think Kat could have killed her father? She'd been in bed beside him that very night. They'd made love not an hour or two before the murder must have occurred. How could Kat have done it?

But Sam knew, deep down, that it was possible. He'd woken up to find her in bed beside him, but she'd been dressed. Or partially so, at least. She hadn't been dressed when he'd fallen asleep.

She could have gotten up and put some clothes on, then climbed back into bed. Easy enough.

But she also could have gotten up, put some clothes on, come down to commit the murder, and then climbed back into bed again.

Sam shuddered to think he might have lain in bed with a murderer all night. Shuddered again to think he might have made love to one several times afterward.

Just as Sam was about to dart up the stairs, Kat stopped short, her neck craned to the side. She walked to the far wall, beside the door to the prototype room, and slid her hand over the surface. She stopped at what looked like a tiny notch, an imperfection in the concrete. Sam couldn't make out much from a distance, but Kat played at the notch with her finger, then pressed against the wall and examined it closely.

Looking frustrated, she turned toward Sam and walked briskly to the door. Sam took the stairs two at a time, nearly stumbling twice on the dark, slick concrete. He slid out the door at the top and into a room down the hall, peering around the jamb as Kat came out of the stairway, looked around quickly, then slipped away down the hall.

She'd been up to something down there, something she hadn't wanted anyone else to know about. Sam didn't want to think that Kat could be the murderer. And he wasn't willing to admit to himself that she was a suspect.

But he had to admit that, in that moment, it didn't look good.

**41**

Sam's mind reeled. He wandered through the halls at random. If he heard a noise, he turned down another hallway. He didn't know where he was going. He just knew he didn't want to see anyone else right then. He needed to be alone. He needed to think.

Everyone had a motive of one kind or another. Thomas and Christa, Cress, Brandon. All of them had been treated badly by Nestrom. And Cress had supposedly been cut out of Nestrom's will.

What about Kat? Did she have a motive? Sam didn't know. He realized in that moment that he barely knew the woman he'd been sharing a bed with for the last two nights. Their connection had been so natural since the first moments on the train, and her beauty had so captivated Sam that in the whirlwind of events since then he hadn't stopped to think about it. He wasn't usually one to fall for a pretty face, but between the connection and Kat's beauty, Sam had fallen hard.

A bad habit of his.

Sam heard a noise and turned down another random hallway. For the first time, the labyrinth of passages was working to his advantage. He was good and lost in the massive house, but he would worry about that later. He had more important things to worry about at the moment. Like solving this murder.

They all had a motive. But who had had the opportunity?

Every single one of them had the chance. None of them had a real alibi for that night. Assuming Christa and Thomas would vouch for each other, they all claimed to have been alone in their rooms.

Or maybe they had worked together, two of them acting as a team. Maybe there were two killers, not just one. Thomas and Christa were a natural pair, as were the twins, Brandon and—a lump rose in Sam's throat—Kat. Brandon and Cress could have done it, the two disgruntled black sheep. Or Christa and Kat, Cress and Christa. Any combinations was possible.

But how would they have accessed the workshop? Kat had access. Sam had seen it with his own eyes. And Kat had lied to his face about it. How many of the others had access? And did Phillip not know about it, or had he lied to Sam, too? Was he a part of the plot, or just an unwitting accomplice?

Sam heard voices ahead in the hall. He stopped to listen, to see if he could recognize them, but it was just two members of the staff talking about their work schedules.

The voices were getting closer. Staff or not, Sam preferred not to be seen. With no hallways nearby, Sam ducked through a thick wooden door to his left and closed it quietly behind him.

Phillip. Sam hadn't thought much about Phillip, but he was a suspect, too. He'd had the opportunity. He had access to the workshop. He was the one to find the body. But why would he want to kill his employer? Sam had seen no evidence of mistreatment. And Phillip seemed to have nothing to gain from

Nestrom's death. What's more, with Nestrom gone, Phillip could wind up out of a job. What motive could he have had for murder?

There was still one last piece of the puzzle to work out. There were plenty of motives. Plenty of opportunity. And Sam had theories on both. But what were the means? How had Nestrom died?

On that front, he was still stumped. He'd found no evidence of struggle on the body. No scratches or bruises on his skin, no skin or blood under his fingernails. No marks on his neck where someone may have choked him or strangled him with something. No signs of blunt force trauma or puncture wounds on his head or his chest. None of the usual signs of murder by physical means. Forensic analysis would no doubt turn up something more conclusive, but Sam wasn't about to stick around long enough for the police to get involved.

Poison was an option, of course. The white-collar killer. The ladies' choice. But that usually left visible signs, as well. A blue tinge to the lips, a red ring around the eyes, a yellow haze in the sclera. Perhaps a bubble of foaming spittle around the mouth or signs of vomiting. Sam had seen none of that in this case.

The only things at all unusual about the body were the indentation above one ear and the dark spot above the other. Sam had assumed those were from the glasses, but were they? He'd worn one of the prototypes himself and had no evidence of those kinds of marks on his face. That didn't rule out the possibility, but it made it less likely.

And what about the prototypes? At least one was missing. That much was clear from the naming of the videos on the thumb drive. It seemed likely that the killer had taken it, or had wanted to take it, at least. That prototype—all the prototypes, really—were worth billions of dollars.

Enough for someone to kill for.

Sam had to get into the workshop. He had to watch that final video on the first thumb drive he'd found. It may hold all the answers he needed. And after that, he had to see what was on the new thumb drive.

And he had to do it alone. Without Kat.

The only question was how.

**42**

Sam pressed one ear to the thick wooden door. He still heard the voices of the staff members he'd fled a few moments ago. He couldn't make out what they were saying, but they must have decided to stop in front of the door for a chat. Sam would have to wait until they left before making his exit.

He turned and looked for the first time at the room he'd stepped into. He'd never seen it before, but that wasn't saying much. He had no idea how many rooms the house had, but he was quite sure he'd only been in a fraction of them.

This one was much smaller than the others. Perhaps twenty feet square, it was little bigger than the main room in Sam's apartment back in the city. Granted, that was by far the largest room in the apartment, but the dimensions seemed almost quaint in Nestrom's house.

Like seemingly every other room, a fireplace was set into one wall. There must have been a hundred fireplaces in the house. Unusual for such a modern structure, but beautiful and comforting, nonetheless. The fires gave the home a coziness that helped to offset the frigidity of all the concrete and glass.

And like seemingly every other fireplace in the house, this one was well-tended and blazing. The room was warm, but the fireplace was small enough that the air wasn't stuffy.

The space itself was sparsely furnished. The walls were unadorned, the only decoration a chest-high wainscoting that circled the room, white wood with cream-painted wall above. The effect was clean and warm and modern, and unlike anything Sam had seen elsewhere in the house.

Two overstuffed black leather recliners sat side-by-side in the center of the room, a square end table between them. Aside from the orange glow of the fire, the only light in the room came from a small lamp that stood on the small table.

On the wall in front of the recliners hung the largest flat-screen television Sam had ever seen. It covered nearly the entire wall, and had to have been at least a hundred inches, probably more. There was a switch on the wall on one side of the screen. When Sam flicked the switch, the television pulled back into the wall with a soft hum until the face of the screen was recessed from the wall, revealing two small grooves running along the sides of the recessed cavity on either side of the screen. As Sam watched, a thin, rigid cover slid down from the ceiling. So cleverly had the installation been built that, once the cover was in place, Sam couldn't tell there was anything behind it, even from only a foot away. Even the wainscoting continued across the cover in a line that seemed unbroken from the rest of the room.

Sam turned toward the end table. The surface was bare, save for the lamp, but there was a small drawer in the front. The only thing inside was a remote control. He pressed the power button.

Immediately, the cover over the television slid back up, the massive flat-screen pushed forward again, and the lamp on the end table dimmed. The screen flickered to life as Sam propped himself on the edge of one of the recliners.

On screen, an image came up, warbly and choppy, like someone had paused an old video. Sam examined the remote and found the play button.

The footage was old and grainy, taken with a low-resolution camera. The sound filled the room, soft but clear, but the audio quality was as poor as the video, mostly background hiss.

On the screen, a woman carved a mound of clay with a set of wooden knives. The clay sat on a round platform, a kind of lockable Lazy Susan. She would step on something off-camera—it must have been some kind of pedal—and the mound of clay would rotate slowly. Then she would release her foot and the round platform would lock in place again.

The woman looked to be in her mid-twenties, at most, though she could easily have passed for nineteen. Her blonde hair was smooth and shiny, tousled and twisted into a haphazard pile on her head, held in place by two crossed paintbrushes. The nonchalance of the hairstyle added to the woman's beauty, which radiated from the screen.

Sam had no doubt about who he was watching. That radiance was unique and hereditary. The woman on the screen had to have been Kat's mother.

The camera slid to one side, bobbing and weaving into odd, artistic angles, first playing with the spin of the clay, then with the light coming through the windows behind the woman, then focusing on her hands, in close-up, as she worked her wooden sculpting knives over the slick, wet clay. Her hands were coated in grey clay sludge, but the effect was to make them somehow seem more refined, more delicate, more powerful.

All the while, the woman's voice spoke, a rapid-fire commentary about her process, her thinking.

"The first stages of the sculpting process are exploratory," she said. "I'm searching the clay for the piece that lives inside."

"Something lives inside the clay? How does it breathe?"

Nestrom's voice, teasing the woman. His wife? Girlfriend? Sam didn't know when they married.

The woman's face was open, but focused. She didn't take Nestrom's bait.

"You can mock it all you want, but there is something alive inside here, just as there's something alive inside that code you're always writing. It's a metaphor, of course, but it's also a truth."

"What lives inside clay or code?" Sam could hear the smile in Nestrom's voice. He'd certainly never heard that tone when the man had been alive.

The woman stared straight into the camera. Her eyes blazed with intensity. "Ideas," she said. "Passion. Purpose." Her eyes flicked to a point behind the camera. She was looking at Nestrom, her head tilted to one side. "Love." A faint smile played at her lips then.

Sam's breath caught in his chest. With a strand of escaped hair laying over one cheek, the light from the windows framing her in an angelic glow that matched the beauty radiating from her, Sam could barely breathe. Like her daughter, Kat's mother's beauty was breathtaking.

Nestrom must have thought so, too, for the camera stayed on the woman's face long after she turned back to her work. It zoomed closer until her face filled the screen, huge on the wall.

Then it went black.

The video ended, and Sam was kicked out to a loading screen, a bunch of files in a list. They all had filenames like the ones on the thumb drive, strings of numbers representing the year, month, and day. The file Sam had just watched was from June of 1987. He scrolled through the files to the end. The last video on the list was dated from February 1996. Sam clicked on it.

The resolution this time was much better. Even on the large screen, the detail was crisp and sharp. A video camera with resolution that good in the mid-nineties must have cost a fortune.

The video opened with a tight shot of a pair of crystal blue eyes, wet and limpid, with thin lines shining away from the outer corners over the temples. The eyelids and cheekbones were pallid. Dark slashes carved below red rims. The eyes themselves were unfocused and dull, staring straight ahead, away from the camera, unseeing.

"Do you have anything you'd like to say?" Nestrom's voice, but barely recognizable. Hoarse, quiet, halting. Choked.

With what seemed a great effort, the eyes turned to the camera operator, then to the camera lens itself.

"To who?"

"To anyone."

The eyes looked away from the lens again, looked straight ahead. The camera pulled back a bit to reveal the whole face. Kat's mother lay in bed, propped against a pillow. Sam could see the telltale collar of a hospital gown across her chest.

"Georgie?" said Nestrom.

The woman's eyebrows lifted slightly. Her head lolled against the pillow, her eyes moving with it, as if to move her eyes alone required too much effort, too much coordination.

"Last words, you mean?"

Silence, then the camera wavered, shook. Sam could see compassion in the woman's eyes, but her body didn't move. A hitching sob came from off-camera.

"It's okay, love," the woman said, her voice a rasping whisper. "You'll be okay."

"How can you say that?" The camera shook. "Where you go, I go, remember?" Nestrom's voice was just a whisper. "You're my life, Georgie."

The woman looked straight ahead again.

"The kids will be your life now."

Nestrom's voice became hard. "They're the reason—"

"No." The woman closed her eyes and rolled her head back and forth against the pillow, the movement seeming to cost her a great deal of energy. The movements slowed and stopped, like a spinning top slowing, slowing until it collapsed on the table. "No, they're not," the woman said, her eyes still closed. "Don't say that."

Nestrom stayed silent.

The woman opened her eyes, turned them toward him, beyond the camera. "Please don't think that."

Nestrom didn't respond. After a few more moments, the camera shook again and Sam could hear Nestrom's quiet sobbing.

"Please don't go, Georgie," he whispered through his sobs.

The woman's eyes held that same compassion, but behind it Sam could see a vast empty desert of fatigue and sadness.

The eyes lost focus, slid away from the camera, and stared forward once again.

"I wish I didn't have to," she said.

## 43

Sam stood at the base of the stairs to the workshop, in front of the glass vestibule.

By the time he'd finished watching videos in the theater room, the two staff members had moved away from the door. He'd peeked out, seen no one, and slunk his way into the stairwell and down to the workshop.

There had been a lot of videos on the television upstairs. The earliest was from 1985, just a couple of years before the sculpting video. It seemed to have been made the night Nestrom and his wife, Georgianna, had met.

Sam wasn't sure how that had been captured on film. Nestrom had been filming. Maybe he'd been an amateur film buff, crazy about the new camcorders that had come out only a few years before. The vintage, retro equipment sold for hundreds of dollars these days on eBay and Etsy, but back in the early eighties, they were brand new. Nestrom had gotten one somehow. Maybe he was one of those enthusiasts who filmed everything, all the time.

Including, in a stroke of luck, the night he met his future wife. A brash, snarky, beautiful young Georgianna giving Nestrom shit for hiding behind a camera lens, until he finally set the camera down and stepped in front of it. In contrast to Georgie's poised beauty, Nestrom was gangly, geeky, and so, so young. Baby-faced. And yet he was confident and handsome in a nerdy way, a way that would be popular forty years later, but wasn't back then in the eighties. Except to Georgie, who was very clearly interested in, if not immediately smitten by, the odd young man with the camcorder.

Sam had jumped around in the files. There were lots of videos of Nestrom and Georgie in her art studio or out for a walk in a field or a forest, with Nestrom behind the lens. A few flipped the pattern, when Georgie took the camera and snuck up on Nestrom while he hacked away at some green-on-black code scrawled over a boxy computer monitor.

Then the kids came. First, Christa. Several videos showed her and Georgie together. Sam watched as she was a baby, then a toddler, then a precocious six or seven year old. Birthdays and first steps and, as Phillip had said, all the Christmases.

But Georgie was always the main subject, the star of the show. And for every video with Christa in it, there were three without her, with only Georgie.

And then the twins came, Kat and Brandon.

And Georgie changed.

Her smile dimmed a touch. Her radiance glowed a shade less bright. She was still beautiful and still young, but she would sit when before she had stood, walk when before she had run. She would use the arm of a chair to lever herself up or reach behind to grip a sideboard for balance. As the videos progressed, her hair grew thinner, coarser, duller. Her skin grew sallow. Where in earlier videos she had been vivacious and indomitable, in these Sam watched her become sickly, cautious and frail.

All leading up to that final video, the one in the hospital bed. The one that must have been made just before Georgie died.

And Nestrom blamed his children for her death. That much was obvious from his exchange with Georgie at the end. Maybe she'd gotten sick somehow after giving birth to Kat and Brandon. Or maybe she'd had some condition, cancer or something, that coincided with the pregnancy. If that were true, if Nestrom blamed his kids for the death of the woman who was clearly the most important person in the world to him, it would explain his treatment of his children in the years since Georgie died. It wouldn't excuse it, but it would explain it.

What was harder to explain was exactly why Sam had come down to the workshop with absolutely no clue how to open the doors. He hadn't summoned Phillip because he didn't want anyone to know he was down there. And he didn't want Phillip hanging around, waiting to see if Sam needed anything. Sam could have dismissed him, perhaps, but Phillip was still a suspect. Sam didn't want any suspect getting wind of what he knew.

Which, at the moment, wasn't a whole lot.

But he had the original thumb drive. That last video, taken the night Nestrom died, would undoubtedly tell Sam a lot.

And he had the new thumb drive, the one from Nestrom's necklace.

He needed to get into the workshop to see what was on those drives.

Why the hell hadn't he packed his laptop for the train ride? He'd thought about it on the way out his apartment door. But he hadn't planned on his trip lasting for days, and he was looking forward to unplugging for a few hours.

It didn't matter. The only computer in the house, as far as Sam knew, was behind two walls made of glass, with layer upon layer of security guarding them.

He paced back and forth in the small space before the glass

vestibule, pulling his fingers through his hair. How could he get inside? He could try to lift a thumbprint, either from Phillip or from Kat. Lift it from a used glass with a piece of tape, then press it onto a medical glove? Would that work? Would the oils from the fingerprint transfer from tape to glove well enough to fool a sensor?

Worked on TV. Probably wouldn't work in real life, but it might be worth a shot.

But then he'd have to fool the voice recognition. Could he just record Kat's voice? Would she have to say something specific to get through the security door? Some kind of passcode or identifying phrase?

Probably. He'd have to figure out what the phrase was, then somehow trick Kat into saying it in casual conversation while he secretly recorded her.

"Oh for fuck's sake," Sam muttered. His voice sounded loud in the small space, even with the stairwell curling up above him. "Great, now I'm talking to myself." His derision echoed in his ears.

He paced back and forth. He was going to have to go to Phillip, maybe even bring him on as a confidant. He didn't want to, but Phillip seemed the least likely to be involved in the murder. He had no motive that Sam could see. Sam would have to convince Phillip to open the door for him, then guard the staircase while Sam worked, just for an excuse to get Phillip out of the room.

Sam paced and pulled his hair and racked his brain, then shook his head. "There's no other way," he said under his breath. "Unless you want to open for me," he said, louder, crying to the heavens. "Unless you want to let me in yourself, Dr. Nestrom."

He really was going crazy now. Too many days trapped in this wacky house with six murder suspects and a corpse.

"Would you like me to let you in, instead, Sam Davis?"

Sam jumped at the sound, and he had to fight the instinct to sprint up the stairs in fright. Adrenaline pumped through his veins. He could feel it pulsing in his forearms as he clenched and unclenched his fists and waited for his heart to stop hammering in his ears.

When he regained his senses, he realized something.

He recognized that voice.

He recognized it from the videos he'd just watched.

Georgianna Nestrom. Kat's mother. Like Christa had said when Phillip first opened the workshop for them to look at Nestrom's corpse.

Nestrom had recreated his wife's voice for the AI behind the security system.

"Would you—" Sam's voice was scratchy and dry. He cleared his throat. "Would you open the door for me?"

"You can open it yourself, Sam," the voice said. "Put your thumb on the scanner."

Sam did. The outer door clicked open.

As soon as it clicked shut behind him again, the inner door of the glass vestibule clicked open.

He was inside the workshop.

But how?

"Dr. Nestrom granted access to you at 11:46PM on December 24," the voice said.

Before he died. Why the hell would Nestrom do that?

"Who else has access to the workshop?"

"In addition to you, Phillip Beroulis, Katerina Nestrom, Brandon Nestrom, Cressida Nestrom, Christa Crowell, and Thomas Crowell all have access to the workshop."

"Nestrom granted everyone access?" Sam hissed to himself. He couldn't believe it. Why the hell would Nestrom do that?

"Dr. Nestrom granted access to you, Phillip, and Thomas. Access for the others was created separately."

"By who?"

"Unknown," said the voice. "Access was granted manually, not by voice command."

"Manually? You mean, by typing it in or something?"

"Access was granted via command line."

Someone had hacked into Nestrom's impenetrable system and given access to Kat, Brandon, Cress, and Christa. Did that mean one of them had done it? Had they given access to everyone else just to hide their tracks?

Or had Phillip or Thomas done it? They already had access. Maybe they had access to the system, too, and could grant access to the others to help with some plan to kill Nestrom.

And why the hell had Nestrom granted access to Sam before he died?

For that matter, why had he had a hand-written note to Sam in his pocket? He'd never met Sam before that night.

And the video, calling Sam out by name, asking him to take the information straight to the police. Nestrom must have done all that on Christmas Eve, late at night, between dinner and his death.

But why?

Sam let out a heavy sigh. Why the hell did it seem like every time he solved one problem, ten others cropped up?

It didn't matter. Through some miracle, he was inside the workshop. Alone. Now, at least, he could look at the thumb drives in solitude.

As long as no one else decided to come down while he did.

**44**

Sam had been methodical. He'd loaded the first thumb drive and gone through each video in sequence, starting with the earliest.

After watching the first few from start to finish, he'd scrubbed through the rest, one by one. There were so many to watch, and they all showed the same thing. Product test after product test.

It was fascinating to watch Nestrom's progress. Even just in the thumbnail view from the scrubber, Sam could see the breakthroughs when they happened. When the cameras on the glasses stabilized, the heads-up display started to work. Once Nestrom figured out the parallax issues and the image blending between the views for each eye.

And then Nestrom introduced more functions and more information. He tried to visualize them in the screen, but it made everything an incomprehensible jumble. Prototype after prototype, iteration after iteration, test after test, Sam watched as Nestrom tried again and again to get that part right.

He stopped at the video where that problem was resolved. It was a turning point in the development process, when things changed from just a great device along the lines everyone expected to a groundbreaking new technology. Nestrom knew it, too. He added a section at the end of the testing video where he discussed what he'd learned and where he intended to go. Sam watched it all the way through, riveted by Nestrom's barely restrained excitement.

Nestrom had figured out how to put an image in the subconscious mind of the user by encoding it in the background where the conscious mind couldn't see it, but the subconscious could. The process was essentially subliminal suggestion, like TV commercials used to do, or rock music in the eighties with their satanic messages.

Only those were all bullshit. Nestrom's glasses were real. When he'd been wearing the prototype, it was this process of subliminal suggestion—or sensory stacking, as Nestrom called it —that had given Sam an awareness of what was going on elsewhere in the house, up the staircase and in the hallways above them. He listened to Nestrom on the video explaining how the glasses could now tap into the feeds from the cameras and sensors in the house, aggregate the information in real-time, and deliver it through the glasses to the user with this sensory stacking technique. It was a real breakthrough.

Sam checked the filename. The breakthrough had come on December 4 at 3:47PM. Just three weeks ago. Prototype 1201.2. Nestrom had gone through twenty-six more prototypes in three weeks. The man was a machine.

No. He was obsessive, to the detriment of his family and his relationships. He turned his back on his own children, his own life, in order to throw himself into his work.

And this was the man society idolized.

Nestrom quickly explored the implications of the breakthrough and built upon it, stacking information on the other senses, as well. He'd stacked the visual. In later prototypes, he stacked the auditory sense. He even incorporated spatial characteristics into his audio to build a three-dimensional auditory image in the user's mind, essentially stacking a kinesthetic awareness. In later prototypes, he explored the use of subtle haptics to bring a sense of touch into the mix that, he said, produced a significant enhancement in the user experience without breaking through to the user's conscious attention.

Breakthrough after breakthrough, innovation after innovation. It was amazing to watch.

Sam went on through the videos, his own excitement mounting as he worked his way toward the last one, the one from Christmas morning. The one where Nestrom was killed.

Only that video wasn't there anymore.

Sam was positive he had seen it.

But now it was gone.

Sam double-checked the filenames. He looked for hidden files. Went to the command line and did a search for any video that had been recorded after 2AM on Christmas Day.

There were none.

The last video Sam could find was the README file recorded for him at 1:02AM on Christmas morning.

That couldn't be right. Sam distinctly remembered another recording. He was absolutely sure of it. Had he somehow erased it accidentally? He checked the trash folder on the laptop and found nothing.

He ejected the thumb drive, pulled it out of the port, and pushed it back in, hoping that the video would reappear when the drive reloaded.

Still nothing.

He pulled the drive out again, ready to try the process once more, then stopped himself. Doing the same thing over and over wouldn't help. It would only drive Sam nuts. Where could the video have gone? If it had been deleted, there had to be a way to recover it. But how?

Sam twirled the thumb drive between his thumb and fore-finger. The chromed metal stick spun like an airplane propeller as he flicked it with his middle finger again and again. He stared down at the spinning object, barely aware it was moving, barely aware he was making it move. His mind spun as fast as the thumb drive, searching for an explanation.

Sam frowned. He stopped the twirling and let the thumb drive rest in his palm, looked at it for a long moment.

Something seemed off.

The thumb drive was about an inch long, made of chromed metal, with a silver connector at one end. Just a normal, average thumb drive.

But something about it nagged at Sam's brain. It didn't fit with his memory.

He thought back to when he was examining Nestrom's corpse in the gardener's shed, when he'd first discovered the thumb drive and the odd note. In his memory, the drive wasn't shiny. It was dull, like brushed nickel.

And it wasn't long. He distinctly remembered putting it into the laptop port the first time. He could barely see the drive beneath his thumb. All he could see was the connector sticking out.

To check the suspicion forming in his mind, he moved as if he were inserting the drive in his palm into the computer. Fully half of the thumb drive stuck out behind Sam's thumb.

This was the wrong thumb drive.

How the hell could he have mixed up the drives? Up until a short while ago when he'd found the new thumb drive, he'd only ever seen one. How could he have mixed it up with a different one?

He sighed in frustration, but pushed the concern to the back of his mind. It didn't matter. The video was gone. One more mystery in an endless string of them. Sam could worry about it later.

For now, he had another thumb drive to investigate.

He slid the blade-thin drive into the laptop port.

Unlike the other drive, which held hundreds of files, this drive had only two files on it. One was another video named README.mp4. The other was a file named "20221226_0222_1238.0_2.mp4".

December 26 at 2:22AM? That was earlier that day, a full twenty-four hours after Nestrom was killed. How the hell could there be a video from that time? And how the hell could it be on the thumb drive that was tied around the neck of Nestrom's corpse in the gardener's shed?

2AM. Where had Sam been at 2AM?

He'd been here, in the workshop with Kat.

Trying on the prototype glasses.

Sam felt a chill run down his spine. He needed to watch that video.

But he needed to stay methodical. Not let his emotions, his excitement, get the better of him. That was the number two rule his parents had taught him about running a job. "Reassess and be resourceful," they would say. "Keep your mind open and work through your options."

The number one rule was never to lose your humanity, never forget that the people working with you and the people huddled scared in front of you were human beings with lives and families. Number two was never to let your emotions get the better of you, keep your mind open and calm and look for opportunities with what you had around you.

Sam opened the README file. Nestrom's face filled the screen. He looked haggard, disheveled, much older than his years. Older than he'd looked at dinner not two nights ago. His eyes focused on the camera. Despite his appearance, his grey eyes were sharp as knives.

"I know who you are," he said.

That chill ran down Sam's spine again, then came back up and around for another pass.

"You must have known I would find out. After I rattled off all that information about you and your parents at dinner, your fears had to have been confirmed." He pushed his face closer to the lens, his nose and cheeks distorting slightly. "But I don't care."

He leaned back again, a smug, toothless smile on his lips. "Surprised? Hm?" Nestrom shrugged. "I know who you are and I don't care. You're a thief. Fine. Take what you came for. But here's what I want in return." He leaned forward again. "Find my killer. You know by now who the suspects are."

His pale eyes grew hard as diamonds. "Find my killer," he said, his voice a low growl, "and ruin them."

**45**

The door to the prototype room closed quietly behind Sam as he stepped back into the workshop. He'd searched the room from top to bottom, found every prototype in sequence except prototype 1237.6.

And now he knew there was one more missing prototype. Prototype 1238.0. The one in the second video on the new thumb drive Sam had found.

That was the latest prototype. The last one Nestrom ever worked on. But the killer had to have stolen 1237.6. It was the one with the missing slot at the assembly station. Did the killer even know 1238.0 existed? It seemed unlikely, or they would have ransacked the workshop trying to find it. Could that have been what Kat was looking for?

It was possible the killer had actually stolen 1238.0, and 1237.6 had simply gone missing somewhere. But that seemed even more unlikely. As meticulous as Nestrom obviously was, he wouldn't have misplaced a recent prototype. Hell, he had every prototype he'd ever made carefully catalogued and stored in felt-lined slots in a climate-controlled room attached to his workshop. He wouldn't go to all that trouble for thousands of prototypes and then misplace one of his most recent versions.

No, someone had taken 1237.6. And maybe they'd taken 1238.0, as well.

But Sam had a feeling they hadn't.

Sam had a feeling the killer didn't know 1238.0 even existed.

Which meant it had to be there, somewhere in the workshop.

Sam looked around the room and blew out a heavy breath. He didn't know where to start. He and Kat had already searched the room thoroughly, and then gone over it again. They'd uncovered every place where something could be stored or hidden, unlocked every drawer and cabinet. There was no sign of any missing prototypes.

He pulled his hand through his hair and turned in a slow circle. The situation kept getting weirder and weirder and he was running out of time. The snowstorm had passed. The plows were working around the clock to clear the roads and the police would be there soon. Tomorrow afternoon, probably, or the following morning, at the latest. And once they came, they'd lock down the entire house. Between the cops and Nestech's legal and security teams, Sam wouldn't be able to go anywhere without more than one set of eyes watching every move.

He needed to figure this thing out, fast.

His eyes dragged over the workshop as he turned, not really seeing anything, not really focusing at all. The desk with Nestrom's laptop. The couch. The four work tables. The glass vestibule leading to the stairs. The computer terminal in the corner. The door to the prototype room.

Something caught Sam's eye, broke through to his conscious brain. A tiny mark in the wall, one that looked like yet another of the hundreds of imperfections in the concrete.

Only Kat had been studying that particular imperfection earlier.

So Sam studied it, too.

Even from up close, it was unobtrusive. It really did look like just another imperfection. Except upon close examination, this imperfection kept going. Most of the tiny hollows scattered at random over the concrete walls of the workshop and the staircase dug into the wall and scooped back around. They were indentations, like someone had stuck their thumb into the concrete before it dried. But this particular indentation dug quite a bit further than most. It looked more like someone had pushed a small egg halfway into the concrete, rather than their thumb.

Sam bent down to study the indentation more closely. The face of it was like all the others, a wide, oblong dish. Unlike the other indentations, though, this one canted at an angle into the wall so that the left side was much deeper than the right. Most unusual of all was a small slot at the deepest point, a slot that pushed even deeper into the wall.

Sam felt along the surface of the indentation. The texture was moderately rough, like the rest of the concrete wall. A pleasant texture, just rough enough to be interesting, not rough enough to be distracting.

The slot was partially hidden in the shadow cast by the deep side of the indentation. Sam shined the flashlight of his phone into the darkness.

The slot was deep enough that Sam couldn't see the bottom of it. The sides were smooth and even. That meant it wasn't formed by accident. It had to have been deliberately and carefully cut into the wall.

But why? What was the point of a slot in the wall? Was it for ventilation? The vestiges of a switch or button that had been ripped out of the wall? Some kind of peep hole?

No, those ideas made no sense. One tiny slot would be

useless for ventilation in a room as big as the workshop. And Nestrom had enough money and OCD to patch it over if he'd ripped something out of the wall.

As for a peep hole, Nestrom would never allow a peep hole in his workshop. If someone else had put it there, Nestrom would have found it and plugged it. And if he were the only one with access, why would he need a peep hole in his own workshop?

Only he wasn't the only one with access. Phillip and Thomas —and now Sam—had it, too. Nestrom had granted them access on purpose. And now Kat and the others also had access. How long had that been the case? Was Nestrom aware of that before he died?

Maybe the peep hole wasn't for someone else to spy on Nestrom. Maybe it was for Nestrom to spy on someone else.

That didn't really add up either. Why would Nestrom want to spy on someone in his own workshop? He'd be more likely to kick them out than to spy on them.

Whatever the reason for its existence, if that really was a peep hole, that meant there was a space behind it. Somewhere to peep from.

Which meant there had to be a way to access it.

Sam examined the wall around the slot more closely, looking for seams or cracks. He tapped on the wall at intervals but heard only the thin knock of knuckles on concrete. Nothing to indicate a space behind the wall or a false front of any kind. He held open the door to the prototype room with his foot, examined the doorway closely to see if there was any kind of entrance or opening that might be hidden there, something that a peeper could slide into to get behind the walls.

Nothing.

He didn't know the layout of the house well enough to know if there could be another access point. It was possible that an adjoining room or an external wall or even a basement crawl space could allow entry. Without detailed blueprints, scanning equipment, or lots of time to explore, Sam wouldn't be able to figure it before the crowds arrived.

At the thought of blueprints, Sam searched the library station, shuffling through the stack of papers and diagrams on the table in the center of the workshop. It was a long shot, and it didn't pay off. The only blueprints there were schematics of the prototypes.

He went back into the prototype room, the door snicking shut behind him. The prototype room extended straight away from the workshop, but it ran parallel to whatever might be behind the peep hole. If there was any kind of space behind the hole, it would share at least part of a wall with the prototype room. Sam ran his hands along that wall, searching with his eyes and feeling with his hands for any means of entry, a crack or seam, a button or lever.

Unlike the rest of the workshop, this wall was perfectly smooth.

Sam heard muffled voices on the other side of the prototype door. He pressed his ear against it. He could hear the voices well enough to identify a deep voice and a higher-pitched voice, but he couldn't hear what they were saying.

He wanted to open the door, open it enough to make out the words, but doing so risked detection. The last thing he wanted anyone to know was that Sam could access the workshop. He wanted to keep that information to himself, for the time being.

But he had to know who was there. And what they were saying.

Sam took a deep breath. He pushed the button that activated the latch bolt. Thankfully, Nestrom's attention to detail included deadening just about every mechanical noise in the workshop. The latch bolt slipped open with barely a sound.

Sam waited, heart pulsing in his ears, waiting for whoever

was on the other side of the wall to push open the door, having heard the latch, no matter how faint. He waited to be discovered.

Nothing happened.

He released the breath he'd been holding, then pulled in another, long and slow. He pulled back on the door, bracing with his other hand on the inside to be sure the door didn't open more than the tiniest crack.

"...doesn't matter even if it is here somewhere. No one will find it."

Sam recognized Brandon's voice. It was loud, close.

"Someone will eventually find it. You know they will. They'll tear this place apart."

And that was Kat's voice.

"Thomas won't allow it. Company property remember? Once the cops are gone, no one will be allowed in this room again."

"Yeah, right," said Kat. "Thomas will tear the place down with his own hands if he thinks there's money to be made from it."

"By the time that happens, we'll be too far ahead. They'll be playing catch-up forever."

Sam pulled the door a tiny bit wider, wide enough for him to see into the workshop with one eye. He could see the glass vestibule. He could see the edge of the two workbenches closest to the door, the computer station and the optical station.

He couldn't see Kat or Brandon.

He opened the door a crack wider. Now he could see the library station and the assembly station. But still no Kat or Brandon.

He opened the door another crack wider.

"Why do you keep playing with that hole?"

Brandon's voice seemed deafening in Sam's ear. He'd opened the door wide enough that he could see the back of Brandon's left shoulder.

They were standing right beside the door.

Sam's breath caught. He pushed the door shut again, leaving

it open just enough to hear their voices. He held his breath, waiting for the moment when they would sneak up on the door to the prototype room, tense themselves on the outside, then bust through and grab Sam, throw him to the floor in the workshop and set upon him with blows and questions.

That moment never came.

"There's something here," said Kat.

Sam let out his held breath, letting it out in a slow, quiet hiss like the air from a bicycle tire. His heart was beating so loud in his ears, he had trouble hearing Kat's voice.

"There's nothing there," said Brandon. "It's just a mark on the wall."

"No, there's something in there," Kat said. "An opening. Like a keyhole or something."

"A keyhole?"

The voices stopped, long enough that Sam considered cracking the door open again to see what was happening. He had just tensed his muscles to do so when Brandon spoke again.

"It's just a crack," he said. "An air bubble or something. Something from when they poured the concrete. It's nothing."

"Hmm." Kat didn't sound convinced.

"Look, he's not down here, okay? Just like I said he wouldn't be. He can't get in here on his own, and Phillip said he hadn't let him in."

"He's got to be around here somewhere."

"Well, he's not down here, so I don't give a shit where he is. And I'm starving. Let's go eat dinner. Little narc's probably hiking through the snow trying to report to the police and earn his fucking junior deputy badge."

The voices grew fainter.

"He's not like that."

Sam heard the glass door open.

"Just because he's good in bed doesn't mean he's not like that. Even little narcs can have big—"

The door clicked shut, cutting off the sounds of their voices.

Sam waited, counting slowly to twenty in his head. He cracked the door open just enough to see the glass vestibule.

It was empty.

He cracked the door open a bit further, then a bit more. He wasn't taking any chances. They could have made it seem like they'd left, but snuck back inside, baiting Sam to come out.

Bit by bit, he opened the door wider.

He saw no one.

The workshop was empty again.

## 46

Sam went back to the imperfection in the wall, kicking himself.

What had his parents always taught him? Rule number two was to keep your mind open to all possibilities.

A keyhole? Not a peephole, but a keyhole?

Why hadn't he thought of that sooner?

Sam lit the flashlight on his phone and examined the slot once more. The opening was tall and thin. Exactly like a keyhole. But it was taller and wider than most keys. If it was a keyhole, the key would have to be unusually large. More rectangular than key-shaped. Like a key card or one of those RFID keys. Almost like the new thumb drive Sam had been looking at. Something blade-like and thin.

A jolt went through Sam like a lightning strike.

Something blade-like and thin, but not like the new thumb drive Sam had found.

More like the pendant he'd found with it.

He pulled the pendant out of his pocket. It seemed to be about the right thickness and about the right height. He held the square end, the end with the hole in it. The side that would open the beer bottles. The edges of the hole rubbed against his thumb as he slid the pointy end into the slot in the wall.

Nothing happened.

The pendant slid in just fine. It was the right thickness, the right height. But it knocked into something hard inside the slot and wouldn't go any further.

Sam took it out and slid it in again. Same thing. The pendant hit whatever was blocking it and wouldn't budge. He pushed on it, twisted the pendant against the sides of the slot. Nothing.

He pulled it out with a sigh. Might as well try the other end.

He flipped the pendant around, now holding the pointy end and pushing the bottle opener side into the slot. Again, it fit perfectly, width and height. With just the slightest resistance, it slid into the slot to the point where it had stopped before, knocking against something inside. Sam pushed a touch harder.

The pendant slid in further, and Sam heard a click. A jolt of excitement set Sam's heart racing. He tugged on the pendant, but it wouldn't budge. Sam couldn't push it in further and he couldn't pull it out again.

Something must have slid through the bottle opener, through the hole, locking the pendant in place.

Sam took a deep breath, then twisted the pendant to the left.

Nothing happened.

He twisted it to the right.

To his shock, the key twisted a full ninety degrees, laying horizontal in the slot.

That should have been impossible. The slot was nowhere near wide enough for the pendant to lay flat.

Sam grabbed his phone and shined the flashlight into the dark hole.

What had been a tall, thin slot was now a wide, wedge-shaped one. Whatever had pushed into the bottle opener was gone now. Sam pulled the pendant free with no resistance.

He pushed on the wall around the indentation, expecting it to swing open with some kind of cleverly hidden door.

Nothing happened.

But Sam had figured it out. He'd gotten the pendant, put it into the slot, and twisted it open. That couldn't have been a coincidence.

He shined his light into the slot again. The left side of it was smooth. Sam could see a small dark metal rectangle, like a deadbolt, set flush into the side. That must have been what caught the pendant earlier. It must have retracted when Sam twisted the pendant.

The end of the slot was a small flat rectangle, but the right side flared out from it, forming the wedge shape.

Only that side wasn't smooth like the other. Toward the far end, in the back, there was some kind of opening in the side of the wedge. Sam opened the camera on his phone, zoomed in to get a closer look at the inside of the slot.

There was definitely an opening on the inside of the wedge. Some kind of triangular depression in the side. Sam zoomed in more, turned the phone for a better angle. From that viewpoint, he could see that the depression was more pyramidal than triangular.

Clearly something was meant to fit in there. Sam looked at the pendant again. It was flat on both sides. Nothing stuck out at all. Certainly nothing pyramidal.

Maybe the pointed end was supposed to fit into the depression? Sam pushed and pulled on the pendant with his thumbs, trying to get it to bend in some way that would fit the depression. But the pendant was smooth, solid metal. It wouldn't budge.

He looked at the side with the bottle opener, the weird Christmas tree shape, a rectangle superimposed on a triangle. He thought about the deadbolt that had caught inside it. It must have fit into the right angles of the rectangle. Maybe the triangle fit the pyramidal opening in the wedge.

But that was impossible. The deadbolt had come out of the hole to fit into the bottle opener. There was nothing coming out of the wedge. It was just a pyramidal hole. Something had to fit inside it, or something had to come out of the wall to fit inside the triangle on the bottle opener.

Sam examined the slot again, looking on the left side, beside the deadbolt, to see if there was another sliding piece there that might fit through the triangle in the bottle opener and into the pyramidal hole on the other side.

All he saw was a smooth surface. Nothing there.

Something was still missing, some crucial piece to the puzzle.

Sam sighed. He was getting really tired of that feeling.

**47**



"The prodigal narc returns," said Brandon when Sam entered the dining room.

Sam frowned at him.

Christa and Cress were in their usual seats on the far side of the table. Brandon and Kat sat across from them. Sam was surprised to see that Thomas had settled into Nestrom's seat at the head of the table. Unlike when Brandon had tried to usurp it the previous night, the staff seemed to accept the new arrangement, taking away Thomas's empty plate and refilling his wine glass without complaint.

"Where have you been, Sam?" said Kat, standing to greet him, a worried look on her face. "I looked all over for you."

"I got lost somewhere in the house," Sam said, giving a crooked smile. "Took a wrong turn and couldn't find my way out of the maze. When I finally escaped, I checked in the billiard room, but no one was in there. I thought dinner was at eight."

"Brandon finally convinced Phillip to serve at seven," said

Thomas as he sipped from his wine glass and stared down at his phone.

"The first thing he set his mind to that actually succeeded," said Christa.

Thomas looked up at Sam. "I can ask Phillip to bring you a plate of endive salad. We can wait for the entrée."

"No we can't," said Brandon.

"That's okay," said Sam as he took a seat beside Kat. "I can skip the salad. But, thank you."

"Lost in the maze, huh?" said Brandon. He glanced at Kat. "Find any cheese?"

"You're making even less sense than usual, brother," drawled Christa, "and that's saying something."

Thomas tapped on his phone as the staff served the main course, a pork chop with a green sauce, mashed potatoes, and glazed carrots. As the scent of the hot food hit Sam's nostrils, his stomach growled loudly. He realized that he hadn't eaten in hours. Kat smiled at him and squeezed his leg.

She couldn't possibly be a murderer, could she? Could a killer have a smile that heart-melting?

"The roads are opening faster than expected," said Thomas. "Apparently a dead body is enough to get the city to change their road-clearing priorities. Our legal and sec teams will be here first thing in the morning. We expect the police to be here by noon."

"Won't the police be here at the same time as your corporate monkeys?" asked Cress. "They're all using the same roads."

Thomas gave Cress a curt smile. "The corporate monkeys are flying in by helicopter."

"Flying monkeys?" said Brandon with a grin. "Guess that makes you the wicked witch."

After dinner, Sam was surprised when everyone stayed together, adjourning to the parlor. But, unlike on Christmas Eve, when the mood had been relaxed, almost festive, the air that night was humming with tension. Cress and Brandon sat on the couch in front of the fire as they had before, cigars in hand, but they didn't light them. Brandon turned his over and over like a rotisserie skewer, while Cress twiddled hers between her fingers. They both stared into the flames with distant eyes.

Thomas sat beside them, tapping away on his phone, as usual, his unlit cigar in his lap.

Christa, Kat, and Sam sat at the card table. Kat shuffled the deck again and again, the cards riffling and snapping as she interleaved their edges, then joined them with a bridge. No one suggested a game. No one offered a snarky comment. Christa sat back in her chair, lost in her thoughts, while Kat stared down at the cards.

*Riffle, snap.*

*Riffle, snap.*

*Riffle, snap.*

Sam found his gaze drawn to Kat's hands, mesmerized by the rhythmic sounds and movements. He could smell the subtle scent of her perfume. The skin of her hands was soft and smooth. His thoughts ran to the rest of her skin, soft and smooth and sweet-scented all over her body. He thought about feeling that skin later, the two of them alone in the bedroom.

But was Kat the killer?

The thought hit him like a cold shower.

She had the motive. Her life with Nestrom was no rosier than anyone else's.

She had the opportunity. She'd been with Sam that night, but he'd been fast asleep until early morning. She could have slipped away in the middle of the night and killed Nestrom, then come back into bed with Sam.

Which put her in the same group as every other person in that room. Motive and opportunity.

Sam's skin went cold at the thought.

But what were the means?

Sam watched Kat shuffle the cards over and over.

*Riffle, snap.*

Her long, graceful fingers straightened the deck, turning it over and cutting it for another shuffle.

*Riffle, snap.*

Her rings gleamed in the light from overhead. Sam hadn't noticed Kat's rings before. He'd been too busy noticing other parts of her.

*Riffle, snap.*

She wore a ring on her left index finger, a silver ring with delicate diamond-set leaves. On the middle finger of that hand she wore one of those rings that looks like three rings jumbled over the top of each other, gold, silver, and rose gold.

*Riffle, snap.*

On the middle finger of her right hand, she wore a wide gold ring with cutouts in the shape of butterflies. Beside that on her ring finger was what would have looked like a wedding ring, if it weren't on the wrong hand. Delicate twisting stalks of rose gold with diamond leaves. Kat must really like plants. Or diamonds. In the center of the ring was an opalescent stone, beautiful but understated, cut in an elegant octagonal shape.

Kat noticed him looking at her ring. "It's called an eighty-eight cut," she said. "Eight sides, eighty-eight facets."

Sam had never seen that shape before. Of course, he was not exactly a jewelry connoisseur, but the shape seemed unique.

"Supposed to be good luck, in Asian cultures. Something about the number eight bringing good fortune."

The skin on the back of Sam's neck prickled. A wave of energy flooded through him.

"What's wrong?" asked Kat. She was looking at him strangely, her hands stopped in mid-shuffle.

Sam cleared his throat. He could feel a the hair stand up on his neck. "What do you mean?" He tried his best to will his voice to be steady and calm.

"You jumped, then your face got all weird, like you'd seen a ghost or something."

"You're white as a sheet," said Christa. "Did the pork disagree with you?"

Sam took a deep breath, trying to slow his racing heart.

"What's the matter, narc?" said Brandon. "Too much excitement for you?"

Sam jumped. Brandon was standing right next to him, unlit cigar clutched in his hand like a knife handle. Sam hadn't heard him approach.

"I'm fine." Sam shifted in his chair and tried to smile reassuringly, but wasn't sure if he pulled it off. He was pretty sure he hadn't, in fact. "I just nodded off for a second, I think."

Christa let out a heavy sigh. "Well I can certainly understand why." She stood up. "Are we just going to sit here, or are we going to do something?"

Her question was met with a rousing chorus of indifference.

"Alright, then," she said. "Let's go, Thomas. I can think of plenty of things to do in the bedroom."

They left together. Brandon flopped back down on the couch beside Cress.

Kat straightened the cards meticulously, set them down neatly in the center of the table. She turned her beautiful, bottomless eyes toward Sam with that look that turned his mind to jelly.

"I can think of a few things, too," she said, her voice low and sultry.

As she led him out of the room and up the stairs, Sam could

barely think at all. He'd just figured out how to unlock the hidden door in the workshop. And he was running out of time.

But it was too risky to sneak around with everyone still awake. He'd have to wait until later.

He let Kat pull him into the bedroom, kick the door shut, and wrap him in her arms. Her skin was soft and smooth, her scent was sweet.

For the moment, Sam had plenty to keep him occupied.

# 48



Kat had been fast asleep when Sam slipped out of the bedroom, her body naked and relaxed on the covers, the lines of her figure outlined by the pale moonlight through a part in the curtains. The night sky was clear, the moon and stars bright. For a wistful moment, Sam had wanted nothing more than to spend the hours until morning sketching Kat again.

But the police would be there at noon.

And Sam had to make sure he wasn't.

He gathered his clothes in his arms and waited until he was outside in the hallway to pull them on. He didn't want to risk waking Kat. He pulled on his shoes and socks and slipped through the dark hallways as quickly and quietly as he could. As he opened the door to the staff hallway, he heard laughter and voices. His heart leapt into his throat. He jumped back and pushed the door shut again. After a long, tense moment, he cracked the door and peered down the hallway.

Light spilled from an open doorway at the far end. Sam

could hear low voices drifting down the still and silent hall. Someone must be in the kitchen enjoying a late-night snack. Or maybe someone from the staff was assigned to stay up all night on the off chance one of the family would need something. Wouldn't surprise Sam. More useless waste of staff time to serve the whims of the rich.

Sam slipped through the door and down the hallway to the outside. He shivered as a gust of cold wind whipped past, knifing through him and chilling him to his core. At least he'd worn his shoes this time. He wished he'd worn his coat, too.

He moved quickly, slipping into the gardener's shed, using his phone as a light source. No sense risking detection by turning on the overhead lights. He uncovered Nestrom's right hand, picked it up in his. Sam still shivered every time he held the cold, hard flesh. He turned the hand over in his to better access the diamond.

But the diamond was gone.

All Sam saw was the gold bezel, the pyramidal indentation empty where the trillion-cut diamond should have been.

"Strange place to spend an evening," came a low voice from the darkness in the corner.

Sam jumped, pointed his phone toward the sound. Brandon sat on the seat of a riding lawn mower, a shovel in one hand.

In the other, he held his mother's diamond.

"Look what I found," he said, holding the stone up into the weak light from Sam's phone. Brandon admired the diamond almost casually, a slight smirk on his face. The jewel shone as its facets caught the light, prismed it into brilliant whites and reds and blues.

"Beautiful, isn't it?" said Brandon. "Beautiful and... unusual, right? An unusual shape." Brandon stood and slipped the diamond into his pocket. He tapped the ground with the butt of the shovel as he stalked toward Sam. "But just the right shape for that hole in the wall in the workshop, don't you think?"

He smirked again as he took Sam's phone and tossed it in the corner.

Sam had never wanted so badly to wipe a smirk off someone's face.

**49**

DECEMBER 27, 1:19AM

Brandon and Sam made their way wordlessly down to the workshop. Thankfully, Brandon had left the shovel behind in the gardener's shed. Sam wasn't exactly the type for a fistfight. He preferred brains to brawn. But at least he didn't need to worry about being brained from behind by a shovel.

Brandon unlocked the doors to the workshop with another smirk toward Sam.

"We've had access since we were in high school," Brandon said. "You don't think we wouldn't have figured out how to break into the one room in the entire house our father didn't want us to go? Any self-respecting kid would have done the same. Besides," he shrugged, "my sister's a computer genius."

He arched an eyebrow at the surprise on Sam's face.

"You didn't know that?" Brandon snorted. "Guess you guys don't really talk much, do you?"

He led them to the wall where the lock still sat half-open, the wedge shape waiting like a hungry mouth for a key to swallow. Sam hadn't been able to figure out how to close it back up. He figured it was designed to be opened all the way or not opened at all.

"Thanks for cracking it open this far," said Brandon. "Been trying to figure it out for years, ever since my father installed the fucking thing." He pulled the diamond from his pocket, tossed it in the air and caught it in his palm, held it up between thumb and forefinger. "Soon as I saw the hole, I knew what to do." He held out his other hand. "Give me the thing."

"What thing?"

Brandon's face darkened. "Don't dick around. I am not in the mood."

"You give me the diamond, I'll open the door."

"I think you're confused about who's calling the shots here."

Sam shrugged. "The way I see it, this is a partnership. You've got the diamond, I've got the key. We need each other."

"See, there's the confusion. I don't need you. I need the key." He flapped his fingers. "Give it to me or I'll beat you senseless and take it from you."

It was tough to argue with that logic. With a sigh, Sam pulled the pendant from his pocket and held it up. Brandon snatched at it, but Sam pulled it away.

"Give me the diamond."

"My nephew is far too nice," said a voice from behind Sam. He looked over his shoulder and saw Cress coming through the doors. She held a gun in her hand. "I'm not."

So it was down to Cress and Brandon. One of them was Nestrom's killer.

And now Sam was in a soundproof workshop, alone with the two of them.

And Cress had a gun.

"I would have killed you the moment I saw you," said Cress.

While Sam's attention was focused on Cress, Brandon stole the pendant from his hand.

"Or at least knocked you out." She glanced at Brandon. "So

much simpler when they're knocked out, dear boy. Have I taught you nothing?" Brandon shrugged and grinned.

Sam's heart dropped.

Cress had a gun. Brandon had the pendant *and* the diamond.

And Sam had zero leverage.

Cress motioned toward Sam with the gun, waving him away from the locked door. While Brandon fumbled with the diamond, Cress kept the gun trained on Sam, but her eyes were fixed on Brandon. She was blocking Sam's path to the vestibule, but he edged closer to the prototype room. He didn't have a plan, but he at least wanted an option, a place to hide.

Brandon finally managed to fit the diamond into the hole in the pendant. It slipped into place with a click, just as it had fit into the ring on Nestrom's dead finger.

A makeshift key.

A brilliantly clever makeshift key.

As Brandon set the key into the lock, Sam could see the wedge fold shut around it. Brandon pressed in with his thumb. There was no sound as the key snapped in, but when the lock released it, Sam knew the door was open. Brandon tossed the key aside on the counter, practically bouncing with glee.

Cress stepped closer to the hidden door as Brandon pushed against it with both hands. With Cress distracted, Sam darted into the prototype room and held the door shut behind him. He stood with his back against it, pressing hard with his legs to hold it tight, expecting Cress to start shooting or Brandon to try to break in any moment.

They didn't.

No shooting or banging or shouting. No teeth-shattering jerk from Brandon's body slamming against the outside of the door, trying to barge inside.

Sam heard nothing, felt nothing at all.

He cracked the door open and peeked into the workshop.

Cress and Brandon were gone.

He opened the door wider and poked his head around it.

The workshop was empty, the hidden door closed.

Seizing his chance, Sam dashed out of the prototype room and toward the glass vestibule to make his escape.

When a gleam of refracted light caught his eye.

The diamond. It was still sitting on the counter, in the pendant, where Brandon had carelessly left it behind.

With a hard gulp, eyes trained on the hidden door for any sign of opening, Sam raced over to the counter and grabbed the pendant and diamond. He turned back on a dime, like running wind sprints in gym class, burst through the glass doors and out of the workshop.

And nearly tackled Kat on the stairs.

**50**

"What are you doing?" Kat said. "Why are you running?"

In the cold and dark of the stairwell, breath hitching in his chest, Sam explained as quickly as he could what had happened. The pendant and the diamond, Brandon and Cress and the gun.

He couldn't see Kat's face in the shadows, but he could feel her mood shift with the news.

"You're going the wrong way," she said. Her voice was as hard as the concrete walls and as cold as the night air. "We're going back down there. Together."

"Shouldn't we get—"

"Now," she said, pushing past him and down the stairs.

Sam had never heard Kat speak like that. And he wasn't about to argue.

Kat opened the security doors to the workshop without a word and stomped straight to the hidden door.

"Open it."

The tone in her voice left no room for dissent.

Sam pushed the diamond out of the pendant. He twisted the empty pendant in the lock, moving it into the wedge shape. He popped the diamond back into the hole in the pendant and unlocked the door the rest of the way, marveling again at the cleverness of the mechanism.

Sam pocketed the key as soon as the lock released it, trying to make the gesture as casual and unobtrusive as possible. Kat didn't seem to notice. She stepped up to the door, pressing with both hands.

"Wait," said Sam, one hand on Kat's shoulder. "They've got a gun."

Kat didn't say a word in response to Sam. Gone was her entrancing smile, the gentleness of her features. Her mouth was set in a hard line and fire burned in her eyes.

Sam was scared of what Brandon and Cress might do. They were both more than a little unhinged.

But in that moment, Kat was even more fearsome.

He hung back while she pushed the door open.

"You fucking asshole," she said, standing in the open doorway.

Sam couldn't see past her, but he heard Brandon's voice. "Oh, hey, sis," he said. "I was wondering when you'd get here."

Sam stepped toward the door, but Kat stepped further into the room and shut the door behind her.

She shut the door in Sam's face.

Left him all alone in the workshop while she went inside the hidden room with Brandon and Cress.

Sam couldn't have been more surprised if she'd turned in the doorway and slapped him in the face. He didn't quite know what to do with himself. He still needed to get into that room, needed to see what was in there.

He needed to find the last prototype.

Did Brandon and Cress already have it? Did they even know

it existed? Or were they just curious to see what was in the room they'd been unable to open for so long?

No. Cress wouldn't have brought a gun if she was just curious. She wouldn't have gotten up in the middle of the night. She would only have done those things if she thought there was something valuable in there.

They had to know what they'd find in there. Or at least what to look for.

And Cress had shown no compunctions about threatening violence. Was she the killer? Had she killed her own brother?

And why was Kat so willing to go into a closed room with the two of them? Did she think that because they were family, she would be safe? Was she that naive?

Sam felt closer than ever to answers, but still felt like they were dangling in front of him, hidden in a fog, tantalizingly near, but still just out of reach.

He had to get into that room.

He had to get past Cress and Brandon.

He had to keep Kat safe.

He needed a plan. He was looking around the empty workshop, taking stock of his options, when the lights went out.

# 51

DECEMBER 27, 1:49AM

In the workshop, deep underground, the darkness was absolute.

Sam felt in his pockets for his phone, cursed as he remembered that Brandon had tossed it in the corner of the gardener's shed.

He couldn't see his hand in front of his face. He held it up, knew it was there, but could see nothing. He felt incorporeal, insane, like he were falling down a deep, deep pit, endlessly falling toward an unseen, unknown end.

But that was just his fear talking.

He was in the workshop. Alone in the dark. In a room behind him were three people, two of whom could be killers.

Two of whom could be intending to kill Sam.

He could run. Run for the glass doors and escape, go and get help. Get Phillip or Christa or Thomas.

But he didn't want to risk leaving Kat. Who knew what could happen while Sam was gone? And what if he couldn't get back into the workshop? Kat would be at the mercy of a killer. Or two. Sam wouldn't do that to her.

He sighed, the sound shockingly loud in his ears. The workshop was dead quiet, and the darkness was debilitating. Why weren't the safety lights on, the blue lights that had been running when Sam had come into the workshop with Kat the other night?

Sam shook his head. The other night was only last night. Twenty-four hours ago. It seemed like an eternity. And he couldn't lose himself in what-ifs. Whoever had cut the power had cut all of it. Sam needed to act. Now.

In the dark, in his mind, Sam constructed a map of the workshop, a blueprint of the space. He did his best to orient himself within that mental map. When the lights went out, he'd been facing... what? The glass vestibule? The back wall? Or the hidden door?

No, he'd been facing the back wall.

Which meant that the assembly station was directly ahead of him.

And on it, a collection of prototypes.

Prototypes that might help him see in the dark.

Sam took a confident step to his right to move around the library station.

And banged into a waist-high countertop. Hard.

He bit his lip to keep himself from crying out, his hip screaming in pain. He rubbed it hard with the heel of his hand.

Damn. He must have been facing the glass vestibule when the lights went out. His mental map had been painfully wrong.

He reached out, touched the countertop he'd run into. That had to be the library station.

He slid his hand further over the counter, feeling along until he encountered something on the cool, smooth surface. Stacks of papers. Lying flat.

Definitely the library station.

He moved his hand back to the edge of the countertop and kept it there, sliding it along as he moved gingerly around the station to the other side. He reached across what he figured would be the aisle, expecting to feel the assembly station.

And found a wall instead.

Sam cursed softly under his breath. How could he have been to the side of the library station?

There was no way to see where he was. The damn dark was so thick, he lost his bearings with each step, his eyes searching desperately for any point of reference to latch on to.

Maybe his eyes were the problem. He shut them, and tuned in to his other senses.

He could feel a gentle breath of cool air against the sweat beading on his forehead, could smell the faint plastic-and-metal scent of electronic components. He could hear the depth of the space around him: the closeness of the wall, the subtle difference between the sound of the volume of air beside the wall and the sound of the air where the wall ended and the living space began.

He focused on those sounds, those sounds and the touch of his hand as he shuffled around the library station, half-step by half-step. He pushed all preconceived notions of where he was out of his mind, opening and emptying his mind completely.

Left hand on the countertop, right hand reaching out. Feeling everything. Taking everything in.

His right hand slid along the cool concrete wall, then fell into empty space.

His left hand felt the corner of the library station.

He turned left, keeping his hand on the counter.

His right hand still found nothing. Just empty air.

He reached further, stretching out.

Until he felt another countertop, felt further to make sure. Feeling forward and back, he marked the countertop edge, then stepped over to it.

He was at the assembly station.

Or so he believed.

He released the breath he'd been holding and opened his eyes. They were met with the same impenetrable wall of darkness.

He had to be careful here. If he really was at the assembly station, there would be a lot of delicate equipment on the countertop in front of him. The last thing he wanted was to knock something off with his clumsy fumbling in the dark, shattering it on the concrete floor beneath him, making a lot of noise and potentially drawing attention. From the killers in the room behind him.

Sam shuffled to his left, running his hand along the edge of the counter until he found the corner. He shuffled back to his right, counting his steps until he found the far corner. With this shuffling measurement in mind, he moved back to his left until he stood in what he thought was the center of the workstation.

Eyes squeezed shut again, he saw colors. Only the colors of behind his eyelids, from the squeezing, but it was something to latch on to. Something to remind him that his eyes still worked.

And shutting his eyes helped him to concentrate, to visualize in detail exactly what he remembered, what was on the assembly station and where it sat in relation to everything else. There had been some electrical testing equipment in the front right corner, a couple of metal boxes with electrical probes attached, red and black wires and metal leads in neat coils beside each box.

Sam reached out with his right hand, slowly feeling along the surface until he came upon a cool, smooth surface. He explored gently, carefully with his fingers. Felt the edges of a metal box. Felt a coil of wire, then another.

Good. He'd found the equipment.

On the other side of the table, he remembered a bunch of eyeglass parts and tools in trays.

He felt his way along the countertop until he found one plastic tray, then another, then two more.

Okay, he was in the right place and he had his bearings. He'd found the equipment on the right and the parts on the left.

What he wanted was in the center.

The prototypes.

Sam worked his hands slowly toward the center of the table, then away from himself toward the back of the workstation. That's where the tray of prototypes had been.

He felt for it, gently tapping with his fingertips, methodically exploring the space in the dark, careful not to move to far, too fast, so as not to knock anything to the floor.

He felt nothing.

Empty space.

Sam expanded his search, felt to one side, then the other, trying to ignore the feeling of panic clawing up his throat, like a hand reaching up to strangle him, its grip tightening, tightening.

On his left, he felt the plastic trays again. On his right, the electrical testing equipment.

There was nothing between them.

The prototypes were gone.

## 52

DECEMBER 27, 2:09AM

"Oh, Saa-am."

Brandon's sing-song voice came over some kind of speaker in the workshop.

In the still darkness, it pierced the silence like an ice pick.

The voice dropped to a low, sinister pitch. "I see you, Sam."

Instinctively, Sam ducked down low, crouched between the workstations.

"No, no, Samuel. You can't hide from me anymore." He could hear the smile in Brandon's voice. "I see everything now."

Shit.

Brandon could be bluffing, just trying to scare Sam.

Or he could be wearing a prototype.

Maybe even the latest prototype.

But would he know it even existed? Had he found it laying on the counter in the hidden room, or in an unlocked drawer or cabinet?

The details were irrelevant. Sam had to assume he was wearing one of the prototypes, and it didn't really matter which one. Whether it was the latest prototype or one of the prototypes from the assembly station, they were all incredibly powerful devices. Devices that let Brandon see in the dark. Devices that would help Brandon make short work of finding Sam in the ink-dark workshop.

Finding him and killing him.

Panic was no longer clawing at Sam's throat. Now it was choking him to death.

He closed his eyes again, forced himself to pull in deep, calming breaths.

His parents had taught him the technique as a way to calm himself during a job. In the heat of the moment, it seemed like madness to stop to breathe deliberately. But your goal is to keep breathing for as long as possible. You might as well use your breath to your advantage while you do.

Long, slow count to four on the in breath. Hold for four. Long, slow count to four on the out breath. Hold for four. Repeat.

Slowly, the throttling grip of panic loosened. Sam's chest relaxed. His heartbeat slowed.

He took stock of his situation.

Two killers in a room behind him, wearing sophisticated equipment and armed with at least one weapon.

A dark room full of things Sam could run into, things that could hurt him.

But very little he could use to hurt Brandon or Cress.

They would come out any minute, he was sure, to do Sam in. What could he do to defend himself? Throw an eyeglass frame at them? Stab them with a screwdriver? Zap them with electrical leads?

No, Sam needed to even the playing field.

He needed a prototype for himself.

With the prototypes from the assembly station gone, that meant all the remaining prototypes were in the prototype room.

Right next to Brandon and Cress.

Sam could make a break for it. Dash through the dark into the prototype room to gear up before Brandon and Cress came out to find him.

He shook his head slowly.

It had taken him forever just to move around a table. If he tried to go all the way to the prototype room, odds were that he'd wind up with a broken leg, lying on the floor right in front of Brandon when he came out.

Sam continued his deliberate breathing, eyes closed. He sensed the open space to his right. The living space, where Nestrom's couch and desk were.

At least there he'd have room to move, with a wall between himself and the others.

He didn't have many other options.

Sam didn't hesitate. He stayed in his crouch and scuttled into the open space, his hands out in front of him, feeling for unexpected obstacles. Thankfully, this time his bearings were true. His outstretched hands found the cushions of the couch instead of the corner of a table or something equally painful.

With a grateful sigh, he sat on the floor, his back against the couch.

Reassess. Reassess and be resourceful.

Now he was in a more open space. Still blinded by darkness. Still woefully under-equipped. Still completely unarmed. But he'd removed one set of obstacles.

He was still facing two people—two killers—with far greater advantages.

What about Kat? Had Brandon tied her up in the corner? Knocked her out unconscious? Killed her in cold blood? Was she struggling to distract Brandon and Cress, to give Sam some advantage?

"You know I can still see you, right?" called Brandon's voice over the speaker again. "Do you really think a wall is gonna block my vision?"

Sam cursed under his breath.

"By the way," called Brandon again, "in case you hadn't figured it out, I'm wearing the glasses." The speaker clicked off, then came on again. "The special glasses." Clicked off, then on again. "My father's fancy, high-tech glasses." Brandon's voice grew fainter, as if he were speaking to someone behind him. "What? I don't know. He's a fucking dumbass. I want to make sure he—"

The speaker clicked off. Silence rushed in, joining the darkness.

Brandon was right. Hiding behind a wall was no advantage at all for Sam.

He wouldn't win with tactics. He needed a strategy.

He had open space, but he still couldn't see. And it was too hard to get to the prototype room in the dark.

He needed light.

He tried to recall if he'd seen a flashlight when he and Kat had searched the workshop. Nothing sprang to mind.

Reassess and be resourceful.

The wall was no protection, but he had the open space. At least he could move without banging into things.

What else was around him?

The couch. The desk. The chair. The laptop.

The laptop.

Battery-powered.

Large glowing screen.

He could grab the laptop, use it to light his way while he ran to the prototype room.

He scuttled toward the desk. His hand, outstretched before him, found the chair. Sam wheeled it to the side, felt in front of him for the laptop on the desk.

He found it, pulled the power cord out of the jack, turned.

And heard a noise, loud in the dark silence.

A door swinging open.

"Sam, Sam, Sam," called Brandon, his voice muffled slightly by the wall. "So foolish. So naive."

Sam sank into the chair.

"I do admire your pluck, though."

This was the end, then. Brandon had emerged, wearing a prototype.

He was coming to kill Sam.

Sam pushed the laptop back onto the desk, not caring about the noise he made. The laptop banged onto the surface, slid across it. Clattered into something.

Clattered into something.

Sam's heart rate spiked as he reached out in the dark, feeling for the laptop, feeling around it, searching for what he hoped might be there.

His stomach flipped when his hands closed around a tiny plastic object.

A prototype.

The same prototype Sam had worn the night before.

"But now," said Brandon, his voice closer, just on the other side of the wall, "like a typical houseguest, you've overstayed your welcome."

Sam put on the glasses, waited while they booted up.

"It's time for you to go," said Brandon.

Sam counted the moments, praying that he still had time.

**53**

DECEMBER 27, 2:13AM


The laptop screen filled the air with a cold, blue light. Sam shivered. With the power off, the air had already gone frigid. The icy blue glow made it feel even colder.

Nestrom's face appeared on the screen.

"Documenting the time," said Nestrom, holding up the clock from the desk. "It's possible that many people will see this video..."

Nestrom's voice droned on, his face filling the screen, but Sam wasn't paying attention.

He was watching the shadows.

Through the viewscreen of Sam's glasses, Brandon appeared life-size and to scale, as if Sam were looking at Brandon in real life. He was just on the other side of the wall.

Cress came out of the room behind him.

Holding her gun.

The inky darkness was gone. All the objects, all the people in the room were as plainly visible as if the lights were on and the walls were made of glass.

Sam knew that if he took the glasses off, he'd be blind again in an instant.

And he knew that Brandon was seeing him as clearly as he saw Brandon.

At least now the playing field was level.

Except for one thing: Brandon didn't know it.

Brandon rounded the corner of the wall, stood in the center of the room, walking slowly toward the laptop.

"...No passwords or administrator restrictions," droned Nestrom on the video. "Should you see fit to copy and distribute this video, that's your..."

"Clever," said Brandon. "But if you think seeing my father's face again will trigger some kind of breakdown, you are sadly mistaken."

"...I won't stop you," Nestrom continued. "I'm sure it will interest plenty of people..."

Brandon took another step forward. "I didn't care when I killed him, why would I care now?"

"...You might even make some money from it..."

Sam crouched under the desk. He wasn't hiding. There was no point in hiding. The glasses made it impossible.

He was waiting.

But he needed a distraction. He had hoped Nestrom would provide it.

"...if you're watching this, it means I'm dead..."

In his glasses, Sam could see the feed from the laptop, playing the first video Sam and Kat had watched. In it, Nestrom's face grew larger as he leaned toward the camera.

"...I'm dead, and someone in my household killed me..."

Brandon stopped a few steps from the laptop. He said nothing, just stared at the screen, his face blank.

"Fuck you, brother," said Cress as she stepped around the wall. She pointed her gun at the laptop screen.

At her brother's face.
And fired.

## 54

Even in the large workshop, the sound of the gunshot was deafening.

Sam's ears rang, a high-pitched squeal that speared through his brain behind his watering eyes. The smell of gunsmoke stung his nostrils.

But he had no time to worry about any of those things.

Cress had given him the distraction he needed.

He'd been crouched under the desk, his hands on the rolling desk chair, heels braced against the wall behind him, waiting for Brandon to come closer. He hadn't come as close as Sam had hoped, but Sam couldn't wait any longer.

With all the strength his legs could muster, he exploded out of his crouch, pistoning his legs like a bobsledder at the top of the track. He drove the chair across the concrete floor, thrust it hard at Brandon, laying his own body nearly flat to put every ounce of power into the impact.

The chair back caught Brandon in the stomach, folding him in half. A fraction of a second later, the base of the chair took out

Brandon's legs. Brandon's body tumbled forward and landed on Sam's back, flattening Sam to the cold concrete as the chair wheeled wildly away.

Sam heard a soft grunt. He didn't know if the grunt came from Brandon or from himself. In that moment he didn't care.

In that moment, the world around him was darkness once more.

The impact with Brandon had knocked Sam's glasses off his face. He heard them clatter across the floor in front of him.

Brandon swore behind him, worked his legs over Sam's back, trying to scramble forward.

Sam twisted around, his legs pinned beneath Brandon's surprisingly heavy torso. He grabbed one of Brandon's feet.

Brandon's other foot kicked Sam in the ear. A dull whine filled his brain, joining with the high-pitched squeal from the gunshot in an off-key chorus of pain. His ear burned and felt wet at the same time.

Despite the pain, Sam gripped Brandon's foot. The other foot flailed around in the darkness, trying to make solid contact again with Sam's head.

Trying, but missing.

That meant Brandon had lost his glasses, too.

Level playing field.

Sam tightened his grip on Brandon's foot and twisted hard, twisted inward, toward Brandon's other leg. Ankles and knees were made to twist outward. They didn't twist inward quite so easily.

Brandon howled in pain.

Sam twisted harder.

The howl became a scream. Brandon rolled off of Sam, pulled Sam over with him until Brandon was on his back, Sam beside him, still twisting his foot.

Sam didn't know where Brandon's head was, but he knew it was on the ground somewhere. Instead of kicking down as

Brandon had done, Sam swung his foot parallel to the ground. Better chance of hitting something that way.

Brandon's scream cut off with a dull thud and a low moan.

Sam seized the opportunity. He scrambled to his knees and dove toward where the moan had come from, fists swinging.

They found Brandon's chest and neck, not his head.

Before Sam could adjust, Brandon threw him off, threw him hard toward the far wall, sent Sam sliding backward along the ground. He threw his arms out to slow himself, to keep his head from banging into the concrete wall. His hand knocked into something, something small and light. It clattered across the floor toward the corner by the desk.

The glasses.

Sam scrambled to his knees, ready to dive toward the clattering sound, but Brandon caught him by the ankle first. Sam spun around, butt on the floor, turning his foot before Brandon's grip could tighten around his ankle. He kicked out, this time kicking straight down toward his other foot.

The heavy grunt told him he'd caught Brandon full in the chest.

But Brandon's grip didn't loosen.

Sam kicked out again, higher, felt his heel catch Brandon in the throat, his toes strike Brandon's chin. Another grunt told him the kick had been solid.

Sam pushed off from the floor with his arms, jerking his body with his hips, stretching backward toward the corner. Still, Brandon's grip on Sam's ankle didn't loosen.

Sam kicked again, a kick in the chest.

Another kick.

Then another, this one aimed higher.

Sam felt Brandon's head snap sideways from the impact.

One more kick toward the head, and finally Brandon's grip loosened.

Sam leapt backward. His ankle came free, and he scrabbled

like a crab across the slick floor. Somewhere in the distance in his mind, he knew that the slickness came from blood, both Brandon's and his own.

He searched in the dark with his hands, searching for what he hoped was a prototype. Leveling the playing field was all well and good when you were at a disadvantage. But Sam wanted the advantage now. He was tired of scrambling in the dark.

He flipped onto his knees, his hands searching wildly along the ground as he crawled forward, His palms became as slick as the floor. Behind him, he heard Brandon's groans turn to angry growls. He would be on Sam again in an instant.

Sam swept his hands wider along the floor, covering more ground, careful to keep his palms open, his hands loose. The last thing he wanted was to knock the glasses away with a hasty sweep.

"Fuggnn ashhhull," muttered Brandon. Apparently one of Sam's kicks had caught him in the mouth, made it hard for Brandon to speak.

He knew Brandon was eager to return the favor.

Sam had only seconds to search, seconds before he'd have to stop looking for the glasses and focus on defending himself once more. He steeled himself for another struggle in the dark.

His hand knocked into something, knocked it toward his other hand. Sam grabbed it, hands shaking, sat back on his knees, felt the object in his hands.

The glasses.

# 55

DECEMBER 27, 2:19AM

Relief flooded over Sam as he put the glasses on, the Nestrom logo floating in the air in front of him as they booted up. His body protesting at the movement, he pressed his back against the cold, concrete wall and levered himself to his feet. Interminable seconds passed while he stared at that damn pale blue letter N in his glasses, pulsing rapidly with his heartbeat.

When the image in the glasses resolved, the view was rimmed with an orange border. Some kind of icon, like someone giving a karate kick, hovered in the periphery of Sam's vision for a moment, then faded. Other than that, the view was clear and crisp. The only clue that the room was actually pitch black was a slight dimming of the view, a slight vignette around the edges. Like looking at the world through a tinted window.

Otherwise, the glasses showed him everything. Brandon on the ground in front of him. Cress, unmoving, on the floor to Sam's left. A second prototype just a couple feet away. Sam picked it up and slipped it in his pocket.

He watched as Brandon struggled and slipped and failed to

get to his knees. Blood covered his mouth, and the side of his face was already starting to swell.

Cress lay crumpled in a heap at the base of the wall, the desk chair beside her. Her eyes were closed and she wasn't moving, but Sam could see her chest rising and falling with her breaths. Knocked out somehow. Knocked over by the chair, maybe, when it came loose in the struggle.

Her gun lay on the floor at the end of the wall, out of easy reach for her, even if she were to wake up. The gun glowed in Sam's glasses in the same orange color that rimmed the view. Some kind of overlay that highlighted weapons, perhaps?

He stepped carefully, staying clear of Brandon and making sure not to slip in the puddle of blood beneath him.

It was too far from Brandon. The blood had to be Sam's. Sam felt his face, checking his mouth and his nose. When he put his hand to his ear, he found the source of the bleeding. The side of his neck and jaw was sticky and wet and hot. Blood ran down onto his shirt.

Brandon must have sensed that the fight was over, that he'd lost his advantage. He'd stopped trying to get up, just lay on his back in the dark.

Sam sensed movement behind him, behind the wall. He looked over his shoulder. The glasses let him see through the wall, to see Kat emerge from the hidden room.

"In here, Kat," called Sam. "It's okay. It's safe to come out."

Even with his head turned back toward Brandon, Sam could still sense Kat behind the wall. The way she moved, smooth and sure, she must have been wearing a prototype of her own.

He kicked Brandon's foot. "You're as bad at murder as you are at pool."

Brandon mumbled something that Sam couldn't make out.

"He always was a slow study," said Kat as she came around the corner.

"Guess killing your father must have been beginner's luck."

"That's not entirely true," said Kat.

The orange glow around the edge of Sam's glasses screen flashed. The gun on the floor was still glowing orange, but now Kat's form glowed, too, as she stooped to pick it up.

She leaned casually against the wall, pointed the gun at Sam, and smiled that damn, irresistible smile. "He had some help."

## 56

Sam's stomach somersaulted, then dropped to the floor.

Kat was one of them. One of the killers.

Kat nudged Cress with her foot, keeping the gun pointed squarely at Sam.

"Did you kill my aunt?"

"Your aunt—" Sam swallowed hard. His tongue felt like a desert, his throat like sandpaper. "Your aunt tried to kill me."

"That's no excuse."

Sam couldn't tell if Kat was fucking with him or not. In that moment, it didn't seem like the most important question to ask.

"Are you going to kill me?"

"God, I hope not," Kat said. "I'm really starting to like you."

Through his glasses, Sam sensed three figures coming down the stairs toward the workshop. They were just fuzzy blobs at first, but after a moment he could see them more clearly.

Thomas, Christa, and Phillip.

Somehow, Sam didn't think they were coming to rescue him.

Phillip turned at the doorway and fiddled with something on

the wall. The lights came on, momentarily blinding Sam. He pulled off his glasses and shoved them in his pocket, rubbing his eyes without thinking. Pain shot through his skull. Brandon must have caught him in the face at some point. The bridge of his nose was tender, and he could feel some swelling around one eye.

Thomas came around the corner and surveyed the scene with obvious disgust.

"Goddamn it," he said. "I thought we agreed there would be no more mess."

Cress groaned as she stirred on the floor. Christa bent down to help her sit up against the wall.

"You wanted to get into the room," said Brandon, his words slow and muffled, but discernible as he probed his jaw gingerly with his fingertips. "I got into the room."

"I didn't tell you to destroy the place in the process."

Brandon shrugged, then winced in pain. "You didn't say not to."

Thomas sighed. "And your face is a horror show," he said to Brandon.

"Even more than usual," Christa chimed in.

Thomas set his hands on his hips, his face pulled into a deep frown. "How are we going to explain that to the police?"

"Let that asshole explain it," Brandon said with a deathly stare toward Sam. "He's one of them, anyway."

"I am not one of them," said Sam with a sigh. "And you were trying to kill me."

"I wasn't going to kill you."

"She tried to shoot me," said Sam, pointing toward Cress.

"If I were trying to shoot you," Cress said, "you'd be shot." She winced and pressed her hand to the back of her head, checked it for blood. "I was shooting at my brother."

"You turned out the lights. You stalked me through the dark."

Sam gestured toward Brandon. "And you said you were going to kill me."

Thomas glared at Brandon.

"I never said that," said Brandon, holding up his hands defensively. Then he thought for a moment. "I don't think I said that. But even if I did, I was just trying to scare him."

"Seems like it worked," said Christa. "You scared him just enough to beat the shit out of you."

"That," said Brandon, rubbing his jaw, "was luck."

Sam opened his mouth to respond, then closed it again. Wasn't worth the trouble.

And from the dubious looks on the faces of the others, there was no need.

Thomas surveyed the room. "Shit," he muttered, pulling out his phone. "I'm going to need to fly in a crew to clean this mess up before the police get here."

"How are they going to do that without the police noticing?" asked Kat. "You decided to let them come down here, remember? If we'd gone with my plan—"

"If we'd gone with your plan," Thomas interrupted, "we'd have no defense when they found out we were lying. And they would find out, Kat." His voice softened as he looked up at her, saw the hurt on her face. "They always find out. At least this way, we can make some excuse."

"Like what?" scoffed Cress. "We say we decided to tidy up a bit to make things easier for them?"

Thomas shrugged and shook his head. "I don't know. A previously scheduled cleaning crew. We say the room was regularly cleaned every morning."

"Even Christmas Day?" said Cress.

"It doesn't matter." Sam could hear the strain in Thomas' voice. "It'll be a minor detail that we can somehow sweep under the rug."

"If the broom is made of dollar bills, you can sweep anything away," said Kat.

Thomas didn't look up from his phone at her comment, but his mouth hardened into a thin line.

Sam stared at each of them. The entire family was there, plus Phillip, who stood patiently to one side, hands clasped in front of him. None of them seemed remotely surprised to be awake in the middle of the night. None of them seemed remotely curious as to why Brandon and Sam were covered in blood, or why Cress had been found on the floor, or why she'd shot out the screen of a laptop. They all acted as calmly as if they were sitting down to dinner.

Including Kat.

Sam's heart ached when he looked at her. So beautiful, so full of life and fun.

But she was a murderer. Or a willing accessory, at least.

"You can put the gun down, Kat," Sam said softly. "I'm not going to run away. And I'm not going to hurt anyone."

"Bullshit," said Brandon. "Shoot him, Kat."

"Do not shoot him, Kat," said Thomas without looking up from his phone. "The last thing we need is another corpse to explain."

"I appreciate your compassion," said Sam.

"Give me the gun," said Brandon, holding out his hand. "I'll kill him and bury his body in the snow. They won't find him for months."

"And what happens when they do find him?"

Brandon shrugged. "I'll dissolve him in acid before then, like Dahmer."

"You watch too much Netflix," said Kat.

"Or not enough," said Christa. "Dahmer got caught in the end."

"No one is killing anyone," said Thomas.

"Anyone else." Cress smiled sweetly at Thomas from the floor as his eyes slid to hers.

"Phillip," said Thomas, returning his attention back to his phone, thumbs tapping away, "would you please help my brother-in-law get cleaned up? We need to see what his injuries look like so we can invent an excuse for him."

"What about *his* injuries?" said Brandon, pointing to Sam.

"His injuries are more easily explained," said Thomas, his tone all business.

"In other words," said Christa, "he kicked your ass with barely a scratch."

Cress cackled. Brandon balled up his fists.

Sam's injuries felt like more than a scratch, and he didn't like them goading Brandon. The last thing Sam wanted was to amp Brandon up any more. He was already volatile.

"Brandon held his own well enough," Sam said, touching his neck and ear.

His words had the effect Sam had hoped for. Brandon lifted his chin smugly toward Christa and Cress.

"But if you're trying to get away with all this," Sam continued, "you're going to need a lot more than a cleaning crew and some flimsy excuses."

"Oh, really," said Thomas without looking up. "What makes you say that?"

"Because there's a video that proves you killed Nestrom. All of you."

That got their attention. Thomas' thumbs stopped tapping. The room fell dead silent.

All eyes were on Sam.

"And none of you even know where it is," he said.

**57**

DECEMBER 27, 2:33AM

Once Sam's words had sunk in, the silence in the room shattered. The cacophony of so many different voices all talking at once, shouting and arguing with each other, took its place. Only Phillip was silent, his face set in his usual mask of stoic professionalism.

The whole family had been in on it. Nestrom had correctly assumed that someone in his household would kill him. But even he didn't seem to suspect that they would all work together to plot his demise.

Sam still hadn't worked out the full story, but he had a pretty good idea of how it had gone down. Now he just needed to figure out how to get himself out of the picture, and to take what he came for in the process.

He slipped a prototype out of his pocket and put them on. Of all the amazing capabilities the glasses had, there was one in particular that Sam was grateful for in that moment.

Sound attenuation.

As soon as he put on the glasses, the din of everyone's

arguing quieted. He could still hear it, could hear the individual voices even more clearly than before. But the volume had been turned down to a level that didn't instantly give Sam a headache.

The glasses really were incredible.

"Enough," said Thomas over the noise. The talking did not quiet. "Enough," he shouted.

The others finally heard him. Their chatter silenced, and all eyes looked to Thomas, then to where Thomas was staring. At Sam.

The silence stretched on, as conspicuous as the uproar had been a moment before. Thomas' eyes narrowed, appraising Sam, gauging his opponent. As meek and subservient as Thomas had seemed in front of Nestrom, Sam could see now that he was a formidable man, the kind of person Sam would not want to meet across a conference room table with a high-stakes business contract on the line. He wondered, even, if all the meekness had been an act, a role that Thomas played around Nestrom. It was a time-honored tradition to manage your own boss. Maybe Thomas had just been giving Nestrom what Nestrom wanted so that Thomas would be free to do what he liked with the company.

Under Thomas's quiet stare, Sam could feel himself being evaluated. He could feel Thomas trying to decide what leverage Sam held. What weaknesses did he have? What could Thomas offer him? And most importantly, what did Sam want?

That one, Sam knew, Thomas would never guess.

"Okay, Sam," said Thomas, a charming smile on his face, one that did not dim the predatory gleam in his eyes. "Let's say we believe you."

"It's the truth," said Sam.

Thomas's smile didn't waver. "Let's say we believe you have this magical video, somehow proving us all guilty of murder. What would you do with it? Take it to the police, like my father-in-law told you to do?" Thomas shrugged. "Nestech's lawyers are the best in the world. They can explain away one video. If that's all you have, the case wouldn't even make it to trial."

Sam chuckled. "I wouldn't take it to the police, Thomas."

Thomas nodded. "Of course not. So you take it to the press or you post it online. Try to win in the court of public opinion. Try to drag the Nestrom name through the mud and bring Nestech down with it." Thomas smiled even broader. "We'd win again. The public has a short memory, and Nestech devices are in every pocket, used all day, every day. The public loves Nestech. Your story would promote our brand. All publicity is good publicity, after all. We'd run some damage control, issue a statement or two, talk about deep fakes and fake news for a while. We'd sell more products, and the story would become a distant memory within a week. Hell, if worse came to worst, we could even come up with something to distract the press. Pay a celebrity to dump their girlfriend or help a dictator bomb their own people."

"You would do that just to kill a story?"

"We killed a man," said Thomas.

These people were even crazier than Sam had thought. He looked around at all of their faces. All of them stared back at him. Not one seemed to feel enough shame to avert their eyes.

Not even Kat.

"I wouldn't take it to the press," Sam said.

"Then what, Sam?" said Thomas. "Blackmail? Extortion? I thought you were better than that, but okay. Name your price. And dream big, son, because once you're paid, you'll be on the run forever. If I catch even a rumor of your whereabouts after this, I'll kill you myself."

"I think you're misunderstanding how blackmail works."

"I think you're misunderstanding how serious we all are." Thomas's voice raised in volume. His face reddened. "This is our livelihood. This is our lives, our future. And I will not let some arrogant stray off the train"—he darted a glare toward Kat

—"ruin it for us. We just killed one asshole. I won't let another one get in the way."

"I'm not going to blackmail you," said Sam.

"Then what, Sam?" Thomas shouted, throwing his hands in the air in exasperation. "What do you want from us?"

Sam stuffed his hands in his pockets and shrugged. "I want you to let me go."

## 58

DECEMBER 27, 2:40AM

Sam waited while they processed what he'd said, shivering in the chill of the workshop as the sweat from his struggle with Brandon cooled on his skin. He could see the gears turning behind their eyes, trying to figure out his angle. Thomas, in particular, peered at Sam with an intensity that made Sam feel like his soul was being X-rayed. Like Thomas could see right through him.

"You want us to let you go?" Thomas said. "What do you mean?"

Sam shrugged again, his hands balled into fists in his pockets. "I mean just that. I want you to let me leave this house. Before the police arrive."

"We're not keeping you here," said Kat. "If you want to leave, just leave." She stepped toward him. "Is that what you want?"

Sam thought he could see hurt in Kat's eyes, but he may have been imagining it.

"I want you to act as though I never existed," he said, staring into Kat's eyes, "as though you never met me, never heard of me."

This time, he knew he wasn't imagining it. His words had hurt Kat. Sam didn't want that, but he didn't want to sleep with a murderer, either.

He pulled his eyes away, shifted them to Thomas, who regarded Sam with cool detachment. "You want us to lie to the police."

"There's no trace of my being here, not in any way that the police would notice. There won't be any awkward questions or inconsistencies. Which is more than I can say for others." Sam looked at Brandon, who raised his middle finger in return.

"How do we know you won't turn us in as soon as you get back home, or wherever it is you're going?" asked Christa.

"If I do, you'll defend yourselves, just as Thomas said. But it would be a hell of a lot easier if you never had to. It's worth the risk to let me go."

"Why don't you want the police to know you were here?" asked Thomas.

Sam sighed. "You remember what Dr. Nestrom said at dinner, about my family?"

"That your parents were a couple of two-bit thieves who got caught?" said Cress, her voice straining as she struggled to stand. Christa and Kat bent to help her up. "He also said your father is dead and your mother is already in jail."

Sam clenched his jaw, biting back a defensive retort. "Given my family history, I'd just as soon not give the police any reason to wonder about me," said Sam.

"Afraid to spoil your illustrious criminology career?" said Brandon. He pulled himself to his feet, as well. Sam did not offer to help him up.

"It wouldn't look good for me to be found at a murder scene," said Sam.

"It's not a murder scene," said Thomas. "It's the scene of the unfortunate, untimely death of a great, great man, and the holiday gathering place of his heartbroken, grieving family."

"Just let me go, and you can spin any story you want, without complications."

Thomas stared at Sam in silence. Sam felt the skin on the back of his neck crawl. He was nervous. If Thomas didn't go for this, for whatever reason, Sam didn't have a backup plan.

"Okay, fine," said Thomas. "Deal. But I want you to destroy that video right now, while we're watching."

Sam shook his head. "Kat's the best with computers here, right?" Everyone nodded. "I'll give her instructions at the door. She can delete the video when I leave."

"What if the instructions are fake?" said Brandon.

"I'll go out the back and leave on foot. As long as Kat follows my instructions right away, you'll still be able to catch me if they're fake. I won't have gotten far."

All eyes turned back to Thomas, who stood, arms crossed, tapping his lower lip with his index finger.

"We can't trust him, Thomas," said Brandon, wincing as he stepped forward. "He's just trying to trick us."

"What else are we going to do?" said Christa. "Keep him around and let him speak with the police in private? What do you think he'll tell them? That we all sat around and played gin rummy while our father's corpse cooled in the gardener's shed?"

"That is pretty much what happened," said Cress, drily.

"We have to get rid of him, then," said Brandon.

"What, kill him?" said Kat.

"If we have to, then so be it," said Brandon, squaring his shoulders toward Sam. "He's giving us no choice."

"No one is killing anyone," said Thomas.

Brandon immediately backed down, like an obedient attack dog. Thomas stepped closer to Sam, looking him straight in the eyes.

"What is it you really want?" Thomas mused, almost to himself. "Money?"

"I have money," said Sam.

"Revenge, then?"

"I'd never even met you people before three days ago."

"That doesn't mean you couldn't have something against us," said Cress. "We're a prominent family. Maybe you're crazy and you think we're responsible for your father's death or something."

"Yeah," said Sam. He dropped his voice to a husky whisper. "And I'm Batman."

Thomas stared at Sam a moment longer. "Okay, Sam," he said. "We'll let you go. And we won't mention you to the police."

Brandon and Cress protested. Even Christa seemed surprised.

Sam flicked his eyes to Kat's face. She looked back with her big, beautiful eyes. Sam felt a stab in his chest at the sadness he saw there. Sincere sadness, it seemed.

He hoped it was sincere, anyway, because he felt it, too. Kat was so lovely, inside and out.

If only she weren't a murderer.

"We'll escort you out," said Thomas, gesturing to one side. Sam walked past them all into the main workshop area, toward the assembly station. He glanced at the electrical testing equipment, at the different probes lying there. In the light, he could see there were several different shapes, from pointed probes to probes with flat, circular tips.

Something triggered in his mind.

He stopped and turned. The others were trailing him in a line, Thomas leading the way. They all stopped short in front of him.

"I do have one question," Sam said. Thomas raised one eyebrow. "How did you actually kill Nestrom? I couldn't find any clues on his body."

"You want us to tell you how we committed murder?" said Thomas. "Why would we do that?"

"What's the harm?"

"I don't know," said Brandon, "maybe that you'll stab us all in the back and turn us in to the police."

"Didn't we just have that conversation?" said Sam. "I'm not going to turn you in. But I do want to know how you did it."

"You're the criminology whiz," said Cress. "You tell us."

"What's your theory?" said Thomas, a faint smile on his lips.

"You all have access to the workshop," said Sam. "I figure Phillip or Thomas let you in the first time—"

"Phillip?" said Cress. "He's just the help." Phillip bowed solemnly in acknowledgement. Sam couldn't tell, but there had to have been sarcasm behind the gesture.

"Okay," Sam continued. "Thomas let you in and Kat somehow hacked into the system to grant access to everyone else."

"My genius sister," said Brandon. He tried to put his arm around her, but cried out when he lifted it. He glared hard at Sam as he rubbed his shoulder.

"Wasn't easy," said Kat. "But I learned from the best." She almost looked remorseful when she said it.

Almost.

"And then someone came down on Christmas morning when Nestrom was in here working, killed him, and stole the prototype." He looked at Thomas. "That is the motive, I assume? You want to bring the prototype to market now, and Nestrom wanted to wait?"

"Business is business," said Thomas.

"Plus, he was a fucking asshole," said Cress, "who deserved to die a long time ago."

"That fucking asshole was funding your very lavish lifestyle," Sam said.

"And never let us forget it." Christa spoke under her breath, but Sam could hear her clearly with the sound enhancement from the glasses he wore.

"But how did you do it?" said Sam. "All I could find on the

body were some marks on his temples where the glasses had rubbed against his skin."

"Those weren't rub marks," said Kat.

Brandon stood at the assembly station. He turned a dial on the testing machine, flicked a switch, and held up two of the electrical leads. They were long and thin, with flat, circular ends. He tapped them together and they sparked, sending a tiny smoke cloud into the air with a soft sizzling sound.

What a horrible way to die.

"I would have thought electrocution would leave more of a mark," Sam said.

"It's not strong enough to electrocute anyone," scoffed Brandon.

"Dr. Nestrom's brain had unusual activity patterns," said Thomas. "Scientists have been asking to study it for years, thinking it could be the cause of his unique genius."

"I think he'd just shocked himself too many times," said Kat, "tinkering with all kinds of electrical devices. The damage probably built up over time."

"Seizures?"

"Episodes," said Kat. "Tiny ones, mostly. A twitch in his cheek or a moment of uncontrolled blinking. But they occasionally built up to larger effects. And the possibility of something much worse."

"All we did was help it along," said Brandon, touching off another sparking smoke cloud.

They'd induced a grand mal seizure. Another horrible way to die.

And yet Nestrom's corpse wore such a peaceful relaxed expression. Sam thought about the picture he'd found in Nestrom's pocket, and about the diamond in the pendant in his own pocket. Nestrom loved his wife, even so many years after her death.

Perhaps he was ready to die.

Maybe he was even looking forward to it.

**59**

Sam led them through the house and into the staff quarters, the whole group following like a school field trip. Through the window set into the door, Sam could see the hallway that led to the outside. To his freedom. To his success.

He turned to Thomas. "I'd like to be alone with Kat for a moment, if that's okay. She can walk me to the door by herself."

Thomas looked at Kat, who nodded, then back at Sam for a long moment. "Fine," he said. He held out his hand to Sam. His skin was smooth and dry, cool and soft. His handshake was firm. He leaned toward Sam. "Remember our agreement," he said. "There will be repercussions should it be broken."

Sam had no doubt about that. He would not want to make an enemy of Thomas Crowell.

Though, in truth, he was about to.

Sam pushed open the door to the back hallway, held it open for Kat. Brandon stepped up to Sam, nose to nose, chest puffed. "We'll be watching," he said. He was trying to be intimidating, but the blooming bruises on his jaw and face undermined the impact of his threatening tone. Sam clapped him on one shoulder. Brandon winced and shrank back.

Thomas whispered something to Kat. She nodded and passed through the door. It swung closed behind them both. Over his shoulder, Sam could see the others, four faces bunched together in the window, with Phillip looking on impassively in the background.

The light from several dim wall sconces lent the hallway a firelight glow. Sam and Kat walked slowly, in no hurry, like two people who had just met, had just spent a long, lovely evening in conversation at a bar and were now ambling toward their reluctant goodbyes.

And it was a reluctant goodbye for Sam. He really had been falling for Kat. There was so much to love about her. Her wit, her intelligence, her compassion, her beauty. He'd only known her for a few days, but in that time he'd seen only one real flaw.

Unfortunately, it was a big one.

Kat's hand sought Sam's. She twined her fingers in his, squeezed, pulled him closer to her. In the cold air of the hallway, Sam could feel her warmth, like a small sun walking beside him. He wanted to curl up in that warmth, close his eyes and sleep in it, bask in the glow of that small sun.

"You don't have to leave," she said. "Whatever is bothering you, we can work it out."

Emotions warred within Sam. He wanted to believe her. He wished they could work it out.

But he didn't think he could.

"It was you, wasn't it?" Sam said. "You're the one who killed him?"

Kat didn't look up at him, but she pulled him closer to her as they walked.

"Brandon, actually," she said, her voice soft. "I was the diversion."

Sam nodded slowly. "Any regrets?"

Kat looked through the window at the far end of the hallway and let out a long, heavy sigh.

"Of course I have regrets," she said. "I killed my father." She gave a short, rueful laugh. Sam saw her eyes shining in the soft light. "Not exactly how I saw my life working out." She stared down at the floor again, her hair falling down, blocking her face from Sam's view. "But you didn't live with him, Sam. You didn't grow up with him."

She turned her head and stared at him. Her tears magnified her eyes, enhanced them. Sam nearly lost himself in those dark, bottomless eyes again. He wanted to. He wanted nothing more than to forget everything he'd learned and just live the rest of his life in blissful ignorance by Kat's side.

"He was not a good father," Kat said. "He was not a good man."

Once again, cold reality brought Sam from his daydreams. "But did he deserve to die? To be murdered?" Kat shook her head and looked away. "You have money, Kat, right? You could have just moved away and started your own life, away from your father."

"I tried that." Kat tilted her head and smiled at Sam. His heart nearly stopped again. "You have no idea about us, do you? Who we are or what we've done?"

Sam shook his head. They reached the door and stopped. Sam could feel the cold seeping through the glass window from the frigid night air.

"I'm so used to sycophants, people telling me what they think I want to hear because they work for me, or because they know who my father is. It's nice to meet someone who isn't interested in me for what they think I can give them."

Again, Sam's heart melted in Kat's eyes, in her smile. Again, Sam pulled himself back. She was a murderer. Nothing could change that fact.

Of course, he and his parents were thieves. But even among

criminals, there were distinctions. There were lines that, once crossed, separated you forever.

"I want you to know why I did what I did," said Kat.

"Why you killed your father?"

"Why I felt like I had to."

Sam let out a deep sigh. "I don't need your confession, Kat. I'm not a cop and I'm not a priest."

"No, but you are a friend," she said, taking Sam's hand in hers again. "And I was hoping we could be more."

Her voice lifted in a question. Sam didn't respond, didn't even make eye contact. He didn't trust himself to.

"Please, just let me tell you my side of things," Kat said. "Then, you can go. If you still want to."

Sam didn't want to hear Kat's side of the story. He knew whatever she said would just sow doubt in his mind, and he didn't want things to be harder than they already were. But he nodded anyway. How could he refuse?

"After my mother died," Kat said, "my father pulled back more and more from the company. Became more of a recluse. Eventually, he hired other people to run it for him. When Christa and Thomas married, he bought Thomas's fintech startup and made Thomas CEO of Nestech. Christa was stuck because of that.

"At first, I think she thought she could change my father. She'd known him the longest, before my mother died. She could actually remember when he was happy. I think she thought she could bring him around." Her mouth set in a line. "But it didn't work out that way. Things just got worse."

"Where were you?"

"Gone. Brandon and I left as soon as we were old enough. He went gallivanting around the world, and I started my own tech company, a security firm."

"What kind of security?"

"Hardware and software," said Kat. "Everything from cameras and keypads to firewalls and encryption."

"So you got out," said Sam. "Why come back to kill your father?"

"I got out, but I didn't stay out." Kat looked out the window, stared through her own reflection at the dark night. "When my company started to take off, my father bought it. Hostile takeover."

For a father who didn't seem to care much about his kids, he interfered in their lives an awful lot.

"So I started another company. Video games, this time. Something as far away from my father's interests as I could get."

"Still a tech company."

Kat laughed. "I'm not going to start manufacturing push pins," she said. "I have to work with my skills and interests, after all."

"Let me guess. He bought that one, too?"

"Nestech's brand new gaming division," Kat nodded, "the cornerstone of their subscription services division." She stared out the window again. "So I started a third company. Augmented reality and virtual reality." She turned to Sam. "Headsets. Glasses and goggles." Her mouth twisted at the corner. "It's a hot market right now."

"So I hear."

"But he didn't buy me out this time." Her smile turned hard. "This time he just stole my work."

"Stole it? How?"

Kat shrugged. "I still don't know, exactly. I think he might have paid off one of my execs, but I can't prove it yet. He definitely didn't hack my systems."

"How do you know that?"

"I owned a security company, remember?"

"Is that how you got yourself into the workshop?"

She sniffed with derision. "I wrote the fucking code he was using."

"You'd think he would have known that was a risk."

"He did," she said. "I'm sure he did. We'd been playing cat and mouse with the security on the workshop since I was in grade school." Her voice grew quiet. "I think he wanted me to break in."

"But why would he steal your ideas? Why not just buy the company again?"

"He was already working on the same tech, as it turns out, so it would have made more sense for him to buy it. But then I would have just started another one." She stared out the window again. "He didn't care about the tech. It was me he wanted."

"I heard he tried to hire you to run Nestech."

"My guess is that he was trying to ruin my reputation. Drive that company into the ground so that no investor would work with me on any other ones. So I couldn't start a new venture. Then he'd have me by the balls." She gave Sam that twisted smile. "So to speak."

"So you came back and killed him."

Kat shook her head slowly. "He was killing me."

"But he wanted you to run his company. That must have felt good."

"He just wanted to control me. Look at how he treated Thomas. There's no way I would go back to that."

"So was it your idea? To get everyone together to kill Nestrom?"

"Actually, that was Aunt Cress."

Sam nodded. "The will."

"The will," Kat nodded back. "She called us all, got us all to come here for Christmas." She sighed. "I wouldn't have done it on my own, Sam," she said. "I don't think any of us would have. But all of us together? We all had reasons. You said it yourself.

With all of us together, and the snowstorm, there was nothing to stop us."

Sam furrowed his brow. "What were Phillip's reasons?" Sam still couldn't place a motive for Phillip. Unless he was getting paid off somehow.

"Phillip?" Kat laughed. "Phillip was just doing his job. He's probably as shocked as you are by all of this shit. He's just too professional to show it."

And still Phillip hadn't quit. Unbelievable.

"Okay," said Sam, "then why did you bring me here?"

Kat's eyebrows shot up with surprise. She laughed, a clear, ringing note that seemed to reverberate through the hall like a struck bell ringing.

"Because I like you, Sam," she said. She stepped closer, put her arms around his shoulders. "I like you a lot."

She slid her fingers into his hair, pulled his head to hers. Sam knew he should resist. Part of him wanted to resist.

But more of him didn't.

Kat kissed him, deeply. All the pain, all the anguish, all the anger and frustration—and, yes, love—he could feel it all in the heat of her kiss, in the strength of her embrace.

Sam let himself go, let himself fall into the pure passion he felt whenever he was with Kat.

One last time.

"Please don't go, Sam," Kat whispered, her face pressed against his neck.

It took every ounce of self-discipline Sam possessed to push Kat gently away. He held his palm against her cheek, stroked her still-wet lips with his thumb. "I'm sorry," he said, looking deep into her eyes the way one looks at the ocean as a plane carries you away from it. "Truly."

Sam heard the door at the far end of the hallway burst open.

**60**

DECEMBER 27, 3:22AM

The sound of the door banging against the wall reverberated in the hallway like a pistol shot. Sam had expected it to be Brandon, stalking toward Sam out of some misbegotten brotherly instinct to protect his sister. He was surprised to hear Thomas's voice, instead.

"Very clever," said Thomas when he reached Sam and Kat. "It almost worked, too."

"What almost worked?" said Sam.

Thomas held out his hand. "Give them to me, Sam."

"Give what to you?"

"The glasses."

Sam's heart dropped. He'd been so close.

"The glasses?" he whispered.

He cursed himself in his mind. If he hadn't stopped to listen to Kat, he'd be long gone by now.

Thomas pointed toward the glasses on Sam's face. "You thought you could just walk out with them?"

Sam, stunned, said nothing.

"And you," Thomas turned to Kat. "Were you just going to let him?"

"I wasn't thinking about it," Kat said.

"You weren't thinking at all."

"I didn't even realize I was still wearing them," said Sam. It was partly the truth. He'd forgotten all about the glasses once he and Kat started talking.

"I'm sure," Thomas said, clearly not believing Sam. "Have you given Kat the instructions?"

"In the hidden room," he said to Kat. "There's a video file on the computer in there." He tapped the glasses he still wore. "The glasses have an auto-record setting."

"How do you know that?" asked Kat.

"Because I saw the recording from the first time I wore them." It had been the second video on the new thumb drive.

"So the video evidence of the murder is a video you've been filming this whole fucking time?" said Thomas. "We just gave you the evidence against us?"

Kat folded her arms across her chest. "See?" She lifted her chin toward Thomas. "I told you I deleted the other video." She looked at Sam admiringly, shaking her head.

"And you switched the thumb drives," said Sam.

Kat nodded.

Sam pulled the glasses off of his face, stared down at them in his hands. He folded the earpieces closed, and smiled.

It really was an amazing device.

Thomas snatched them from Sam's hand.

"Get the fuck out," he snarled. "And you better hope I never see you again."

He stomped halfway down the hallway, then turned. "Let's go, Kat. You've got *more* evidence to destroy."

With one last long look, Kat walked slowly away. Sam

watched her go. She looked back once, at the door, before Thomas pulled her away with the others.

And then Sam was alone.

He turned toward the outer door, looked at himself in the reflection of the window, a dark, shadowed image, like a villain in a horror movie.

But Sam was no villain.

A criminal, yes. But not a villain.

He smiled as he pulled the second pair of glasses from his pocket. He looked at the prototype number etched on the side.

1238.0.

Sam slid them on, waited while they booted up. When the blue Nestrom logo had faded and Sam could see the world around him, inside in the hallway and outside in the night, when he could see the shapes of the others below him in the workshop, he was ready.

He lay his hand against his pocket, double-checking. Felt the thin, rectangular shape of the thumb drive there.

"Georgie," he said, "confirm that a copy of the video from the last test has downloaded to the thumb drive."

He needed to make sure the copy had downloaded before he got out of wi-fi range. The second thumb drive was more than just a storage device. It had wi-fi capabilities, as well. He didn't know how Nestrom made it work, but that was how Sam's test had wound up on the drive when it was hanging from the neck of Nestrom's corpse. Nestrom must have been using the newest prototype to help record and analyze data from the prior version. Training AI on previous iterations of itself.

Sam expected to hear the voice of Kat's mother, Georgie, confirm the video transfer. Instead, he heard a man's voice.

"Confirmed, Sam," it said. "Test 3 video copied. Start time 2:19AM. Duration 64 minutes."

Sam smiled, "Thank you, Dr. Nestrom."

Nestrom had uploaded his own voice to the AI assistant before he died.

Of course he had.

"No, Sam," Nestrom's voice said. "Thank you."

Sam grinned as he pushed through the door into the cold night.

**61**



DECEMBER 29, 2:03PM

When the reinforced metal door buzzed and the guard pulled it open, Cameron Hauk stepped dutifully into the antechamber. The door slammed shut behind him.

Lined with a small bank of dented, lockless metal lockers on one side and large, reinforced glass windows on the other, the room was little bigger than a small bathroom at the Nestrom house. The floor was lined with beige linoleum of an age and style that seemed sticky and dirty even when it was freshly cleaned. The walls were painted the same numb beige, the only accent the moldy pea color of the window trim.

Cam set the few items he'd brought into one of the lockers and held his arms out to the side as another guard patted him down, the fourth pat down since he'd arrived at the facility. Security was tight. It was a prison, after all.

Through the windows, he could see his mother already seated at a table in the visitation room, her silver-streaked black hair stark and beautiful against the garish orange of her prison jumpsuit.

"Hey, Sue," Cam said to the guard, "I brought in some of those horehound candies you like. Left them out front with Terry."

"You're the best, Cam," said Sue as she felt along Cam's arms and the sides of his torso.

"You know you can get them online, right?"

"You know I barely can turn on my computer right?"

Cam laughed. "Maybe I'll set up a subscription for you, get them delivered for you every month."

"Then they won't be special," Sue said as she squatted to feel along Cam's legs. "And I'll gain a hundred pounds." She stood and put one hand on the soft folds of her belly. "A hundred more pounds."

"You still look beautiful to me, Sue," said Cam with a wink and a grin.

Sue arched one eyebrow. She was short and heavyset, her skin a mottled sable, her dark eyes shining like she'd just drunk a triple shot of espresso. She'd been there since Cam's mother had been transferred in five years earlier, and her sharp humor hadn't dulled a bit in all that time. Cam didn't think he could say the same if he had to spend his days as a prison guard between these drab, mind-numbing walls. He wasn't sure who had it worse, Sue or his mother. One was being punished against her will. The other had chosen to punish herself.

"You and your momma," Sue shook her head. "The two of you could charm the skin off a snake."

"I just call it like I see it."

"Uh huh." She gave Cam a dubious smirk, pulled a ring of keys from a retractable metal cable on her hip, and turned to unlock the door to the visitation room. "All that charm ain't gonna stop Terry from eating them candies himself before I even get out there."

Cam dropped his arms and jerked his chin over his shoulder. "Check my locker," he said.

Sue pointed at him with a mischievous grin. "You dog." She pulled open the door to the visitation room. "You spoil me."

"You look after my mother, Sue," said Cam. "I could bring you candies for the rest of my life and it still wouldn't be enough to thank you for that."

Sue's cheeks blushed. "Go on, get. Get in there," she said, her voice thick. "Don't keep your momma waiting."

The visitation room had a door at each end—one for visitors, one for inmates—and held six or seven round tables, generously spaced throughout the sparse, long room. Each table was made of metal coated with orange plastic and bolted to the floor. Four benches, also bolted down, circled each table in gentle quarter-arcs. The look of it reminded Cam of an elementary school. The musty, institutional smell of it reminded Cam of some of the older buildings on his college campus. Antiseptic and mold mixed with flickering hope and endless boredom.

The room was empty except for a lone guard in the far corner and one other inmate seated to Cam's left as he walked in, a slender blonde with a gator's mouth tattooed on her neck and wrinkles on her face that belied her youth. She had a visitor of her own. Cam waved as he walked by, and the inmate returned his wave with a friendly smile.

Cam nodded toward the guard as he sat down opposite his mother. The guard gave a small smile and lifted his chin in response.

"You look happy," said Cam's mother.

"I'm always happy when I get to see you."

"Damn right you are."

She held out her right hand, curled her middle and ring fingers down to her palm, and set her hand down on her side of the table. Cam repeated the gesture on his side.

Sign language for *I love you.*

Visitors weren't allowed to make physical contact with the inmates. Doing so was grounds for revocation of visitation privileges. As friendly as Cam and his mother were with them, the guards were there to do a job, not to make friends. Paulina Hauk received no special dispensation, no treatment that fell outside the bounds of the rules, rules that applied equally to everyone. The guards had too much integrity for that, and Cam knew that his mother wouldn't have wanted it any other way.

That didn't mean she wasn't treated well. Within the bounds of the rules, there was a lot of latitude for interpretation, and Paulie was a favorite among guards and inmates alike. She was hard not to love.

But rules were rules, and Cam was not about to make his mother's life in prison more difficult by breaking them.

He'd find a way to take advantage of the system, instead.

"Missed you Sunday," Paulie said. "Did you have a good Christmas?"

"The snowstorm shut the trains shut down on my way here. Ended up spending the holiday with someone I met on the way."

"What a shocker," Paulie laughed. "Where's your sketchbook? I want to see why my future daughter-in-law looks like."

Cam sighed. "No wedding this time, mom," he said.

"What did she do?" She furrowed her brow. "What did *you* do?"

"It was definitely her." Cam glanced at the guard in the corner and gave his mother a pointed stare. She nodded slowly.

"Did this star-crossed lover have a name?"

"Kat," said Cam, annoyed by the quiet wistfulness in his voice. "Kat Nestrom."

Paulie whistled, soft and low. "It's all over the papers. Sad story." She nodded, thinking. "No evidence of foul play, they say."

"No evidence? That's good to hear."

"They say he had a seizure. Some kind of brain condition. The family is donating his brain to science for study."

"They're very generous people," Cam said.

Paulie's eyebrows lifted. "How generous?"

"Pretty generous," he said, "once they have the right motivation." He glanced up at the guard, who was staring blankly over the tops of their heads. "In fact," Cam let a smile tug at one corner of his mouth, "they have no idea how generous they can be."

Paulie smiled back. "Sometimes people just need a little push to get them to do the right thing." She took a deep breath and pushed her arms against the table, stretching, her eyes drifting behind Cam. She nodded toward the inmate at the other table. "Mazie says she's going to propose to her lady there."

Cam looked over his shoulder. The blonde inmate and her visitor, a tall, thick woman with straight brown hair down almost to her belt, were staring intensely at each other, their fingertips an inch apart on the table, as if they were aching for nothing more than one simple touch.

"Good for them," said Cam.

"Yes, but not so good for Chicky." She looked at Cam. "Mazie's girlfriend. Gonna be uncomfortable in the yard when she finds out."

"Good to know you're keeping busy, mom," said Cam. He rubbed his hands aimlessly on the table, the surface smooth and clean. "Any mention in the papers of Sam Davis?"

"Not that I recall."

"Oh, ok."

"Why would Sam be in the papers?"

"Sam was at the Nestrom's for the holiday." At his mother's raised eyebrows, Cam added, "I needed the backstory. Nestrom was bound to be a digger."

Paulie nodded slowly. "Sam Davis," she mused. "I've always liked that name. Very forgettable."

"Oh, Sam is unforgettable," Cam grinned, "but very hard to get in touch with."

"Sounds like an interesting guy." She smiled at Cam, and a look came into her eyes, a motherly look, that broke Cam's heart. He wished that, just once, he could give his mother a hug. It had been fifteen years since he'd last hugged her. Her punishment did not fit her crimes, in Cam's opinion, and it didn't impact just the criminal. Not the one with the conviction, at least. It impacted everyone who loved her. And that was a large group of people.

Paulie's eyes moved over Cam's shoulder again. He turned to see Mazie and her visitor stand. Sue held the door open for the visitor to leave while Mazie stayed rooted in place until the door was shut and locked again. A third guard came in from the far door and escorted Mazie out, leaving Cam and his mother alone in the room, the guard in the corner their only companion.

"How's school going?" his mother asked.

"It's going well," Cam said. "One more year."

"Sam keeping his grades up?"

"Top of his class."

"And how is our dear friend Mr. Attorney General?"

"Still impressed with Sam's work."

They shared a long look. Cam's mother had been in prison for fifteen years, and for fifteen years Cam had been searching for a way to get her out. Her sentence was sixty years, forty with good behavior. She'd be eighty-one years old by the time she got out.

Cam had no intention of letting it go that long. They had a plan, a long con. A very long con that had a lot of moving parts and a lot of risk. But it was a good plan, if it worked.

Of course, any plan was a good one if it worked.

"Stay patient," said his mother. "Stay positive. Stick to the plan—"

"—until the plan falls apart." Another of his parent's aphorisms. "I will, Mom. I promise."

He looked deep into her pale blue eyes. Paulie Hauk was the most positive, optimistic person Cam had ever known. Even when she'd been sentenced to sixty years, she'd thanked the judge, even thanked the prosecuting attorney before they took her away, thanked them for being open-minded and conscientious in their jobs. Both of them looked almost guilty themselves for sending her to prison.

But in her eyes, Cam could see the suffering. His mother hated confinement, not of her body, but of her spirit. The rules and the routines of prison life stifled that spirit. She had learned to make the best of it by focusing on the people around her, as she always did.

But she was suffering. And Cam couldn't bear to see his mother suffer like that.

~

They spoke for a while longer, Paulie catching Cam up on the prison gossip, Cam telling his mother about the Nestrom family. Cam thanked the guards again as he left, collected his keys and his wallet from Terry at the visitor desk.

He walked slowly through the dingy parking lot snowbanks to his car. Walking out of the prison always felt surreal to him, like walking in a dream. For a few minutes, he couldn't remember whether reality was inside the prison or outside.

The sky was the deep, empty, aching blue that only seems to come after a heavy snowfall. The contrast between the cloudless blue sky and the endless white snow, sparkling in the sunshine, always gave Cam a pain in his chest, like his heart would burst from the beauty and the emptiness of it all.

The pain became more intense from his awareness of his own freedom, and from knowing that his mother couldn't share it.

As he got in his car, Cam thought about Nestrom's glasses, locked away in a safe at his apartment. Not the most secure storage location. If Thomas found out that Cam had taken them, would he send a team to break in and steal them back? He probably would.

No, he definitely would. Cam might have to figure out a better place to keep the glasses until he needed them.

But getting the glasses was just one part of a much larger, much more important plan.

Cam started the car, heard the engine hum to life, and pulled away.

It was time to move on to the next step.

# ACKNOWLEDGMENTS

Great thanks to Kim for her help in editing this novel. The collective groans of a thousand readers have been averted by your keen eyes.

As always, my love and thanks to Holly. Without your support, my love, none of this would be possible.

# ABOUT THE AUTHOR

Kevin Robert Aldrich lives in California and is the author of several romance novels:

If you love heart-pounding romantic suspense, you'll love Bare Trap and Flames of Freedom.

If you like vampires, witches, and forbidden love, get a copy of Spellbound now.

And if you love powerful contemporary romance, try Racing Hearts and Ollie & Alli today.

# MORE FROM THE AUTHOR

To learn more about Kevin Robert Aldrich and stay up-to-date with all of his stories and novels, please visit his website:

www.kevinrobertaldrich.com

To be automatically notified of every new release, join the Kevin Robert Aldrich mailing list at the website above.